Praise for the novels of
Jasmine Haynes

"Deliciously erotic and completely captivating."
—Susan Johnson, *New York Times* bestselling author

"An erotic, emotional adventure of discovery you don't want to miss." —Lora Leigh, #1 *New York Times* bestselling author

"So incredibly hot that I'm trying to find the right words to describe it without having to be edited for content . . . extremely stimulating from the first page to the last! Of course, that means that I loved it! . . . One of the hottest, sexiest erotic books I have read so far."
—*Romance Reader at Heart*

"Sexy." —*Sensual Romance Reviews*

"Delightfully torrid." —*Midwest Book Review*

"More than a fast-paced erotic romance, this is a story of family, filled with memorable characters who will keep you engaged in the plot and the great sex. A good read to warm a winter's night."
—*Romantic Times*

"Bursting with sensuality and eroticism." —*In the Library Reviews*

"The passion is intense, hot, and purely erotic . . . recommended for any reader who likes their stories realistic, hot, captivating, and very, very well written." —*Road to Romance*

"Not your typical romance. This one's going to remain one of my favorites." —*The Romance Studio*

"Jasmine Haynes keeps the plot moving and the love scenes very hot."
—*Just Erotic Romance Reviews*

"A wonderful novel . . . Try this one—you won't be sorry."
—*The Best Reviews*

THE PRINCIPAL'S OFFICE

Jasmine Haynes

HEAT
New York

THE BERKLEY PUBLISHING GROUP
Published by the Penguin Group
Penguin Group (USA) Inc.
375 Hudson Street, New York, New York 10014, USA
Penguin Group (Canada), 90 Eglinton Avenue East, Suite 700, Toronto, Ontario M4P 2Y3, Canada
(a division of Pearson Penguin Canada Inc.)
Penguin Books Ltd., 80 Strand, London WC2R 0RL, England
Penguin Group Ireland, 25 St. Stephen's Green, Dublin 2, Ireland (a division of Penguin Books Ltd.)
Penguin Group (Australia), 250 Camberwell Road, Camberwell, Victoria 3124, Australia
(a division of Pearson Australia Group Pty. Ltd.)
Penguin Books India Pvt. Ltd., 11 Community Centre, Panchsheel Park, New Delhi—110 017, India
Penguin Group (NZ), 67 Apollo Drive, Rosedale, Auckland 0632, New Zealand
(a division of Pearson New Zealand Ltd.)
Penguin Books (South Africa) (Pty.) Ltd., 24 Sturdee Avenue, Rosebank, Johannesburg 2196,
South Africa

Penguin Books Ltd., Registered Offices: 80 Strand, London WC2R 0RL, England

This book is an original publication of The Berkley Publishing Group.

This is a work of fiction. Names, characters, places, and incidents either are the product of the author's imagination or are used fictitiously, and any resemblance to actual persons, living or dead, business establishments, events, or locales is entirely coincidental. The publisher does not have any control over and does not assume any responsibility for author or third-party websites or their content.

PUBLISHING HISTORY
Heat trade paperback edition / February 2012

Library of Congress Cataloging-in-Publication Data

Haynes, Jasmine.
    The principal's office / Jasmine Haynes.
      p. cm.
    ISBN 978-0-425-24716-7
    1. Divorced women—Fiction.   2. Mothers and sons—Fiction.   3. School principals—
Fiction.   I. Title.
    PS3608.A936P75 2012
    813'.6—dc22
                                                                    2011037773

PRINTED IN THE UNITED STATES OF AMERICA

10   9   8   7   6   5   4   3   2   1

To Rita, for all her enthusiasm

ACKNOWLEDGMENTS

Thanks to my special network of friends who support me, brainstorm with me, and encourage me: Bella Andre, Shelley Bates, Jenny Andersen, Jackie Yau, Ellen Higuchi, Kathy Coatney, Pamela Fryer, Rosemary Gunn, and Laurel Jacobson. And of course, to my agent, Lucienne Diver, and my editor, Wendy McCurdy.

PROLOGUE

THE PRETTY BLONDE STARED INTO THE REFRIGERATED JUICE section, like a child in front of a candy store window seeing the very thing she wanted and knew she couldn't have.

She was perfect.

Rand was relatively new to the area, having moved here to start a job last fall, five months ago. But even so, he didn't prowl grocery stores early on Saturday mornings looking for women. He'd needed a couple of items and didn't like waiting in line, so he'd stopped after his run along the canal.

Then he saw her. It was fortune smiling down on him, the law of attraction at work.

Her blond hair fluttered just past her shoulders. Her pretty profile showcased full ruby lips and long lashes several shades darker than her hair. The tight white T-shirt outlined mouthwatering breasts that were more than even his big hands could hold, and her jeans hugged the delectable curve of her ass. She wasn't too thin, yet was well taken care of. Best of all, there was no ring on her finger. He never amused himself with married women. He came from a long line of players, marriage being no barrier whatsoever between them and the objects of their desire. He wasn't about to be like any of them.

She was no sweet young thing, but closer to his age—forty—or possibly a couple of years younger. He preferred his partners to be older, seasoned, more sure of themselves, of who they were and what they wanted. Women who were old enough to appreciate trying something new, something daring.

He was as staid as they come during work hours, with a position that required a quiet, unwavering authority, steadfast diplomacy, and a hell of a lot of psychology. But after hours, his life was his own business. After hours, anything goes.

He smiled as she finally made up her mind and reached for the fridge door. Her breasts plumped with the movement.

Oh yeah, he'd love to get daring with her.

RACHEL STARED AT THE ROWS AND ROWS OF JUICE BOTTLES. SHE was a frugal shopper, buying only what was on sale, because in her mind, the sale price was the real price, and anything else meant you were overpaying. She lived for coupons. Penny-pinching was the only way she could make ends meet. Sure, her ex paid half the boys' expenses since they had dual custody, but the cost of living in the San Francisco Bay Area was astronomical, gas prices had once again skyrocketed, and cable TV and high-speed Internet, not to mention the boys' cell phones, just might bankrupt her. She had a full-time job she enjoyed, with excellent medical benefits, but she was a receptionist. Her salary barely covered standard monthly expenses. Her ex, an accountant, was the real breadwinner. Their house was underwater so they hadn't been able to unload it during the divorce settlement, and they were still waiting for the market to recover. In the meantime, she lived in it. The boys were with her every other week;

teenage boys could eat you out of house and home. For the most part, she made healthy home-cooked meals and only occasionally brought home fast food. It would have been cheaper to buy soda for the boys to drink, but she did her damnedest to make sure they learned good eating habits.

So she wanted that juice, which was on sale at half off, plus she had a coupon. Wouldn't you know, though, the last bottle had twisted at the top of the rollers, stuck fast, and there wasn't a grocery clerk in sight to help her out. Well, she was *not* going to be bested by a damn juice bottle. Yanking open the refrigerator door, she put a foot on the rubberized track, grabbed the edge of the shelf, hauled herself up, and stretched until her fingers just brushed the plastic bottle. If she could knock it a little, dislodge it . . .

"Let me help."

The male voice was deep enough to send a delicious shiver down her spine. She would have gotten out of his way, but she felt him along her side as he leaned into the fridge door with her. His hand on the small of her back set a flame burning low in her belly. She couldn't have moved if her life depended on it. Oh no, this was too good to miss. With barely a stretch, he straightened the bottle and set it rolling down the tracks to her waiting hand.

She was breathless when she turned to look up, and up some more. He was close enough to make her eyes cross, and she couldn't focus sufficiently to take in more than cropped blond hair, piercing blue eyes, and a square, smooth-shaven jaw.

"Thank you" was all she could manage. She didn't want him to move. It had been so long since she'd felt a man this near, breathed in his pure male scent, musky with testosterone and clean workout sweat.

He stepped back out of the fridge slowly, his body caressing the length of hers for what seemed like an eternity, until his heat was replaced by the cool blast of refrigerated air.

"My pleasure," he said in that deep voice, setting her blood rushing through her veins.

She was so used to her ex's average height that, even though she was five-foot-five, this man made her feel petite. Tall and broad, he was a Viking who'd just stepped off his ship. Except for the all-black running outfit. Tight black jogging pants encased his muscled thighs, and the black Lycra shirt framed his powerful chest. She was staring, probably even drooling. In days of old, yeah, he'd have been a Viking or a knight. These days, a cop or a fireman. Or a corporate raider.

The man made her remember how long it had been since she'd had sex. With the divorce and all the stuff that went before, it had been two years. Two *years*. She'd been so busy and worried, she'd hardly noticed. Until *this* man had stood close to her, awakened her.

She realized she must have been staring at him like he was an ice cream cone she was dying to lick.

Too bad she couldn't afford a relationship right now.

"Well, thanks again." With great effort, she tore her eyes away and grabbed her shopping cart. A man was the *last* thing she needed in her life. She had enough trouble managing her sons—teenage boys were murder—not to mention her ex. No sirree Bob, she did not need a man.

Yet she allowed herself one last glance over her shoulder as she wheeled her cart down the meat aisle. He was watching. His gaze turned her hot inside and out.

No, she didn't need another man in her life. But she sure wouldn't mind a little casual sex. At the very least, the Viking was something to fantasize about.

EVERYTHING HAPPENED FOR A REASON. HE'D COME TO *THIS* STORE at *this* time; it had to be to see her. He was a believer in the law of attraction. If you wanted it badly enough, it would come to you, whatever it was. He'd felt the sizzle of her body against his, sensed her desire in the quickening of her breath and the perfume of her hormones. So, when he started his engine as she was exiting the grocery store with her full cart and a young clerk trailing in her wake to load the haul into her minivan, he didn't feel any need to get her phone number or give her his. Law of attraction: He'd find her again.

Or she'd find him.

1

RACHEL DELANEY TUCKED THE GROCERY RECEIPT IN HER accordion file on the kitchen counter. She hadn't broken the piggy bank, but who the hell would ever have thought that canned kidney beans with no added salt would cost three times as much as beans *with* salt? Fewer ingredients costs more to manufacture? Wasn't it just a matter of keying a different recipe into the assembly line? Whatever, her goal was making sure the boys ate healthy when they were with her because they sure didn't when Gary had them.

They were still sleeping when she'd arrived home, so Rachel had carted the groceries in, put them away, and started breakfast. She didn't like wasting the weekends she had with the boys on chores, so she rose early to get the grocery shopping out of the way. She certainly didn't need to go to a gym before they woke up either; she got all the aerobic workout she needed running around at breakneck speed so she could accomplish everything and still have time with Justin and Nathan. She and Gary had dual custody, one week on, one week off. She'd have the boys until

Sunday after supper, at which time she'd drive them over to Gary's. He had an apartment only a couple of miles away. Wherever they were staying, the boys were close to school.

It was a gorgeous day. January in the Bay Area was usually sunny, though this January had seen its fair share of rain. But on this last Saturday of the month, the sun streamed through the kitchen window as she whipped up the eggs and vanilla for French toast. Okay, not such a healthy breakfast, but it was a once-a-month-only treat. Sometimes you had to give kids a treat or they rebelled against anything that was good for them.

Just as she knew it would, the scent of cooking that wafted down the hallway soon garnered sounds from the bedroom end of the house. In his horrific *The Walking Dead* zombie pajamas, Justin led the charge like a bull elephant rather than with a zombielike shuffle. His short brown hair was askew, his face still creased with sleep lines from his pillow. At thirteen he was the shortest in his eighth-grade class and hated it.

"Did you get maple syrup, Mom?"

"Yes, honey. It's on the table." Rachel flipped a thick piece of French toast. Maple syrup was god-awful expensive, but what was the point of eating French toast without it? If you were going to be bad, do it with gusto.

In sweats and a torn T-shirt, his identically cut brown hair as mussed as Justin's, Nathan shuffled into the kitchen with a typical zombie growl. He should have been the one wearing *The Walking Dead* pajamas. He'd had a growth spurt over the last summer just before he started his sophomore year in high school, and he now topped his father's five-foot-ten frame. She hoped the same would come for Justin.

She slapped two pieces of French toast onto their plates. Justin grabbed his, and Nathan did the same, though at a much slower pace.

"You're welcome," she said.

"Thanks, Mom," Justin answered as he slid into his place at the table on the other side of the kitchen island.

"Thanks," Nathan echoed, albeit grudgingly.

Rachel told herself his attitude was due to still being half-asleep, even at just past nine in the morning. But she knew that wasn't the reason. Since the divorce, Nathan had become difficult.

She set another batch of egg-and-vanilla-coated bread in the hot pan. The boys were on their second helping by the time she sat down to eat her first.

"Dad said that if I kept my GPA above a three-point-five," Nathan said around a full mouth, "and I pass the driver's test with no errors, he'll let me have his car in the summer when he buys a new one."

"Please don't talk with your mouth full." The response was automatic, and not for the first time, she cursed inwardly at her ex. Sure, Gary offered the car, but he expected her to pay half the cost for the driving school and the insurance. She'd asked him *not* to talk to Nathan about it until she'd figured out where she'd come up with the extra money.

Nathan would be sixteen at the end of May, but they still hadn't gotten his driver's permit. She was putting it off as long as she could.

"You know, it would take a load off you, Mom. I could run Justin around so you wouldn't have to."

She almost laughed out loud. Right. As soon as he got that license and his dad's car, he'd be off with his friends.

"Honey, thanks very much for the offer, but it's only a ten-minute walk to school. Justin doesn't need you to run him around. I already told you that I can't afford the class and the insurance yet. I need to get more settled in my job."

Another zombie growl rumbled low in Nathan's throat.

Before the divorce, which had become final at the beginning of September, she'd been a homemaker. She didn't have a college education or the computer skills required for something higher paying, but she'd managed to find a decent job as a receptionist at DeKnight Gauges, which was only a short drive from the house. There was opportunity at DKG; she was honing those computer skills she was lacking in. But right now, ends didn't always meet. Thank God Gary paid the mortgage and half the expenses for the boys or she didn't know what she'd have done.

Nathan didn't seem to understand how tight things were.

"Come on, Mom. All the other guys are getting their permits. It'll be six months before you have to start paying insurance anyway."

"Nathan, you can wait a little longer."

"Mom—" he started.

"Let's have a nice breakfast," she cut in. "Who wants another slice?"

"I do," Justin piped up.

Nathan simply muttered something unintelligible. She made him one anyway.

"I won't be able to hold my head up if I start my junior year without a license."

Rachel sighed. He got his drama from his father. "Why don't you get a summer job to help pay for it, then?"

She could hear his teeth grinding all the way across the kitchen. "I can't get a job if I don't have a license to drive there."

"There's the bus," she said calmly. "Or you can look for something close by. You could even do some yard work for the neighbors."

"Do I look like a gardener?" he muttered.

The egg coating sizzled in the pan. She didn't answer his question, sure it was rhetorical. When she was his age, she'd done babysitting, hours and hours of babysitting, to be able to afford extras. Saying that, though, was tantamount to the old I-had-to-walk-five-miles-through-the-snow-to-get-to-school story and meaningless to kids these days.

"We're living in the dark ages," he went on. "I can't even text, and I have to watch every minute I'm on my cell phone. You know, that's why Dad *bought* us these phones for Christmas, so we could *use* them."

They had a family plan. She believed cell phones were for keeping in contact with family, making arrangements for pick-ups, and yes, so she knew where her boys were. They didn't have unlimited minutes or unlimited texting or Internet access, and thank God they didn't or everyone would be texting at the dinner table instead of talking.

Since the divorce, everything was her fault because Gary promised them things for which she couldn't afford to pay her share. There was polo for Nathan and soccer for Justin, the cell phones, the *this*, the *that*. Gary's stock phrase was "If you can convince your mom." She always ended up being the bad guy.

She didn't, however, spew any of that. "Here you go." She slid their plates onto the table, too tired to prompt for a thank-you.

"Everything's about money with you, Mom. You make me crazy with it, just like you did Dad."

It was the closest Nathan had come to saying the divorce was her fault. But he thought it, oh he thought it, every day.

"Let's be pleasant at the breakfast table, Nathan."

"I'm not hungry," he muttered, shoving his plate away. He stomped out of the kitchen and half a minute later, the slam of his bedroom door rocked the house.

Across the table, Justin shoveled another bite of French toast slathered with maple syrup into his mouth. At least he swallowed before he said, "Can I go over to Martin's house?"

It was on the tip of her tongue to say they should spend the day together, doing . . . something. But the fact was, her sons didn't want to spend time with her. They were pissed that she'd driven Gary out of the house, that she nitpicked about every dime she had to spend, that she denied them unlimited texting, and that if they went over on free minutes, there was hell to pay.

"Sure," she said, hearing the weary edge in her voice. "Go to Martin's." She didn't tell him to be home by lunch. Martin's mom would feed him.

Alone in the kitchen, she gathered the plates, scraping the wasted French toast into the garbage.

Maybe she was a hard-ass. Maybe she should work harder to pay her portion of the things they wanted. She hadn't gotten her driver's license until she was eighteen, but it was different for a girl. The other boys at school would make fun of Nathan, call him a kid, tease him. He deserved a mother who understood those issues.

"What happened to us?" she whispered.

For Christmas, the boys had gotten her a dress from the local thrift shop, the tags still on it. She'd loved the leopard print. She'd liked that they were learning the value of money. But there'd been something in Nathan's eyes. Something that wasn't . . . nice. As if the gift was a punishment. She'd pushed the thought out of her head, but sometimes, like this morning, it came back. Her eldest boy was starting to hate her. Her heart turned over in her chest every time she thought about the widening gulf, but she had no idea how to breach it.

Justin called out indistinguishable words, maybe a good-bye, then slammed the front door on his way out. Two minutes later, it slammed again. Nathan. She'd have to call his cell and find out where the hell he was going. He'd been hanging around some guys from the basketball team, going to the games with them. He'd tried out but hadn't made it onto the team. He was determined to give it another shot next year. Rachel hadn't managed to meet these new friends yet, so she didn't have a home number to call just in case.

Sometimes she wondered how much more she could take. Everything was falling apart. Nathan hated her, and while Justin didn't seem perpetually angry, she felt him drifting away during the weeks they weren't at home with her.

For a moment, standing at the kitchen sink, a dirty plate still in her hand, she thought about the man in the grocery store. She thought about what it would be like to drop everything, right this very minute, and sneak out to see him. To see a lover. To have hot, fast sex in the backseat while parked in the far corner of a shopping mall lot. Then dashing back home to finish the cleaning before the boys got home. How utterly sexy. How perfectly delicious. Like running away from it all. Even better for relieving stress than soaking in the tub.

Inside, she felt warm and liquid. She'd never been one to daydream a lot, but right now, she sure could use a fantasy Prince Charming to take her away for a little hot nookie. Just like kids needed treats every once in a while so they didn't rebel, she needed a treat, too. An orgasm. More than one. A lot of them. The Viking had certainly awakened her. She could definitely go for having a vibrator in her drawer for moments like this, when she was suddenly, unexpectedly very much alone.

Hmm, was a sex toy in the budget?

THE WEEKEND HADN'T IMPROVED. THE ANGRY SILENCE CHILLING the house sent Rachel's blood pressure soaring. So yes, in the night, with the boys at Gary's and the house empty, Rachel had resorted to fantasy to take her mind off everything. Otherwise her thoughts just went round and round and round.

Was it bad to start craving a fantasy?

By Monday morning, the result was extreme sexual frustration. One orgasm simply made her crave more. At lunchtime, she decided to go for it, dropping by Santana Row just to see how much a sex toy could actually cost. There was an elegantly disguised shop there that would have just what she wanted. In days of old—i.e., before the divorce—she'd been invited to a pleasure party given by a friend, and the saleslady had worked for the shop. Of course, Rachel hadn't gone to the party. Gary hadn't been feeling well that night and didn't want to be left alone with the boys, especially not for something as debauched as a pleasure party. Not that she'd *told* him. Hell no.

By God, the cheapest model was only fifteen dollars, batteries included. It didn't cost much more than the real maple syrup she bought for the boys. She deserved it. The salesclerk bagged it up in a pretty pink tote, and Rachel stepped out into the bright noon sun.

January was just about to turn into February, yet the day was actually hot, an unheard-of seventy-five degrees, which was relatively cool in the summertime but overheated her now. Looking down to snap her purse closed, she slammed into a solid stalk of human male.

"Oomph." She dropped the pink bag, which landed with a *thunk* on the sidewalk. Dammit. Had she broken her vibrator before she even used it?

"Sorry. Let me get that for you."

Rachel couldn't breathe. That voice. It was him. The Viking. And he was touching her bag, the shop's name, Pleasure Time, clearly printed on it in fancy red scroll.

He rose until he towered over her, and God, her heart started to race.

"We meet again."

"Yes." Did that come out as a squeak? At her back, the shop's window was ablaze with red thongs, sexy brassieres, barely there lingerie. Thank God there were no sex toys on display, but still, her cheeks were as red as the thong panties.

"Buying something for a special occasion?" His voice burrowed deep inside her as he handed over the bag.

He'd realize it was too heavy for lingerie. Did he know the additional merchandise the store carried in a tastefully appointed section in the back? "A gag gift," she said quickly.

He didn't back off, and his heat singed her, a tactile reminder of the way his body had slid along hers as he'd rescued the juice for her in the grocery store. She thought of all the fantasies she'd woven around him, the Viking raider carrying her off, how she'd wanted to touch herself that first night, but she hadn't because the boys were home. But last night, oh yes, last night, she'd succumbed to those fantasies. It wasn't enough. She needed more. She needed the vibrator. The one in the bag he'd retrieved for her.

Yet, in this moment, even *that* wouldn't do. She needed *him*. She could feel her pulse beating at her throat, her breath quickening, the heat burgeoning down low. She'd never been highly sexed—too many other things to worry about, like kids and a depressed husband and money—so why did this man suddenly set her on fire?

"A second accidental meeting deserves a coffee. Join me?"

The sun was hot on her hair. She felt people scurrying around them, heard voices, the traffic on the road, distant honks, the roar of a jet overhead from nearby San José Airport, but it all receded as if suddenly they were alone in the bubble of her personal space. She wanted to say yes so badly that she even opened her mouth. Then she thought of Nathan's anger. She thought of how it would only grow worse if she started dating. God forbid she should ever bring a man home. It wasn't worth it. When she considered the consequences, the vibrator was a steal at fifteen bucks.

"I'm sorry, but I don't date." Then her face flamed anew. It was coffee, not a date. She'd made too much of a presumption.

"I don't date either. Tell you what," he said, his voice quiet, his lips curved in a slight smile. "If we meet again, you'll say yes."

He didn't date? What did that mean? Whatever. The chances they'd meet again were exceedingly low. Twice was coincidental. It was actually a bit freaky that she'd seen him here, since she hadn't been to Santana Row since it first opened. "I really don't think—"

He cut her off with his finger to her lips. "Then don't think. Say yes."

His touch actually made her feel faint with a flare of desire. She'd been married so long, seventeen years, she could barely remember what lust felt like. She'd had two lovers before Gary, but it had all seemed to be fast, unsatisfying fumbling. Even with Gary, had it been like *this*, a burning need deep inside? They said some women burned hotter as they got older. Only months away from her fortieth birthday, maybe she was one of them.

"Move your lips," he murmured, "and say yes."

What was the big deal? It was just coffee. "All right. Coffee. If we meet again."

He smiled, two sexy dimples appearing at the sides of his mouth. "Done." He stepped back, and she missed his warmth. "It's *when*, not *if*, because we will meet again." Then he turned.

"Wait."

He waited, without a word.

"You're not married, are you?"

"No." He looked at her hand. "And neither are you." Then his stride ate up the sidewalk. His black slacks seemed form-fitted to his butt. His muscles rippled beneath his white shirt, and even without a suit jacket, the tie had declared him a businessman. A CEO? Yes, he'd be in charge.

Someone knocked into her arm, apologized, a woman who'd been trying to squeeze past her and a man coming in the opposite direction. Rachel was just standing in the middle of the sidewalk watching the Viking's ass as his tall figure receded.

She hadn't even asked his name. He hadn't asked hers. He was leaving it to chance.

Suddenly Rachel wasn't so sure she wanted to leave everything to chance. Maybe the vibrator wasn't going to be enough. Maybe she was going to need the real thing.

2

"DO YOU WANT TO GO OUT FOR HAPPY HOUR?"

Rachel could only stare at Bree Mason. She was pretty, with long black hair and a tall, slender figure. Bree was DKG's accountant, and she'd just finished checking Rachel's work on the payables and receivables input. It was one of the new skills Rachel was picking up to make herself more marketable.

"Um." For a moment, it was all that came out. Rachel was rarely at a loss for words. Some might even say—like Yvonne Colbert, their inside sales manager—that Rachel talked too much. But not now. It was shock. Because Bree had *never* wanted to go out after hours. She was quiet, kept to herself, and after work, she vanished like a puff of smoke. She didn't socialize. In fact, she didn't talk much at all, and the several times Rachel had asked if she wanted to go to lunch, Bree had always said no. That didn't hurt Rachel's feelings; it was Bree's nature. Rachel accepted that.

At five to five on Tuesday, the factory was quiet; the techs started early and left early. Yvonne was talking softly on the phone in her office. Erin was in Dominic's lab with the door closed. A husband-and-wife team, they'd owned and operated DKG for ten years.

Bree didn't look eager, her expression flat, as if her invitation was completely normal. A couple of times in the past few months, Bree had opened up about her father's illness. He'd passed away a short time ago. Maybe she needed to forget her sorrows for a little while. It certainly wasn't a usual request for her, but it wasn't a usual time either. She needed a friend, and Rachel figured she was the closest thing to a friend Bree had. Yeah, that was it, Bree finally needed her.

Rachel wasn't about to let the opportunity pass by. It might never happen again. "I'm free. My ex has the boys this week."

"Good." Bree started shutting down her computer. Then, her hand hovering over the mouse, she turned.

Rachel suddenly felt nervous under her dark stare. "What?"

"You should go to night school and get your AA degree. You're good with accounting."

It was Rachel's turn to stare. Go to college? She didn't have a moment to spare.

"More money," Bree answered as if Rachel had actually said something.

"I don't have time. The boys. Plus it costs money for books and classes and all that stuff."

"Erin pays educational fees in the line of duty."

"But I'm a receptionist."

"You're my accounting clerk, too."

Bree was helping her acquire some accounting skills, but that didn't make her an *accounting* anything. "I just don't think—" What? That she wasn't capable of it? Rachel admitted to herself that she wasn't the college type. She'd married Gary early, and that was that.

Bree shrugged. "Just a thought." She started closing all her open windows on the computer.

Could she do it? Maybe. Yes, probably. If Gary was good enough for accounting, so was she. But now wasn't the right time, the boys, getting settled, yadda, yadda. It wouldn't solve her immediate problems anyway; Nathan would have a fit if she spent money on school before she paid for his driving lessons. Maybe later she'd think about it, and she pushed the idea aside. "I'll get my purse," Rachel said.

Bree merely smiled and nodded.

Twenty minutes later they were seated in a booth at a nearby restaurant that served happy-hour drinks and provided a free appetizer buffet in their bar area, which was amazing in today's economy where nothing was free anymore. The bartenders were pouring drinks, the music was playing, and the bar was absolutely packed. Thank God they'd gotten the last available booth, even if it was in a corner by the restrooms, because the place was now standing room only. Maybe the restaurant made up for the free food with the amount of alcohol that was flowing. Rachel had elbowed her way through the buffet line, figuring the appetizers could pass for tonight's dinner, and she'd ordered the half-priced white wine.

Their drinks arrived, and Rachel raised her glass. "I want to make a toast," she said above the din. "Here's to how well you handled Denton Marbury."

Even in the bar's dim lighting, Bree's blush was obvious. "Thanks."

Marbury was their outside accountant, a CPA, who did the taxes and other governmental filings. He and Bree had had a little run-in. Even Rachel had heard *that* blowout, with Marbury doing all the blowing, right out of his—*Oops, language.*

"And you actually called him instead of sending an email telling him his services were no longer needed." Rachel marveled. She knew it took a lot of courage, especially since it meant Bree would have to handle the IRS audit coming up in a couple of weeks.

Bree dipped her head, studying the tabletop. "Don't you think I should have done it face-to-face?"

Rachel snorted. "*Drive* over there? What a waste of time. No, a phone call is as face-to-face as you needed to be."

Bree nodded, looking up again. "It was important for me to *say* it. And not let him steamroll over me."

"Well, then, you should be really proud of yourself." Rachel knew all about not sticking up for yourself, wishing you'd handled it differently, et cetera, et cetera.

Finally meeting her gaze, Bree nodded. "I am."

"Good," Rachel said. "Anyway, I know you're going to be taking on more stuff, so anything you need to off-load on me, I'd be happy to do it." It was win-win; Bree got help, and Rachel got clerical accounting experience she could use to beef up her resume.

"I'll find some more for you, don't worry." Bree tucked her hair behind her ear, her face still slightly flushed from Rachel's praise.

"How's everything going with your mom? She doing okay?" Rachel's parents were both living. They were back in the Midwest, so she didn't get to see them often, but she didn't want to even imagine losing one of them.

"My mom's stoic. She'll be fine."

That being Bree's stock line, it wasn't the first time Rachel had heard it. "And you? Are you okay?"

Bree smiled then. It wasn't self-deprecating. It wasn't even sad. "I'm actually pretty good, too. I . . ." She stopped, looked at her hands a moment. "I'm better than when I started crying in front of you. A lot better."

That had happened two months ago, when her father started going downhill fast. Bree hadn't told anyone else at DKG, but she'd confided in Rachel. "I'm glad to hear that." Rachel touched her hand briefly, afraid to hold on too long. Bree was skittish. "I've been worried about you."

"You're a good friend, Rachel."

Not really. Rachel had a feeling that Bree didn't have friends, just work associates. So why had she invited Rachel out? "I get the feeling you want to talk about something."

Again, Bree smiled, then shook her head. "I just thought it would be nice to . . ." She shrugged and raised an eyebrow. "I don't go out a lot . . . with friends. Maybe it's time I started."

Wow. Rachel was honored Bree had chosen her, but she was sort of at a loss as to what to say to keep the conversation going. "I met a man." *Oops.* Rachel almost covered her mouth. She hadn't meant to talk about that with anyone. "But I'm not sure I should date him. I mean, I've been divorced less than six months." Can anyone say motormouth? But then she realized she wanted to talk about it. Bree wouldn't gossip. "The boys wouldn't be happy at all with me dating."

Bree munched thoughtfully on a tortilla chip. Rachel had gotten a small assortment of things from the buffet, but Bree just had the chips. Rachel was eating the rest; after all, it was her dinner.

"Does their dad date?"

Rachel tipped her head. It hadn't occurred to her to even think about it. During the last few years, Gary hadn't had much of a libido. He'd said it was work. He was an accounting manager for a division of some huge conglomerate, and he'd hated his job. He claimed he didn't have anything left over when he got home. Gary and sex? Gary and dating? "I don't think so." Maybe Gary's lack of libido had been part of the reason Rachel's had disappeared. There was only so much rejection you could take before you stopped asking. But it was certainly returning now.

Suddenly she *needed* to talk about her Viking. "I don't know his name. And I don't want a relationship or anything. But sometimes I think about—" She stopped. She didn't know Bree well to reveal her sexual fantasies. In fact, she didn't discuss sex with anyone. It just wasn't something she'd ever done.

With that same look on her face that could have meant anything, Bree said, "If you don't want to have a relationship, then just have sex with him."

It was as if the whole bar went stone quiet. Rachel could have heard a pin drop. Not really, but she was in such complete shock that she felt like she'd lost her hearing. All she could see were a bunch of mouths moving out in the crowd and faces contorted with laughter. "I can't believe you said that."

Bree simply looked at her. "I'm not a saint or anything. If you don't want to have a relationship, it really is okay to just have sex." She opened her purse, pulled something out, and slid it across the table. A square of gold foil.

A condom. Rachel slapped her hand over it before anyone saw. "You carry one in your purse?" She was aghast. Only teenage boys doing a lot of wishful thinking carried around condoms.

Bree laughed. It wasn't that Rachel had never heard her laugh before, it was just . . . different. Bree was different in some way she couldn't pinpoint. Different since her father died. Since that confrontation with Marbury. The laugh was almost natural, even confident.

"I'm not a prude, Rachel. Though I have to admit I'd forgotten I had that condom until today when I was searching for something." She smiled. "Perfect timing." Then Bree leaned close. "But I do believe in being prepared for whatever comes my way. I even have a man. A very good man."

"You have a boyfriend?" Rachel heard the wonder in her voice and was ashamed, because why *shouldn't* Bree have a boyfriend? It was just that Bree had *never* indicated it.

"I've only just started to understand how important he is to me. He's the one who thinks I should have more friends." Bree gave Rachel a look. "Friends like you." She patted Rachel's hand. "So take that"—she gestured toward the condom hidden beneath

Rachel's palm—"and have some fun with this new guy you've met."

"I don't even know his name," Rachel repeated.

"That's even better."

Egad. The things she was learning about Bree, the woman hidden beneath the quiet facade.

"Everyone's a stranger until you get to know them," Bree said, and there was such a look on her face, soft, as if an inner light had switched on. She glowed. "Then all of a sudden, there's so much potential you never had a clue was there."

"I'm happy for you, that you've found someone like that."

Bree blinked, came back from whatever blissful place she'd been in. "Maybe one day you'll suddenly discover how special this man you've met is. Like a bolt of lightning."

Rachel pressed her lips into a flat line. "Yeah, well, not until the boys are older." Until they'd gotten over the anger. Things had to settle down. "But Gary has them every other week." She grinned and waggled her eyebrows. "So who knows what kind of trouble I might get into on my own?"

Could she do it? Have a hot, sexy, but casual affair?

Rachel curled her fingers around the condom, then slid her hand across the table and dropped it down to her purse on the seat.

Yes. Oh yes. She could.

OF COURSE, IF RACHEL WAS GOING TO DO IT, SHE HAD TO FIND HIM again, a next-to-impossible feat. The week had come and gone without a single sighting. So here she was at the grocery store early on Saturday morning, a complete slut because she hoped she'd see him. She could have done the shopping later since Gary had the boys, but no, she thought she'd catch her Viking after his run. Like last time.

No such luck. Rachel slammed the minivan's hatch on the load of groceries. She'd used her new and nifty vibrator every night this week to fantasies of him. There was a particularly delicious one she'd entertained several times. He was a masseur at a posh spa, and while she lay there with nothing but a towel draped over her and slices of cucumber on her eyelids—what did the cucumber do for your eyes?—he'd started a deep tissue massage on her arms and hands, then her feet, her calves, her thighs. Then he'd gone very deep indeed, this complete stranger, touching her in oh so many intimate places.

Years ago, a friend whose wedding she'd been in had taken the bridal party to a resort in Napa the weekend before the big day. The bride even paid for a spa treatment. Rachel's massage therapist was a man, and he'd been good with his hands. There wasn't the least thing sexual about it. He wasn't even attractive; he was too thin, too short, nothing like the Viking. But when she'd told Gary, he'd completely flipped, like she'd committed adultery. He'd gotten even angrier when she didn't understand the gravity of what she'd done, acting as if there was something wrong with her moral fiber. *Don't you know what massage parlors are, for God's sake?* At the time—she was only twenty-five—she'd thought he was right, that there was something wrong with her for not seeing how bad it was to let another man, even a masseur, touch her. She'd actually been a bit inhibited in bed after that, afraid she would do something Gary might find unacceptable.

It was all so long ago. She was completely over that skewed thinking, yet somehow, the very fact that Gary had been outraged turned the episode into a powerful sexual fantasy for her, even today, close to fifteen years later. Go figure why an argument would cause that; she'd been horribly embarrassed and humiliated. She'd never told anyone. Yet now Rachel saw her Viking in the role of sexy masseur, bringing her to orgasm in a compact room with jasmine-scented incense and cucumber slices on her eyes. She could actually feel his hands on her, stroking her, slipping beneath the edge of the towel.

Rachel blew out a breath, and her skin felt flushed. Oh yeah, she'd played that fantasy a few times this week. Maybe she'd use that one again tonight. Oddly enough, the vibrator fantasies didn't relieve the sexual tension. She simply wanted more. And better. With someone else doing the touching. Though it didn't look like she was going to have that anytime soon.

"Whatever," she whispered as she pulled out of the grocery store parking lot. She'd done without before, and as Bree always said about her mom, Rachel was stoic. She'd have to hide the vibrator after tonight. She couldn't risk the boys finding it. She certainly wasn't going to use it while they were in the house. It vibrated too loudly. And she moaned too loudly.

At the corner, about to turn for home, she spied a Starbucks. Expensive coffee drinks were definitely not in her budget, but Yvonne had given her a gift card for Christmas, and it was still unused in her purse. Of course, she could re-gift it, but there wasn't anyone to re-gift it to because it was too small for a family or really-good-friend gift.

Why not treat herself? A vibrator, now a mocha. She was developing a wild streak, and she turned into the parking lot.

The line was long inside, stretching close to the door, and she almost backed out. But there was nothing pressing at home, just laundry and housecleaning and prepping some meals she could freeze for the week. Chili with lots of beans and hamburger with a low fat content was actually healthy, easy to make, and easy to freeze and take out later.

She fished in her purse for the gift card as she waited in line, inching forward. Ah, there it was. She looked up to gauge her progress to the counter.

And straight into a pair of startling blue eyes. He was a head taller than everyone else, his hair blonder, his shoulders wider, his jawline stronger, his features more handsome.

Rachel bit her lip hard. It wasn't possible. She'd have thought the only explanation was that the man had been following her, except he'd arrived first.

When, not if.

She fell into the fantasy all over again, his hands on her, his touch intimate, the lighting low, the jasmine scent laced with a subtle, sexy male aroma, the cool press of cucumbers on her eyelids. She couldn't see; she could only feel.

Heat swept through her body. She'd put on makeup, fixed her hair, worn the tight jeans from last week and a pink T-shirt that showed her peaked nipples even through her bra. She'd dressed for him; now here he was.

And she had a condom in her purse.

3

HE SMILED, SPOKE BRIEFLY TO THE MAN BEHIND HIM, THEN CAME back to her.

"What are you drinking?"

Oh, that voice. Rachel remembered it precisely. Her body reacted accordingly, practically melting for him. "A white chocolate mocha." She had time for a coffee; the groceries would be fine for a bit.

He stepped back. "Get us a seat." Then he returned to his place in line.

Two people were vacating a corner table, and Rachel made a beeline for it. Darn. She shouldn't have let him get the mocha. Now she'd have to pay him back with cash.

Unless she paid him back in other ways. That was a delicious thought.

He was so good-looking. Not like a Brad Pitt or a Matthew McConaughey, but something more rugged. She smiled. *Gladiator.* Or *King Arthur.*

She leaned on the tabletop, chin on her fists, ignoring all the chatter around her. He'd looked yummy in running tights, sexy in shirt and tie, but the jeans molded to his butt were perfection. She wanted to drool. He drew stares with his looks, his height. The young woman taking his order beamed with a hundred watts. He had that effect on people, on women. On her.

His order miraculously appeared as if the clerk had put him ahead of everyone else. Then he was heading toward her, wending through the tables, heads turning in his wake.

"How tall are you?" she asked when he set her cup in front of her.

"Six-four." He sat and still seemed taller, the little chair too spindly for his body.

She loved his height, his width. His power. "Thanks for the coffee." She didn't offer to pay him. It was bold, like turning this into a date.

"My pleasure. I've been saving up for the next time I saw you."

"You're confident."

"I just know what I want."

Her blood fizzed inside her. "And whatever you want just miraculously happens?"

"Law of attraction," he said. "You think about it, you create it."

"Well, that explains why I saw you here. Because I've certainly been doing a lot of thinking." Ooh, she *was* bold. She liked it.

"Then great minds must think alike." He was bold right back at her. "My name's Rand—"

She shot a hand out to cover his mouth. "No names and no personal questions." She didn't think about the intimacy of the gesture, but once his lips were warm against her palm, she suddenly felt hot from the inside out. Her brain short-circuited. She dropped her elbow back to the table. Rand could have been short for Randall, or Randy. Except that he didn't look like a man who would call himself *Randy*. He had more class.

"Does that mean this isn't a date?" he asked, a curve to his lips as if he were about to tease her.

"I told you I don't date."

"I remember."

She flashed him a smile despite her nerves and leaned closer, dropping her voice to repeat herself. "I don't date." He had to lean in, too, to hear her. "But I'm not averse to a one-night stand." She should have gone up in flames. That was beyond bold. A girl should wait for a man to ask. She should hold out. She should—

"It'll be more than one night, I assure you."

Rachel didn't want to hold out. She hadn't been with a man other than Gary in close to twenty years. For so long, everything had been about watching money, making sure Gary wasn't upset, taking care of the boys, appeasing everyone, pleasing everyone. Until suddenly Gary wanted a divorce, no discussion, no counseling, no trial separation, just poof . . . gone. She didn't want to be a martyr or, as Bree had said, a saint. She wanted to be treated like a woman. Sometimes she forgot she was anything but a mother, and that was fine when she was married to Gary, but now, two weeks out of every month, she was alone. She didn't want to be lonely anymore.

"We need to have some ground rules," she said.

"Name them, and I'll tell you if I agree."

She liked that he didn't act the complete pushover simply to get what he wanted. "We don't meet at my house because I have two teenage sons with me every other week."

"My house will work. I don't mind telling you where I live." Then he grinned and leaned forward to say with just a breath of sound. "Or somewhere more public when the mood strikes."

Oh. *Oh.* "Are you kinky?"

His eyes suddenly seemed to gleam. "Very. Does that bother you?"

"I'm not sure." Yet her pulse fluttered with anticipation. "We'll find out."

"Good. Next rule."

She loved the idea that they were mapping out a sex plan in a coffee shop surrounded by chatting people. "You don't call me when it's a week with my sons."

"You can do all the calling at your leisure."

"You mean like just call you up for . . ." She trailed off.

"S-E-X," he mouthed.

That was sexy. Wasn't that a booty call? Yes, she loved it. "Okay."

He hitched his hip for his wallet, pulled out a card, then hesitated. "Can't give you that. Has my name."

"No names," she repeated. She was having fun. This was going to be so good.

Then he tipped his head. "What shall I call you?"

Superslut? Oh, she liked that. She'd never been a slut. But only a slut carried a condom in her purse. Did that make Bree a slut? Or did Rachel have to revise years of snap judgments? Whatever. "Call me Rachel." After all, he wouldn't know it was her real name, but so what if he did?

"Rachel." He tested the sound. "I like it. You can call me . . ." He thought.

Studmuffin. That made her smile. "Rand is fine." Since that was all she'd let him get out.

"Rand it is," he finally said.

She retrieved a scrap of paper and a pen from her purse. "You can write your phone number on here."

His writing was neat and precise. He slid the paper back to her. "Any other rules, Rachel?"

"Protection."

"Absolutely." He raised a brow, waiting for more.

She licked whipped cream off the top of the mocha she'd forgotten and felt a shiver as he watched. What other rules? "You don't tell your buddies about me."

"I don't have *buddies*. I've only lived in the Bay Area for a few months."

"Okay, well, those are the only rules I can think of."

"Then let's talk about my rules."

She hadn't expected him to have rules. He was a man; men didn't need them. Sex was just sex to them. "Okay, shoot."

He drank his coffee. No metrosexual mocha for him, but manly straight black and fragrant. "We experiment."

She glanced around. No one paid them any attention in their corner. "What do you mean by *experiment*?"

He closed in again. "Do you know what vanilla means?"

"Yes." She did watch TV, after all. And she'd bought a vibrator.

"We don't do vanilla. We experiment."

She thought about that. He could ask for anything. "Okay. But I reserve the right to say no."

"Agreed. But you need to push your limits."

The coffee drink was sweet and rich. She realized sex could be, too. "I'll push as long as I'm comfortable. What else?"

"Tell me your fantasies."

"That's a rule?"

"I'm done with the rules. Now I want to know"—he reached over to push her hair back and tapped her temple—"how your mind works."

The touch was slight yet somehow intimate, as if they were the only two people in the room. She thought about the massage fantasy, but she couldn't tell him that one. Because of the way Gary had reacted. Not that she thought the Viking—Rand—would think the same thing, but because it was embarrassing that her husband had had so little faith in her that he thought she'd do something in a massage parlor. "I'm not sure I have any fantasies," she evaded.

"Now, that's another rule."

"What?"

"We only speak the truth."

She snorted. "Well, that's pretty darn scary."

Putting a finger under her chin, he was so close she could see tiny flecks of brown in the blue irises. She could smell him, not soap or aftershave or even toothpaste, but *him*: man, sex, testosterone.

"You tell me your fantasies, and I will make everything we do so good for you, you won't be able to get enough."

She felt herself falling, falling, into his gaze, his thoughts, his mind. He'd said their meeting wasn't coincidence, and she suddenly believed he was right, that this was meant to be, that he was the perfect man and this was the perfect time. She wanted to follow any rule he set down.

Okay, and the first was to give him the truth. "I do have one fantasy." She had others besides the masseur, but they were vanilla, and that wasn't what he was asking for. "But I'm not ready to tell you about it."

"Fair enough." He dropped his hand, picked up his coffee. "But you were at Pleasure Time, and that bag contained more than a pair of sexy panties."

She couldn't help blushing.

"And you said you'd been thinking about us. I'm assuming we weren't just holding hands in those thoughts."

"No. But it didn't qualify as pushing any limits." And imagining him as a Viking raider was a bit too juvenile. She pursed her lips. "I should admit I'm pretty vanilla."

He winked. "Then we've got so many things to try. Let's start with the basics. I'll list a few things. You tell me what appeals to you."

"All right."

"Voyeurism," he said in that low, deep, sexy voice.

She shot a look at the tables close by. No one cared. Besides, the roar of the espresso machine would drown out their words. "You mean like a Peeping Tom?"

"That's negative. I'm talking about watching people who want to be seen."

"Oh." She absently stirred the plastic stick in her mocha and imagined taking a walk at night and passing a house with open curtains. Oh my God, she remembered a story a friend had told her. She hadn't seen Laurie in ages, but she remembered the account Laurie had given.

"What?" he prompted.

"Something a friend once related to me."

"Tell me."

She felt a kick inside. "She lived in an apartment on the third floor, and from her living room she could see straight down into an apartment on the second floor across the way, especially at night, when the lights were on."

"Into the bedroom?"

"No, it was a spare room the woman did her ironing in. One night the woman's boyfriend came in, lifted her dress over her hips, and went down on his knees." She was suddenly wet, thinking of the story, the woman, what her boyfriend was doing. And Rand sitting so very close while she talked about sex.

"He went down on her."

"Yes." Laurie said he went to town. They didn't switch off the lights, and the woman never turned around. She simply stopped ironing and spread her legs wider for him.

Rachel looked at Rand, and it was like that moment on Santana Row, or in the bar when Bree plunked down the condom. Everything faded. There was only him, his eyes on her face, the sound of his breath. And how wet she was between her thighs.

"How did it make you feel?"

She swallowed. "Like I wanted to touch myself."

"Did you go home and do that?"

She hadn't. She wasn't in the habit. She was married, and you weren't supposed to do that anymore because it meant your husband didn't satisfy you. Besides, she'd arrived home to find that Gary had had another bad day at work, and any sexual thrill she might have felt died a very quick death.

"No" was all she told him, because she wasn't going to get into complaining about her ex-husband. Talk about a buzz kill.

He sat back, crossed his arms over his chest, and regarded her. "I can see we're going to need to start tonight."

She gulped. Oh God, yes. Otherwise she'd have to wait another week. But what exactly was she agreeing to? This could be a huge mistake. She could get in over her head. She didn't know him. What if something happened? She was the one who'd said no names, but she hadn't even thought about physical safety. She was a mother, for God's sake. She shouldn't be taking risks like this. They should spend time in public places first.

But that would be too much like dating.

"It will be all right," he said softly, as if everything that suddenly rushed through her mind was written all over her panic-stricken face. "Call a friend. Give her my phone number and address. Check in with her."

She didn't have any friends to call. When things at home had gotten worse, when Gary said he was leaving, during the divorce, she'd lost contact with all her friends. No, that wasn't fair. She'd drawn away because she didn't want to complain all the time. She didn't want to keep saying over and over how angry she was. People got sick of that, even friends. And later, she didn't want to admit to anyone that it was actually a relief not to have to deal with Gary's depression anymore. She'd have felt guilty saying that out loud. Then she'd gone to work, and time became precious.

And . . . she sounded pathetic. Of course, she couldn't have talked to any of her old friends about *this*. But she could call Bree. Bree was a friend, one who'd supplied her with a condom.

"One more thing," he said. "I won't touch you tonight."

She opened her mouth, closed it, opened it again. Like a fish. "Then what's the point?"

He gave her an indulgent-older-brother smile. "Leave that to me. I promise not to disappoint you."

Rachel thought a moment, a *long* moment. Then she retrieved the paper with his phone number. "Write your address on here. I'll call my friend to let her know where I am."

She was going to do this. She was going to be bold. She was going to cut loose.

4

BREE HAD BEEN ENCOURAGING. SHE SAID SHE'D LEAVE HER CELL phone on to take Rachel's call. No matter where she was or what she was doing, Rachel was to contact Bree at ten p.m. If she didn't check in, it was time to bring in the cavalry. Maybe she was being overly cautious, but Rachel felt better knowing Bree had her back, so to speak.

She'd mapped the address in Los Gatos that Rand had given her. For the most part, Los Gatos was a well-to-do little suburb that clung to the foot of the Santa Cruz Mountains. The drive didn't take long, and she arrived five minutes before seven. She was always early for everything, so she sat in her minivan one door down from her destination on the opposite side of the street. The neighborhood was older but well maintained, with huge oaks creating an arbor over the road. Manicured lawns were lined with bushes that would flower beautifully in the spring, and lights blazed in most of the houses. Classical music drifted out from the one she'd parked in front of.

In a neighborhood like this, if she screamed loud enough, she'd be heard.

Rand's home was a Tudor style with a mullioned front window, pitched roof, and dormered windows on the second story. If he'd lived here only a few months, he'd bought in the down market, but the houses could still be pricey. She wondered once again what he did for a living, and if he had kids from a divorce who stayed with him sometimes. The house was certainly more than big enough for one person.

A single lamp was lit in the front window and the porch light was on over the door, but the upstairs windows were dark. She checked her watch. It was seven. They weren't having dinner, just drinks. Of course, he could spike her wine with something, but at some point, you made a decision to either trust or not trust. She had Bree for backup, and that was enough.

She climbed out of the minivan and locked the door. Her attire had been a problem. Not having been on a date with a new man in almost twenty years, she didn't own anything provocative or sexy.

Could that have been part of the problem with her marriage? She'd stopped trying?

It was academic now. She'd chosen to wear the leopard-print dress the boys had bought her for Christmas. Not sexy per se, it nevertheless hugged her breasts, then flared out in a flirty skirt that was see-through if she stood in the light without wearing a slip underneath. She'd paired it with black pumps and topped it with a short black sweater. When she'd twirled in front of the mirror back at home, she'd decided she didn't look half bad.

She stopped for a Mercedes driving past, then crossed the road. By the time she'd rung the bell, her heart was beating hard and fast with nerves.

She wanted and she didn't want. She was scared, and her fear wasn't of a spiked drink or a man who meant her harm. It was of whether she was good enough. For him. For any man.

She was just stepping back off the brick front stoop, getting ready to turn and run, when he opened the door. Rachel couldn't move.

A teal and black shirt made his chest seem broader. The two inches of heel on her shoes only made his height that much more impressive, because she still had to look up, up, and up to meet his gaze. His eyes glowed the same teal as his shirt, as if they'd changed color to match, and his hair was golden in the front hall light.

She was enchanted by him.

"I like your house." The comment was pathetically inane. She should have been scintillating.

"It suits."

"Do you have kids?" she blurted out without thinking.

"I've never been married."

"Oh." She paused, wanting to know why he'd never married, but she was the one who'd said no personal stuff. "Don't you like kids?" That wasn't personal, just general.

He laughed, a hearty sound that carried on the night air. "Yes. I like kids."

She didn't quite know why it was so funny, except that he might think she was fishing because she'd told him she had children. "I was just wondering because the house is so big," she tried to explain.

"It's only twenty-two hundred square feet. I have a home office, a spare bedroom, and a separate living room because sometimes I have to entertain for work. Other than that, it's pretty standard."

He had to entertain. Was he a salesman? "Well, it's very nice." She wanted to roll her eyes at herself. This was *not* going well.

He gave a courtly flourish of his hand. "Come in and see the whole thing."

Said the spider to the fly? Why did she keep thinking like that? She was a worrier, about money, about whether everyone was happy, about everything. *You need to stop, Rachel.* For tonight, she would cease all the worrying.

She followed his lead and stepped inside.

IT WAS NO BIGGER THAN HER HOME, BUT WHERE HERS SEEMED A bit dowdy because they hadn't remodeled since they'd moved in—and it had needed it even then—his was crisp and modern. The kitchen was outfitted with a stainless steel oven and glass cooktop, copper pots hanging on big brass hooks over the center island, shiny black marble counters, and a black fridge with the freezer on the bottom. The rest of the rooms were equally well adorned: white sofa and love seat in the living room, heavy oak furniture in the formal dining room, and hardwood floors everywhere.

His office was equipped with a big wooden desk, a manly leather reading chair, and built-in bookcases crammed with volumes from floor to ceiling. Upstairs, one of the guest bedrooms doubled as a den, with more leather furniture, a large flat screen TV, and an assortment of Blu-ray discs in the cabinet. She couldn't read the titles.

She didn't know if he was rich, but he definitely enjoyed his creature comforts. No kids, no wife, no alimony, he could spend his money as he liked.

Then he led her into the master bedroom. She started to feel uncomfortable again.

He knew it. "Don't worry. I'm not going to tie you to the bed." It was a big bed with a large headboard and bedposts at the head and foot that could be put to good use. "Yet," he added.

She bit her lip until she saw the glint in his eye. "You want to tie me up, don't you?"

He nodded, a cheeky grin growing.

"And you're hoping one of the fantasies I tell you is about being tied to your bed."

He nodded again, and the dimples by his mouth deepened. "And perhaps a little spanking, too."

Somehow that look and his mischievous smile blunted her discomfort. A man with evil intentions just couldn't grin like that. She turned, her skirt flaring. "I've never been spanked." But it sounded kinky and fun. "I'm not into anything painful."

"It can be quite erotic and exciting." He quirked one eyebrow. "The minuscule amount of pain is worth it."

"Hah. That's because you'd be giving it, and I'd be receiving it."

He stepped nearer, closing in on her. She could smell his sexy male scent again. "You'll receive so much more than pain," he said, his voice low and hypnotic.

Oh yes, she knew there were so many delicious things he could show her. But not everything all at once. She flounced away. "Maybe, maybe not. We'll have to see."

His lips curved in a slight smile. "Fair enough." He put out a hand, but didn't touch her. The way he'd promised not to touch her.

His bedroom was heavy dark wood furniture and white walls. The photos on the walls were all nature scenes, no people. In fact, she hadn't seen any family photographs in the house. Here, there were shots of majestic redwoods, Yosemite's Half Dome, and a framed trio of a bear drinking from a backyard fountain. She moved closer to examine the pictures.

"I rented a house in Tahoe, and he visited every day for his morning drink."

She tipped her head to look back at him. "You took all these?"

"Yes. I like the outdoors."

They were good. Like something you'd find in a coffee-table book. She'd noticed some nature pictures downstairs but had given them only a glance. "You're pretty good at photography."

"It simply takes patience. And I have a lot of that." He was looking at her with a subliminal message; he'd be patient with her, too.

He was big, and somehow that very fact made him seem comforting, caring—as if, because of his size, he'd always had to exercise caution in how he dealt with people. She wanted to know more about him. Where he was from, if he had family back there, what hobbies he had besides photography, what books he enjoyed, what movies he liked.

All of that was off-limits. She'd set the rule herself. Yet when did simple conversation blur into personal questioning?

Instead of voicing any of that, she peeked into his bathroom to find white tile with a gray wainscoting, an old-fashioned claw-foot tub, and a wood vanity with a marble sink.

"This doesn't look like you." Too girly.

He was close when he spoke, his breath whispering through her hair. "The house was recently remodeled. I didn't think it worth changing. Though the tub is a little short."

It was too short for him to stretch out, but with the taps on the side, it would be absolutely perfect for two to sit facing each other, his knees along the outsides of hers. Oh yes, she could picture bubbles and candlelight and ruby wineglasses and lots of wet skin.

But she was getting ahead of herself.

"Come out to the deck. I've got wine for us."

She hadn't noticed the outside door, but when he flipped a switch, soft light streamed across a wood deck, chairs, two wine bottles and two glasses, and, by the side of a table, a standing heater that already glowed warm and red in the evening.

"I forgot to ask if you like red or white," he said as he opened the door and waved a hand for her to precede him. "So I put out both."

"Aren't you thoughtful." She felt special. Always the one to ask what someone else wanted, she found it nice to have a man take care of her needs. "I'm not terribly fond of red."

"Then I've got a nice white I think you'll approve of." At the table, he poured two glasses from the same bottle, and she thought again of a spiked drink. Was he trying to reassure her by drinking the same and letting her watch him pour?

Rachel smiled her thanks as she took the glass, then wandered to the railing. Below, the backyard wasn't terribly large, but the grass was green and neat, bordered by a hedge of rhododendrons. "You haven't seen them bloom yet, have you?" The sight would be amazing in a few months when the rainy season was over and the sun was out every day.

"I'm waiting for that, but there are plenty of other things to see in the meantime." He pulled one of the deck chairs closer to the railing and gestured for her to sit.

When she did, he pulled the second chair next to hers. He smelled so good, the scent not an aftershave, just something light and clean and male.

She sipped. The wine wasn't too dry or too sweet, but smooth going down. She didn't have wine at home. It put her to sleep when she had so much to do in the evenings.

"Good?" he asked, taking a larger drink of his own.

"Very. Perfect. What is it?"

"Something I got at one of the smaller wineries down in Paso Robles."

She wanted to ask if he'd gone to the central coast on his own or with a female friend. He wasn't married, but she hadn't asked about other women. Because they weren't dating. It wasn't her business.

"I did a bike trip with a group," he supplied as if he could see the question mark above her head. He stretched out his legs, crossing them at the ankles, and balanced his heels on the bottom rail.

"You're very outdoorsy."

He smiled without looking at her, his gaze on something distant. "Oh yeah."

She knew he was thinking something sexual. The seat cushion was soft, the wine made her mellow, and the heat of his body arced across the short distance between them. She'd forgotten how enticing male heat could be, so much better than the standing heater beside them.

From his second-floor deck, they could see into the yard behind his. The back lights went on, illuminating a hot tub, patio furniture, and a gas barbecue.

"Looks like we're not alone out here," he mused, slouching comfortably in his chair.

The horizontal railings were spaced a foot apart with a clear view into the neighbors' yard. A woman came out. Rachel focused. She was slim but not young, perhaps forty, dark haired, maybe pretty, maybe not—it was hard to tell. Carrying a glass of wine, with a bath towel wrapped around her, she bent to the hot tub's jets and set the water frothing. Then she dropped the towel on a chaise and, buck naked, climbed into the tub.

Rachel turned to Rand. "You're a peeper," she whispered, a touch of awe in her voice. It should have bothered her.

Rand merely tapped his glass to hers. "You're going to be a peeper, too. Unless you walk away right now."

She wasn't even tempted.

"Honey," the woman called, her voice wafting to them on the night air. "Pour yourself a glass of wine if you want one. I left the bottle out."

"Can't she see us up here?" After all, his deck was illuminated, too.

"Oh yeah, she can see us."

It reminded her of Laurie's story, the woman doing her ironing. She hadn't turned out the lights, hadn't closed the curtains, and she'd had to know anyone in the opposite apartments could see her. "You're doing this because of the friend I told you about, aren't you?"

He tipped his head enough to look at her. "It made you hot."

Rachel wet her lips with wine. Yes. It had. He'd listened to everything she'd said and decided to give her the show she'd only heard about but truly wanted to see. No man had ever *listened* like that, never been interested in what got to *her*. True, she didn't have a vast experience with men, and most of what she did have was ancient history. But Rand was giving her something she'd never even known she was lacking: a man who looked after *her* needs.

She wondered if he had a clue how potent a seduction that was.

5

A SCREEN DOOR SLAPPED SHUT IN THE NEIGHBORS' YARD AND *honey* came out. He wasn't wearing a stitch, not even a bath towel, and even at that distance, Rachel made out a rather impressive dangle between his legs. It bounced as he crossed the deck. As with the woman, he wasn't young, but was still in good shape, with short, light-colored hair that could have been gray, or blond like Rand's. She imagined he was rather good-looking.

"Are they married?" she asked.

"I assume so. They have parties sometimes, but for the most part, I only see them. No children."

"Do you always bring your dates up here?" she whispered.

Rand laughed. The man looked up. Rachel wished she had a pair of binoculars so she could make out his face. Then again, sometimes fantasy was better than reality.

"We aren't dating," he reminded her. Then, as she narrowed her eyes, he added, "I haven't had time for a social life up to this point. You're the first woman I've shown my big deck."

She couldn't help the smile, because she *knew* he was making a double entendre. And she was glad she was the only one he'd brought out here.

Once he'd seen them, she expected the man to immediately get in the water, but instead he freshened his wife's wine, folded her towel, and laid it by the edge of the hot tub, then slowly stepped down into the water, steam rising into the cooler air around them.

She had a sudden thought. Standing up, she leaned over the railing, trying to see underneath the deck. Still craning, she glanced back to ask, "Do you have a hot tub?"

"No. Sorry."

"Watching them makes me want hot water."

He waggled his fingers, signaling her back down to her chair. "Oh, we'll find plenty of hot water for you to get into."

The couple sat in the tub, sipping, talking low, then the woman climbed out to sit on the edge, facing them rather than putting her back to them. "It's a little hot in there, honey," she said in an unnecessarily loud voice. "I need to cool off a minute." Her husband laughed, said something Rachel couldn't make out.

She leaned in to Rand, basking in his warmth, his male scent, the square cut of his jaw. "How often do you come out here to watch them?"

"I enjoy a nice glass of wine out here beneath the heater. It helps to relax me."

"Yes, but how often?"

"On weekends. Occasionally during the week."

"Does she always sit naked like that?"

The woman leaned back, scissored her legs in the water, splashed a little on herself, then ran her hand up her abdomen, over her breasts.

"Yes. Like that. They certainly don't try to hide anything."

"You know, she couldn't have been in the water long enough to overheat."

"Probably not," he said, a sly smile creasing his lips.

The woman put her arms up to rub her neck and shoulders, her breasts bobbing with the movement. "Honey," she purred, "rub my neck, would you?" Then she slid down into the water, giving her husband her back.

They could have sat on this side of the tub and not have been so visible, but no, they made sure to sit on the far side, so that her breasts skimmed the water, in full view of Rand's deck. Her sounds of pleasure filled the night.

Rachel was fascinated. They knew they could be seen, yet they didn't care. In fact, Rachel was sure the woman was playing to them, speaking louder than she needed to, even moaning as her husband worked her neck muscles.

She found herself straining closer to Rand, not to whisper, but for the proximity, the intimacy, the scent of man.

"She's playing it up for you tonight," he said, his forearm resting on the arm of his chair. She could have touched him, but she didn't, playing the no-touching game.

"She doesn't usually make that much noise?"

He shook his head, smiling. "Not for a while. I suppose having only me watching was getting a little boring for her. Same old, same old."

The husband worked down her shoulder blades, her spine. She arched and moaned over his ministrations. Then his hands flared out to the sides and around to cup her breasts. He massaged her nipples.

Rachel thought of her fantasy massage and was suddenly wet between the legs. She crossed them, pressed her thighs together. Then she was hot, so very hot. It wasn't the standing heater. It wasn't even her sweater, but she took that off anyway, flinging it back across the table. "How far do they go?" she asked, then sipped her wine as Rand looked at her. He made her throat dry with longing.

Eyes a smoky blue in the shadow of the light behind him, his features were lined by the outdoors, but rugged and so very handsome for those extra lines. "Because you're here, maybe nothing," he said.

She felt a pang of disappointment.

"Then again"—he exhaled with a breath that touched her skin and raised the hairs along her arm—"it might heighten the thrill and they'll show it all to you."

She was suddenly burning up, wanting it all, wanting to watch with him. He was freedom. He was edgy. He was kinky. He was all the naughty things she'd never even dreamed of and suddenly wanted with everything inside her.

Maybe at some point during the evening, she could get him to break his promise about not touching her.

RAND TORVIK HAD WAITED WEEKS FOR THIS MOMENT WITH HER. He'd known it would happen eventually. Law of attraction, like two magnets being drawn together. And he was more than attracted to her. He'd raised his desire to near obsession.

Reaching behind them, he grabbed the wine bottle to refill Rachel's glass. She was leaning so close, he accidentally brushed her nipple with his arm. She was taut. He breathed her in, the piquant scent of aroused woman. Her skin was warm and flushed, her pupils dilated, her nostrils slightly flared with excitement.

She fascinated him far more than the tableau in the hot tub. Over time, he'd become a bit jaded about it. But watching her made it new and thrilling again. She hadn't turned out to be as confident and sure of herself as many women her age were, and he'd found that unexpectedly appealing. There were so many things he could introduce her to: a hot and sexy spanking, sex under the stars, being watched instead of merely watching, a little risk taking. This was just the beginning.

She parted her lips in a small gasp, and Rand glanced into his neighbors' yard. The husband had shoved his wife up, her bare bottom tilted, and pushed his hand between her legs. She leaned on the bath towel he'd laid along the edge for her.

Rand had noted that particular sign of things to come.

"Have they done that before?" Rachel asked, her breath faster, eager.

"Yes."

She pouted. "I want you to see something new, too."

"I am."

"What?"

"You." He leaned in to whisper to her. "Uncross your legs."

Her eyes widened, but she did want he wanted, her gaze all for him, the couple forgotten. He breathed in the luscious perfume of her sex. "Are you wearing panties?"

She nodded, swallowed.

"Take them off."

She gulped. "Right now? While you're watching?"

"I'm sure you can do it without revealing a thing." Which would be even more exhilarating. He liked overt in the neighbors' yard, but up here on his deck, he wanted seduction.

She handed him her wineglass, then, as the neighbor wife filled the night with her musical sounds, Rachel reached beneath her sexy leopard-print dress. She raised her butt, then wriggled until the panties slid down her legs.

"They're not very sexy," she said almost as an apology, her cheeks coloring.

They were bikinis, not string, but not granny panties either. "Let me be the judge." He held out his hand, and she laid the white cotton across his palm.

Then, with her gaze egging him on, he raised them to his nose and drank in the scent of her. He closed his eyes to better memorize her unique aroma, fresh, musky. "Very sexy," he murmured.

"I think I should be worried," she said with a hint of breath-lessness. "You're a peeper *and* a panty sniffer."

"Yeah, and I like to jerk off in the shower every morning, too." He held out a palm. "I have to shave off the hair."

She laughed, getting his reference to the old wives' tale that masturbating would make hair grow on a teenage kid's palms. "I check my sons' hands every morning just to be sure they're not being bad boys like you."

Down in the hot tub, the lady groaned and cried out, "Oh yes," at full volume, as if she realized she was no longer the center of attention and wanted to change that.

"Your lady love is calling," Rachel mocked.

The woman was attractive, but she had nothing on Rachel.

"Have they ever asked you to join them?"

"No. They get off on being watched. I don't even know their last name. We've somehow silently agreed that I'm the voyeur and they are the exhibitionists."

With the brief banter, he sensed she'd lost some of the edge. He wanted it back. "The idea of joining them doesn't tempt me so much as turning the tables and becoming the exhibitionist for them."

"Jerking off for them?"

"Bending you over the railing, lifting your skirt, and letting them watch *us*."

She inhaled with a jerky breath, and he knew he had her again. "Watch," he murmured, letting the word caress her ear.

The neighbor turned his wife and pushed her back on the towel, then spread her legs. Rand knew her pussy would be dripping with desire as her husband went down on her, lapping slowly, languorously, making sure their audience got their fill. She moaned, laced her fingers behind her head to watch her husband and, Rand was sure, to sneak a peek to make sure they were being watched as well.

"Isn't this what you wanted, just like your friend's story?"

"Yes." Rachel's answer was barely a breath.

He'd like nothing more than to run his hand up beneath her dress and test her wetness, but he'd made a promise he wouldn't break. Not even when she begged him to.

"Put your hand between your legs and touch yourself."

She leaned away slightly to look at him, her skin pink with excitement.

"Touch yourself, then let me see how wet your fingers are." He whispered his seduction.

She parted her lips, closed them again without answering, and swallowed.

"I said I wouldn't touch you. I never said I wouldn't ask you to do it for me."

She looked back at the couple cavorting below them. Then she inched her dress over her knees, higher up her legs, and finally slipped a hand between her parted thighs. He was sure he scented a wave of feminine arousal.

"Have you ever masturbated for a man?"

She shook her head, watching the yard across the way while he watched her. Her chest rose and fell, her breasts plump above the dress's neckline, her nipples peaked against the bodice.

"Someday I want to watch you. I want to spread you out on my bed, sit in a chair, and just watch."

He could almost hear the rush of her blood, feel her temperature rising, making the air boil around her. Her hand moved beneath the material. Her eyes drifted closed.

"Let me see," he whispered.

Not mistaking what he wanted, she removed her hand and held out her fingers to him. Her moisture glistened like dew. His mouth watered for a taste of her. But that would constitute touching. Instead he inhaled deeply, then, watching her instead of looking for himself, he said, "Tell me what they're doing."

"He's—" She bit her lip. "I can't."

It was nerves. He didn't figure her for a woman who talked dirty. That was clear in the way she'd described her friend's tale. He wanted to teach her the seduction of a little dirty talk, but for now, she could say it any way that made her feel comfortable. "Use a few euphemisms."

She swallowed. He let his gaze travel the length of her slim throat.

"He's using his tongue and his fingers to touch her G-spot inside."

Thank God she knew about the G-spot. Some women were as clueless as most men. "And he's obviously making her moan."

"Yes. Oh my God"—her eyes flared wide—"he's standing up and making her put him in her mouth."

He wanted to stroke the pearl of her nipple, so hard against her dress. Her bra must be thin, almost sheer. He ached to taste the tight bead. "He's big, isn't he?"

"I don't know how she can take all of him." Her breasts rose, fell, beckoned.

"Would you like to taste him?"

"I—" She swallowed, glanced at him. "I—um—never really liked—um . . ."

So many things he had to teach her. Because he knew he could make her love it. Perhaps it was her husband, his taste, his smell. From the moment Rand had started asking about her fantasies in the coffee shop, the moment the attraction had blossomed to intense desire, he'd known she would fulfill him, his needs. Not only for sex, but for the journey, the things he could show her, the delights he could introduce her to. He was a tutor, a mentor. That's what he thrived on. He'd just never thought to look for it in his sexual encounters, thinking experience was the key to hot sex. He hadn't known what he was missing. She'd opened his eyes, and now he could think of nothing else but teaching her.

"Does she like it?" he queried, his own desire turning his voice husky.

"Yes." She curled a hand around the arm of her chair. "She loves it."

Oh yes. He knew how much his neighbor's wife loved sucking. She could go at it for long, long minutes, until the tub's jets shut off and he could hear the slurp of her desire. He never touched himself while he watched. He waited until later, alone, when he could fit the image of another woman over her face. Since the first time he'd seen her, he'd imagined Rachel in the hot tub.

"I'd like to watch you." And he did now, the heat of her skin, the way she moved in her seat, as if she were dying to touch herself, that with just a little more encouragement, she would touch, because she couldn't help herself, because the view from his deck made her forget all her fears, and his voice drove her mad.

But she didn't slip her hand beneath her dress again. Instead, she told him what she saw. For all he cared, she could have been making it up. It was about her, not them.

"He's dragging her up his body." Her voice held a dreamlike quality. "And he's kissing her. Openmouthed. Like they haven't been married for all these years. Like it's all new." Like *she* hadn't been kissed in all these years; he could almost hear the words. "Now he's pulling her down into the water and turning her around."

Rand knew what came next, what always came next. They didn't deviate. He would push her to her hands on the concrete, a full side view, affording Rand the sight of the man's cock impaling her. But he let Rachel describe it, her voice breathy with every delicious detail. He folded her fingers around the stem of her wineglass, momentarily forgetting his vow not to touch her, until he felt the warmth of her skin. She was so enthralled with the scene that she didn't seem to notice his lapse. "Go on," he urged.

She sipped to wet her parched throat. "He's making her brace herself on the edge of the tub, and he's behind her, spreading her legs. His fingers, he's testing her." She gulped her wine as if she needed some sort of relief. "Now he's holding himself, and stroking her with the tip between her legs like he wants to make sure she's wet enough for him."

She didn't use a single dirty word or describe a body part, and yet she made him as hard as the concrete slab the neighbor lady braced herself on.

"Is that how we look?" she whispered. "Men and women?"

"Tell me how they look."

"Beautiful," she whispered, a reverent note in the one word. "I always thought that position was coarse and . . ." She bit her lip, thinking a long moment. "And dirty."

"Dirty is good."

She parted her lips, watching. "Not that I'm a prude or that I don't like sex."

Not a prude. Just that her partners, her husband, had never shown her the sexiness of being a little dirty. "How many men have you known?"

"Three. And no one since my husband."

He liked women who were willing to experiment. She was the best of everything, older, ready, dying for the experience, yet a babe in the woods.

God, yes, there was so much he could teach her, so many things to show her, so many delights he couldn't wait to introduce her to.

6

"ARE THEY FUCKING YET?"

The word jolted Rachel. The first time she'd ever used it, her mother had washed her mouth out with soap. The boys were strictly forbidden from saying it, though Nathan used it sometimes just to irritate her.

Yet in Rand's deep tone, that word melted her. "Yes."

"Say it. They're *fucking*."

She should be horrified. They were spying. If he was a peeper, then he was a pervert. If he did this, watched his neighbors, he could be capable of anything. Yet the man had seen them. He'd positioned his wife so Rachel and Rand had a clear view of his entry, and the woman had looked over her shoulder, straight at Rachel. She'd cried out only after she'd been sure Rachel was watching.

What's more, Rand made the whole thing about her, not them. He watched her, not them. Told her to describe it for him, using her words to heighten his arousal. His heat enveloped her, his scent intoxicated her, and his voice mesmerized her.

"He's fucking her so hard," she told him, then felt him shift closer, until her skin flushed with his nearness. If he'd ordered her to put her hand on him, she would have. If he'd urged her to make herself come, she couldn't have resisted. But he made it all hotter and more exquisite because of what he didn't ask for.

She'd ached for him to taste her wet fingers. She'd died when he didn't. Yet she was so much nearer to the edge of insanity because he hadn't.

"Now. Tell me what she's doing *now*."

"She's stroking her pussy, her clit." The dirty words enflamed her. *Fuck me, please, fuck me, fuck me, fuck me.*

Two fingers on the base of her glass, he tipped her wine to her lips, made her drink. But he never touched her, never asked to, only watched her drink as if he were drinking *her*. "Tell me more," he whispered.

"Her breasts are bobbing. Now she's pinching her nipple." Rachel felt as if it were her nipple, a streak of lightning from the tip to a secret spot deep inside. She squeezed her legs tight.

"Do you want to come?"

"Yes. Please." She felt teary-eyed with need.

The man slammed home, grunted. The woman cried out, arched back. Pounding flesh, hot, as if it were her own.

"This is how good it can feel," he said, soft, low, enticing.

She'd *never* felt this with Gary. Not with anyone. As if she were this man's sole focus. As if she were the only woman he wanted. The only woman who could make him come. He was hard, his jeans tight around him, his scent musky with sex and need and desire.

The woman screamed with climax, and the man groaned in orgasm, the steam of the tub and their sex rising, shimmering, their forms wavering. She could have come with them if Rand touched her, just her arm, her throat. It didn't even need to be erogenous.

"Go home."

She looked at him, barely able to breathe, let alone understand.

"Go home." His eyes were dark, his gaze unearthly. "Or I'll fuck you right here, right now, against the railing."

God, she wanted it.

"But you're not ready."

She could have cried, because she *needed* it. Yet he was right; she wasn't ready. In the morning, no, even before that, the moment he pulled out, she'd start regretting. She *would* do this, but tonight was the appetizer. Tonight was about *becoming* ready, not *being* ready.

She rose. He didn't walk her out.

When she was at the door leading into his bedroom, he said her name. She turned.

"You might be going home, but we're far from done yet."

His words made her shiver. She left on shaky legs. He hadn't hurt her. He hadn't scared her. She'd scared herself more with how badly she'd wanted him to take her against the railing so the hot tub couple could see. He was kinky. He was probably even perverted. But up there on his deck, he'd made her realize she could be those things, too. That she *wanted* to be those things, with him and for him. She wanted to be *this* man's total focus. She deserved it.

After years of never taking chances, of taking care of everyone else, keeping the peace, always doing what was right and expected of her, what she was *supposed* to do, she wanted to throw caution to the winds.

He would ask for more, stretch her limits. And she would do whatever he wanted.

RAND LAY NAKED ON HIS BED, HIS HANDS STACKED BENEATH HIS head, the door closed against the cold night air, the lights off. His neighbors had lost interest in their performance once Rachel was gone.

She'd reacted perfectly. Telling him everything in an excited, breathy voice, her skin so hot he could feel the warmth she'd emanated without actually touching her.

Dazed, she'd left without her panties. They lay on the bedside table, close enough that he could scent her. From his den window, he'd watched her cross the quiet street. Her equilibrium had returned, and she'd driven off.

He could have had her out on the deck. He didn't want it like that. Not tonight. Oh yes, certainly he wanted that someday, and sooner rather than later, but for tonight, he'd wanted only to whet her appetite, not to overwhelm her and send her running for cover.

She'd had only three lovers, one of them her husband. She hadn't asked his history. If she had, he would have confessed that he'd had more than two dozen lovers. He'd seen the question in her eyes—why had he never married?—but her own rule kept her mum.

The truth was a complicated mess, he supposed. He came from an extended family that prided themselves on never having a divorce among them. Consequently, they had a hell of a lot of bad marriages, a fact brought home the first time he returned from college unexpectedly and caught his father with another woman, right there in the house, right there in his mother's bed. It wasn't a surprise, just an affirmation. He hadn't avoided marriage, he'd simply avoided a *bad* marriage. He'd gone further than that, though, concentrating on his career and seeing only career-focused women, until somehow he'd ended up primarily in casual, transitory relationships. It had never bothered him. His career, which was more a vocation than a mere job, fulfilled him.

It all blended with what Rachel wanted. A casual relationship, yet a way to repair her battered self-esteem after her divorce. He was going to be so good at restoring her sense of worth.

The law of attraction had certainly worked its magic, bringing them together at just the right time. A month or even a couple of weeks earlier, she might not have been ready for him. He might not have seen all the possibilities of becoming her sexual mentor.

The phone rang. His cock hardened. He knew it was her. And he had plans.

"I got home safely," she said to his *hello*.

"Where are you now?"

"Walking into my bedroom." She was on her cell phone.

"Do you have your Bluetooth in?"

"Yes." There was hesitation in her voice.

"Are you still wearing that leopard dress?"

"Yes," she said, again with that wary pause.

He pictured her as she'd appeared earlier, sliding the dress up her thighs to take her panties off for him. "Lay on the bed and pull it to your waist, but no higher."

"Why?"

He heard soft rustles, her breath, which ratchetted up his own sexual tension. "Don't ask, just do."

"Yes, sir," she muttered, but he recognized the breathy anticipation in her voice.

"Tell me how wet you are."

She didn't say anything, and he pictured her hand between her legs. In his life, he'd taught a great many things that had no sexual connotation to people of a great many ages, but he'd never taught a woman how to pleasure herself for him.

"I'm very wet," she whispered.

"Get out the vibrator you bought the other day. You bought it for me, didn't you?"

"I bought it for *me*," she stressed.

He liked the answer, but pushed her anyway. "To use while you were dreaming about me."

"You're pretty sure of yourself. You were nicer in person."

He laughed. Another reason he liked older women: Despite any sexual naïveté she had, she wasn't a pushover. "Would it make you feel better to know that I jack off in the shower to fantasies of you?"

"I thought that was just in general, not about me specifically."

He detected a note of wistfulness in her voice. "Since we met, it's been all about you. And now I want to jack off while listening to you come."

"You mean like phone sex?"

"Not *like* phone sex. *Real* phone sex. Haven't you done it before?"

"With who?"

"Anyone. An anonymous man you met on the Internet. You block your number when you call, then you both get off."

"It sounds like you've been the anonymous man before."

"I have. It's hot." As long as the woman's voice was hot, and she let herself go. "I'm not mainstream. I like different things, and as long as no one gets hurt, they're all good."

"What if they're married women?"

"They don't admit it if they are."

"Isn't that like adultery?"

"No. It's called taking them at their word."

Her questions made him smile. She was either a hard case or she was nervous because she'd never had phone sex before and was afraid she wouldn't be able to come or make him come. He was sure that together they would do both.

"Rachel," he said, his voice a purr. "Fuck me now over the phone. Because your voice makes me hard, and watching you watch my neighbors tonight made me absolutely fucking crazy."

* * *

HIS VOICE MELTED HER. HIS WORDS WORMED THEIR WAY INTO HER chest and wrapped around her heart. God, it was good to be desired.

But she was nervous. She'd never done anything like this. Within the space of a week, she'd bought a vibrator, used it every chance she got, then merrily driven off to a stranger's house and watched someone else have sex. Now this.

He wanted her to fuck him with words. She didn't know how. Yet that word was so . . . sexy. Yes, incredibly sexy. A week ago she would have said *fuck* was just another bad word and yelled at her boys for using it.

"Fuck me," she whispered, testing it on her tongue, testing him.

"Do you know how badly I wanted to touch you tonight, to put my hand beneath that dress? I wanted to make you come, then lick it all off my fingers."

She'd never known a man so carnal, so verbal, so seductive.

"Put your hand between your legs and pretend it's me." He mesmerized her with his voice, his words, until her hand was moving of its own volition. She traced the folds of her sex, pushed inside, trailed a moist finger over her clitoris.

"Tell me," he urged. "Talk to me."

"I'm so wet. I wish you were here. I want to taste you the way she was tasting him."

"You want to suck my cock."

"Yes." She closed her eyes and imagined she could smell his tantalizing, musky sexual scent. "I want to suck you. I want to taste it and like it." She'd never liked doing it for Gary. She wanted to do it for Rand. She didn't care why it was different, whether it was Rand's sensual nature that begged for it versus the routine of marriage dulling her senses. "I want to know how you taste," she murmured, her mouth watering for him.

All the while her fingers moved and circled and dipped until her body was arching off the bed. She panted. "Yes, yes, I want to feel you in my mouth. I want to suck your cock deep, lick it, drain it, swallow you whole." She'd never let Gary come in her mouth, but she was overcome with the need to drink Rand.

"I will be your first, your best. I will make you come until you scream, with my fingers and my mouth and my cock." His voice was like a caress along her skin. Suddenly all the desire of the night, the excitement of watching, the fear of the unknown, then this, a man listening to her masturbate, it was all too much, too fast, and she felt a lightning bolt shoot down to her clitoris, burst with heat, then flash back out to every limb and beyond. She cried out his name as she came.

In her altered state, she believed she heard him shout out, too, and as she floated back down, she thought, *I did it, I really did it*. "Did you come?" she asked, hearing the hint of shyness in her voice.

"Fuck yes." His voice was guttural, sexy, satisfied.

She laughed, feeling almost giddy. "You say *fuck* a lot."

"Only for you. *Fuck* is a good word. It's hot, it's needy. It means a man will do anything."

"As compared to *making love*."

"Making love is good; it's reverent. But it's not desperate. I want you desperate for me like I'm desperate for you. Sex is best when it's fucking desperate, when you can't get enough, when you think about it all the time, when it consumes you. That's when you want to *fuck*."

She felt her heart beat hard and fast in her chest, her head swirling with his words. "But you didn't touch me tonight. If you were desperate, wouldn't you have just done what you wanted to do?" She'd turned down the heating since she was going out, and her bedroom was cool. She felt chilled and pushed her dress down her legs.

"Desperation heightens when you don't get what you want."

God, then she was desperate for him, so desperate.

"Rachel, next time you come here, bring your vibrator."

Oh. *Oh yes.*

The Bluetooth beeped in her ear. Call waiting. It was probably one of the boys. "I have to go." The last vestige of heat from her climax drained away. She thought about explaining, but the phone beeped again, and she realized that cutting him off was better than any explanation. It would add to the desperation he claimed he needed. It would be like that moment in his house when he told her to leave, the uncertainty, until he said he'd fuck her if she didn't go. The push-pull, the up-and-down that made everything hotter.

So she simply tapped on her Bluetooth, hanging up, then answered the other call. "Hey."

"Are you all right?"

It took her two seconds to realize it was Bree. "Oh. Yeah. I'm fine." Better than fine. She glanced at the side table clock. Ten-oh-one. "You're punctual."

"You're my friend."

Rachel understood there was great meaning in that. "Ditto."

"Are you still with him?"

"No."

"Was it good?"

She couldn't explain. Bree could never understand the kinkiness of what she did, the heat of doing it, the surprise, how much she wanted more of it. "It was very good."

"Great. Since you're fine, I have to go. I'm kinda tied up right now." Rachel thought she heard a man's deep chuckle. Bree's boyfriend.

"Thanks for checking on me, Bree."

"I'll do it for *you* anytime." Then Bree was gone. Yet again, there was importance in her words. Bree was giving her something she hadn't given a lot of people. She was telling Rachel she was special.

She removed the Bluetooth, setting it on the bedside table. It was after ten. If the boys were going to call, they would have already. She was alone. Her body was sated. But it would be a week before she could have more.

Was she supposed to call him? Ask for sex? How should it work?

Then, in the dark, Rachel smiled. It would work any way she wanted it to. Because he was desperate for her.

For the first time in a relationship, she was actually in the driver's seat.

7

ON SUNDAY EVENING, THE FRONT DOOR SLAMMED JUST AS RACHEL
was putting the last of the Nathan's folded laundry in his bureau
drawers. She'd have more to do this week; when they went to
their dad's, they took full suitcases and returned with all the
dirties.

"I'm back here," she called. Gary dropped them off after
dinner, so at least, following a day of cleaning and chores, she
wouldn't have to cook.

"Hi, Mom." Justin, on his way to his room.

"Hi, honey." She allowed herself a smile as she mouthed the
greeting, thinking of last night with Rand and watching *honey*.
She did not feel guilty about it now that her sons were home. She
was allowed a separate life when they were gone.

Then Nathan wheeled his suitcase in, leaving it by the closet
door. Her heart lifted when he actually smiled at her. He was
such a beautiful boy, taller than her now, turning into a man
right before her eyes. His hair was a lush brown, and she liked to
think he'd have a strong face in a couple of years. More than any-

thing, she wanted to reach out and push back his hair. But that would be considered babying.

"Mom, look." He thrust a paper at her. She barely had time to read it before he started telling her all about it. "Dad registered me for the driving lessons. He said you could pay your half whenever you get the money. He doesn't care how long it takes. All you have to do is sign this. I can even do the class stuff online. It'll be a piece of cake." His brown eyes sparkled with excitement.

Rachel could barely hold the paper without shaking. She wanted to shriek. Goddamn Gary. He'd put her in an untenable position. Because she either had to smile and lie and say how happy she was for Nathan, or refuse to sign and break his heart.

She turned to close his underwear drawer so he wouldn't see her expression. "Well, isn't that great, honey." She tried not to grit her teeth. "What a wonderful"—fucking asshole—"guy your dad is." Of course, she would never say that word in front of Nathan. But it felt marvelous to think it. She realized Rand was right; it was such a good word. And it had so many meanings beyond just sex.

"Will you sign, Mom?" For a moment, Nathan was her little boy again, begging for a new toy that everyone else had.

If he was guilty of playing her and Gary off against each other, she needed to at least call him on it. "Did you ask your dad to register you for the class, Nathan?"

He looked her straight in the eye. "No, Mom."

"So it was his idea."

"He asked me if I would have my driver's license in time to take the car in the summer, and I said no. So he just looked up the class on the Internet. And he made an appointment at the DMV to get my permit."

She was sure there had been a bit more back-and-forth that Nathan was leaving out. She took the paper anyway. At some point, it was just plain stubbornness not to acquiesce. But she would give Gary a piece of her mind. "Get me a pen."

Nathan scampered to his desk. "Thanks, Mom."

After reading the fine print, she signed and handed it back.

"Can you mail it for me tomorrow?" he asked eagerly.

"Write up the envelope and put a stamp on it, and then yes, I can mail it tomorrow."

He grinned. "You're the best, Mom."

She was, for now. Because he'd gotten what he wanted. But the next time she denied him something, she'd be in the doghouse again.

"Please unpack your suitcase and put the dirties in the hamper."

"Sure, Mom." He dragged the case over and flung it on the bed. One good thing, at least she wouldn't be doing that herself, like she normally did.

"And thanks for changing my sheets, Mom."

Whoa. He was laying it on thick. "You're welcome, Nathan. Would you take out the trash for me tonight?"

"Sure, Mom."

Was it bad to milk it for a few extra chores she usually had to get mad over before he'd do? No. But she was still going to call Gary to tell him how pissed she was.

She ducked into Justin's bedroom. He was already on the computer, and she blew him a kiss. Her baby, he didn't grimace at her. Next year, he'd probably tell her to stop with all the kissy stuff. "Dad's got a girlfriend."

Her jaw dropped, and her heart sank. She wasn't jealous; she just didn't want any fallout from it. "Are you okay with that?"

"Sure. She was nice. Kinda young."

"How young?"

"About twenty-five, I guess."

Good Lord. All that crap about having grown apart and needing to find himself was just that, crap. He'd wanted someone new, someone younger, someone smarter—Rachel stopped herself right there. She didn't care. She didn't have to deal with his moods anymore. She didn't have to tiptoe around the house when he'd had a bad day at work. Except for the money issues, life was better without him. Besides, what Gary did wasn't her business anymore. Unless . . . "Did she spend the night?"

"Nah. She brought some movies over on Saturday." He rolled his eyes. "Chick flicks."

"Well, you were a good kid for watching them. And I'm glad you liked her." She didn't ask the woman's name, what she looked like, nothing, but she wondered how long Gary had known her. Since before the divorce? Had he been keeping her a secret? Rachel wouldn't think about it. It no longer mattered. "Unpack your suitcase, would you, sweetie?"

She went to her own room and closed the door. She didn't want the boys hearing her argue with Gary.

"I'm not even home yet, Rachel." His voice was far away, distorted by the car's Bluetooth. "What did I do now?"

She pursed her lips. "I told you I wasn't ready for Nathan to start driving lessons."

The Bluetooth did not disguise his long-suffering sigh. "I told him to tell you that you could pay me your half later."

"That's not the point, Gary. You didn't call me before you did it." He hadn't even had the decency to tell her; he'd let Nathan come to her with the news.

"Fine. Then don't sign the paper."

"You know I can't do that without sounding like a bitch."

He didn't say anything. Because she was a bitch. In his mind. He probably told his new girlfriend what a bitch his ex-wife was. She wouldn't ask about that, because she *wasn't* a bitch and his love life wasn't her business.

"Look, will you just promise you won't do stuff like this without telling me first?"

He grunted. "Sure. Whatever." He sounded like Nathan. She

wanted to smack him. Damn him. He always took away her choices, made the decision without her, then came off like the good guy riding to the rescue. *She* was Snidely Whiplash.

Since she couldn't smack him the way she wanted to, she rode him a little bit more. "And the garage door still needs fixing. The remote only works intermittently." Gary was supposed to fix the stuff around the house, just like before. Until they sold the place, that was still his responsibility.

"It's just the batteries."

"It's not," she said through gritted teeth. "Both remotes do the same thing." She'd already told him. Just like she'd asked him to fix the hedge trimmer so she could cut back the juniper by the front door. She didn't mind doing the work—she mowed the lawn, did the weeding, even got the boys to help her—but she needed the proper tools. And she damn well wasn't going to buy a new trimmer.

"Fine," he said with an edge. "I'll look at it next week."

"Thanks." She hung up without slamming the phone. He made her so angry. She hated feeling like this, powerless.

She needed some control over her life. She needed a better income. Maybe Bree was right, and she should get a degree, accounting, something she could offer DKG to get a promotion and a raise. Then she'd strip away Gary's power over her.

Rachel looked at the closed bedroom door. All of that would take time, a lot of it. What she needed now was to call Rand, right this minute. Some naughty talk, a shot of him telling her she was hot, that he wanted her bad. That would fix *everything*, a deliciously quick fix that wouldn't last, but whatever.

She stalked to the door and flung it open before she could succumb to temptation. She'd already sworn to herself that she wasn't doing anything with Rand when she had the boys. Not even phone calls.

* * *

FIRST THING THE NEXT MORNING, RACHEL PUT HER TAKE-CONTROL plan into action. "Have you got a minute, Erin?"

"Sure, Rachel, come on in."

Rachel admired her boss more than any woman she knew. Erin was only a little older than Rachel, but she'd done so much. Erin and Dominic DeKnight had owned DKG for ten years. She was the guts and heart while Dominic was the brains and the inspiration. He designed the ultrasonic gauges they produced, but Erin got them manufactured and shipped out the door.

She was pretty, with a slim figure and hair a rich shade of red Rachel envied. And she was married to a hunk of a nice guy. Rachel would have said Erin had it all, except that they'd lost their son a little over a year ago. As much as she groused about her boys, she'd die if she ever lost one of them. She didn't know how Erin survived. But she was strong, and that's what Rachel admired most. Remembering Erin's strength was what had given Rachel the courage to come in here this morning. She could be like Erin. She could take charge. She wouldn't continue to be at Gary's mercy.

Erin's desk faced the door so she could always see what was going on out in the roundhouse, which was how everyone referred to the common area in the center of the building that housed all the business machines, the conference table, and the coffee setup.

Without closing the door, Rachel took the chair opposite.

"What's up?" Erin asked.

"Bree said that you do an education reimbursement."

"Yes. As long as the class has to do with improving your current position." She put her pen down and leaned back in her chair, giving Rachel her full attention.

"I'd like to take some accounting courses to help with the

stuff I'm doing for Bree. And computer basics, too." She was self-taught, but Bree's Excel spreadsheets made her cross-eyed. She was woefully lacking. "San José City College has several classes that would be useful." After the boys went to bed last night, she'd done some research.

"Aren't you a little late for the spring quarter?"

"They have some late-start short courses that there's still time to register for." There were a couple of computer offerings that had looked interesting. They began in April, which gave her time to register at the college, meet with a counselor about getting an AA degree, and even investigate financial aid for whatever DKG didn't cover. Yeah, she'd done a *lot* of planning last night.

"The computer classes are certainly reimbursable," Erin said, nodding, "but we'll have to look at the course descriptions for the accounting ones. However, we'll be supportive in any way that's reasonable. It's great you want to go back to college."

Back? Rachel had never started in the first place. She'd graduated high school, gotten a job just to have a job, but all she'd ever wanted was to be a mother. That was all good, and she didn't regret the decision, but now she needed more. "I can't afford to remain a receptionist."

She almost added that teenage boys were too expensive, but she didn't want to remind Erin about her son. True, Erin had started putting out pictures of Jay, and once in a while she'd suddenly remember something and tell Rachel a little story about him. That had only started happening in the last month or so. Before that, no one even said Jay's name.

Erin's computer pinged. She glanced at the monitor, read a moment, smiled, a funny sort of secret smile, as if she was reading something sexual or seductive. Then she turned back to Rachel. "By the way, Dominic and I are taking a couple of days off next week for Valentine's. Can you hold the fort down in case there's a crisis?"

Rachel realized Erin was offering a vote of confidence in the offhand comment. *Here, I know you can do this.* And Rachel could. "Sure, no problem. Heading somewhere special?"

Erin merely nodded, her smile even bigger, but she didn't mention where they were going.

That was another thing Rachel had noticed happening in the last month or so, how much more affectionate Erin and Dominic had gotten. Secret smiles, more touching, and now this, a romantic trip for Valentine's. Good for them.

Rachel stood. "I'll get to work. Thanks, on the education thing. I'll let you read the course descriptions when I've actually signed up."

"Good." Erin's computer pinged again. And again, she read, then laughed softly to herself and started typing.

Rachel had the oddest urge to rush into engineering and see if Dominic was typing on his computer, too. She was sure they were chatting. She was also pretty darn sure it wasn't anything in the least bit work related.

That made her think of Rand. For the first time ever, she wished she had unlimited texting. Because she'd send him a text right now, something naughty, something provocative. Something that would make him think about her all day long.

THE WEEK WAS INTERMINABLE. RACHEL NEVER THOUGHT SHE'D BE dying for Sunday night when she dropped the boys off at Gary's. But it was only Thursday, with seventy-two hours still to go.

She was definitely having withdrawals. What you couldn't have, you simply couldn't stop thinking about, and she wanted Rand badly. He was so right; desperation peaked when you couldn't get what you needed. She was desperate for him now, sexually frustrated, and snapping at everything.

"Principal Torvik is a dickhead." Nathan tossed his backpack on the kitchen table. He'd gone to another basketball game with his friends. Justin was already in his room doing his homework.

"Watch your language." There, she'd snapped at him, without even a *please.* When disciplining, she strove to be neutral, not angry, but she'd failed.

"Well, he *is.*" Nathan pouted.

"What did the principal do this time?"

Principal Torvik was the bane of Nathan's existence. She imagined the man resembled the short, bald principal on *Buffy the Vampire Slayer,* who barked loudly to make up for his lack of stature. She'd only made it to a couple of parent-teacher days this year and hadn't gotten a chance to meet the new principal yet. In years past, she hadn't missed a single school open house or meeting and had made a point to talk to each of her sons' teachers. She'd also known all the boys' friends, met their parents, mostly because of all the carpooling. There were so many things she didn't get a chance to do since going back to work.

Rachel recognized, however, that while Nathan blamed Principal Torvik, his own behavior was the problem. He'd started mouthing off in class, yet another negative effect of the divorce.

"He took my phone away." Nathan threw himself in a chair, making the spindly legs creak.

"What?" She couldn't afford another phone. "What do you mean he *took* it? Didn't he give it back?" Okay, there was discipline, then there was personal property.

"Yeah. But only at the end of the day. And I had to go into his office and listen to another of his stupid lectures."

She calmed down. He'd gotten the phone back. "About what?"

"Not using my cell phone in class." He rolled his eyes just like Justin did, or maybe Justin did it like Nathan. Then he deepened his voice in imitation of the beleaguered Principal Torvik. "It's disruptive and impolite. Blah, blah, blah."

There was a strict rule at the school that there was no talking or texting on cell phones during class. Rachel agreed with it. She also didn't like the way Nathan was making fun of an authority figure. She was at a loss as to what to do about his increasingly poor attitude, toward her and toward school. "Principal Torvik is right. You know you're not supposed to use your cell phone."

"I wasn't *using* it. I only took a picture to prove that Jonesy was sleeping at his desk."

"That's semantics, Nathan. Whether it's talking, texting, or taking a photo, it's *using* it."

"I don't *have* texting," he snarled.

She closed her eyes. She no longer knew how to have a reasonable discussion with him. If she agreed or said nothing, it was teaching him that bad behavior was acceptable. If she sided with the principal, she was the bad guy. Well, sometimes moms just had to be bad guys.

"The solution is not to use your cell phone in class."

"Geez, Mom, thanks for the advice." He stood up, skidding the chair across the linoleum, and dragged his backpack over the table as he stomped away.

"Please do your homework," she called to his back as he disappeared down the hall. Of course, he didn't answer. She blew out a breath. If she could just figure out what she was doing wrong and fix it. For now, the most effective thing she could come up with was to increase her income so they didn't have these constant money battles. She'd filled out the necessary forms to register for the city college online. The little window had come up, flashing a notice that it would take a few days to process her registration.

When she'd signed the divorce settlement that gave Gary responsibility for paying the full mortgage and property tax bill as long as she paid half the childcare expenses, she'd thought it was a great deal. She hadn't realized she'd need veto power over those expenses so that they weren't constantly fighting about it.

Whatever. She pulled out the frying pan. For some reason, it made her think of Rand. Out of the frying pan and into the fire. Oh, she wanted the fire. She was so ready for the fire. Sunday night. As soon as she dropped the boys off at Gary's.

It was the first time, she realized, that she was completely ready to get rid of the boys for a week.

8

DURING LUNCHTIME ON FRIDAY, RACHEL HAD LEFT RAND A MESsage. "I'm dropping the kids off at seven Sunday night."

It was pretty damn hot when just the sound of a woman's voice on a message made him hard. Rand had started making plans, but he hadn't gotten a chance to call her back until he'd finished his evening hour at the gym. By that time, she didn't answer.

"Come straight to my house after you drop them off," he said over voicemail. That was all. He hadn't told her what to wear, or reminded her to bring her vibrator. He said nothing about what he was going to do to her. But he planned. Big-time. All weekend until it was almost Sunday's appointed hour.

It wasn't a stretch to imagine, having been married to the same man for so many years, especially since she'd gotten married young, that she was inhibited. He would release her. Hell, that sounded like Prince Charming releasing Sleeping Beauty with a kiss, but he had a release of a wholly different nature in mind.

When his doorbell rang, half an hour remained before she was supposed to arrive. Yet he never doubted it was her.

She surprised him. He'd assumed she'd go for sexy, testing her newfound confidence after their last meeting. Instead she wore a flowered dress that covered her knees, and while it was pretty, his grandmother would have worn it. Her lips were painted a pale kissable pink that made him want to take her mouth. But not yet. That would come later.

"You are absolutely *fucking* perfect." He gave her the filthy word because he'd already taught her how good it was. "The schoolmarm I'm going to debauch."

She laughed. Without the smile, she could appear a bit somber. "Oh God, what are you going to make me do tonight? Watch again?" She shook her head. "No, you've probably fixed it so they'll be watching me this time."

"You're beginning to know me well." She was also right, what he had planned would involve watching, but he would be the one doing it.

She sobered a moment. "I don't know you at all." Her gaze tracked the features of his face. "That's what makes it exciting."

"Then let's begin." He stepped back to let her in. "Upstairs."

She carried a large purse slung over her shoulder. It could contain her vibrator. If not, he'd bought a spare. She wore low-heeled pumps, and he enjoyed the sway of her ass as he followed her up the stairs.

"Why did you wear that dress?"

Her hand trailing the banister, she spoke over her shoulder. "This is who I am with the boys and at work. I wanted to come here and have you change me into another woman."

Could she know how her words meshed precisely with all his plans for her? Oh, the law of attraction, they were *meant* to find each other. He wondered what she wore beneath the pretty flowered material. "Did your sons ask why you dressed up?"

She laughed again. "I know you told me to come straight here, but I dropped them off early and went back home to change."

He reached up and swatted her ass. She squealed, then punc-tuated it with a giggle.

"That's for not following orders," he said.

She gave him a wide-eyed look as she headed along the upstairs hall. "Are you a dom or something?"

So she'd been doing some Internet research. "No. I'm your teacher. We also demand that our orders be obeyed."

"Guess I'll just lie about it next time," she said flippantly, then stepped into his bedroom.

He'd closed the blinds over the back windows, lit a couple of scented candles, and left on only the lamp next to his reading chair. He sometimes liked to watch the sunset, but for now, he'd shifted the chair to face the bed. On the side table was a glass of red wine for him, and by the bed, a glass of white for her. The comforter was gone, leaving just the sheets and four pillows on the bed.

"Drink," he said. "It will help your nerves."

"I'm not nervous." Her pulse fluttered at her throat, belying her words, and she took a long swallow of the wine.

"Now remove your clothes."

Her skin flushed, and her breasts rose with a sharp intake of breath. "Just like that? No preliminaries?"

He settled himself in his reading chair. "What kind of pre-liminaries would you like?"

She set her purse on the bedside table next to the wineglass. "I don't know. You're rushing me."

He propped one ankle on the opposite knee and leisurely sipped his wine. "I'm not rushing at all. I'm so hot and hard just thinking about seeing you naked that you're lucky I haven't already ripped off your clothes."

She gasped, stared at him, a mischievous smile blossoming on her lips as she put her fingers to the button at her throat. "Well, if you put it like that."

She was pleased. His tone had been mild, but the words desperate, a perfect combination.

"Did you bring your vibrator?"

She nodded.

"We're going to need that, too. Why don't you start by tossing it in the center of the bed."

She eyed him. "I've never known a man who's quite so specific about what he wants."

She'd known very few men at all. He was lucky. He could train her. "You haven't known any *real* men," he said with inflection.

"True, true," she murmured, probably thinking he couldn't hear, as she rummaged around in her bag.

The vibrator bounced when she threw it on the bed. A very feminine pink, darker than her shade of lipstick, and plain. No rotating beads or pleasure bumps. It would do the trick nicely.

"Do you want me to perform a striptease?"

"I want whatever makes you wet and hot."

She rolled her lips between her teeth, thinking, then she swallowed. "I want to stand right in front of you," she said softly, hesitantly. He knew her desires warred with her fears, all the things a woman worried about. *Will he think I'm fat, will he like my breasts, will he think I'm pretty and gorgeous?*

"God, yes," he whispered. "I want to see every inch of you revealed up close. I want to smell you. I want to see the moisture on your skin and the glisten of your pussy."

He wanted to make himself crazy. Before he ever got to touch her.

HOW DID HE DO THAT? SHE WAS DRUNK, BUT IT WASN'T THE WINE. She was wet, but it wasn't a touch. It was the honey in his words. It was the lick of his gaze. Her skin felt pebbled with nervous goose bumps, yet his silver tongue went a long way toward quashing all those nerves. With just a look, he made her feel desirable rather than ridiculous.

She hadn't undressed for a man other than her husband in so many years, she'd forgotten what it felt like, the anticipation, the goose bumps, the nerves. Yet for Rand, her fingers went to the buttons of her matronly dress. She wanted to tear them free, almost as if she were freeing herself. Instead she slipped them loose slowly, one after another, watching his eyes as the irises deepened with desire to a darker hue.

She'd thought long and hard about what to wear tonight. She'd found that on the outside she wanted to look like what she was: a mom, a receptionist, an ex-wife. But underneath, she was all woman.

"Jesus Christ." The curse fell from his lips, and she gloried it in. "You're not wearing a bra."

She shook her head. "No." Then she stepped out of her shoes and pushed the dress over her hips. The material puddled at her feet.

"Fuck."

There was such reverence in that word. Such desperation.

"I would have fucked you on the stairs if I'd known you were completely naked under there."

He banished any nerves that still lingered. She continued to marvel over how he could do that.

Leaning close, he inhaled. "I can smell how wet you are."

With his nearness, she got wetter. She wanted him to touch her, lick her, make her come. But she let him be her teacher. "What do you want me to do now?"

"I want you on the bed. I want you to spread your legs for me. To touch yourself for me."

She swallowed. She'd known that was coming. Touching herself was for the dark of the night, when she was all alone. When she could let herself go, and scream and moan and toss her head on the pillow the way she never had when she was with Gary. It was too . . . embarrassing, like letting someone else see your innermost self.

Rand wanted it. Rachel wondered if she could give it to him, or if she'd freeze at the last moment, but she had to try.

She climbed on the bed, a heavy piece of furniture with a dark wood headboard and bedposts with decorative finials. He'd taken off the comforter to make sure her body didn't get lost in the thickness of it, and he could see every detail unhindered. She angled herself so that he could see her most private parts, then, taking a deep breath for courage, she rolled to her back and spread her legs.

"God, you're pretty."

He had such a way of speaking. He must have seduced a thousand women. Rachel pulled one of the plump pillows beneath her head so she could see him. "Is this how you want me?"

"Yes." He tugged at his belt, unzipped his jeans. Then he looked at her again. "I'm going to stroke myself while I watch you," he said, as if it were a warning. "But first, I want you to show me how wet you are."

She let him look.

"Go on, touch yourself," he urged.

She tunneled her fingers between the lips of her sex. She couldn't have imagined Mrs. Delaney doing this. But Rachel, the hot, sexy woman, oh yes. It was terrifying, amazing. Fire danced in Rand's eyes as he watched her circle her clitoris with a finger. She was wet like never before, hot like the coals burning at the very center of a conflagration. She closed her eyes and lifted her hips to meet the caress of her fingers. Moaning, she gave herself up to touch and feel.

Then she had to see him again. She'd thought she could do this for him by pretending she was alone. But she needed to see.

His hair was dark blond in the lamp's light, and his features were granite. His cock was a prominent bulge against his white briefs, visible through the open zipper of his jeans.

"The vibrator," he said.

She felt around on the bed, found it, twisted the base to High, then put it to the button of her clit. "Oh," she murmured. Then louder, "Oh yes, yes." She rotated her hips, playing the vibrator over herself with the movement of her body.

"You have no idea how beautiful you are." Shoving his briefs down to bare himself, he rubbed his cock. *Cock.* It wasn't a sweet word, but so elemental, so perfect, just like *clit* and *pussy* and *fuck.*

For a moment she closed her eyes and concentrated only on the sensation, the rise of her body, the heat flowing through her. She braced a hand against the headboard and bore down on the vibrator. She didn't care that she moaned and panted and groaned. She didn't care how undignified it all was.

Then she came back to him, opening her eyes.

"What were you thinking about?" His cock was big and hard in his hand as he stroked. She felt breathless watching, giddy that she had done that to him.

"I was thinking about you."

"Liar. I want your fantasies. Close your eyes, fuck yourself with the vibrator, and tell me what you think about when you're alone. Tell me what makes you the hottest."

He was a beguiler, a hypnotist, a magician. He made it easy to admit anything.

She still couldn't tell him about the massage. Even after all this time, and perhaps because of Rand's easy acceptance of everything, the memory of Gary's treatment of her was raw all over again. She couldn't admit to how she'd allowed Gary to make her feel immoral.

But there were other fantasies she'd had over the years. In the past few days, with sex consuming her, they'd come back. She'd done a lot more fantasizing than she'd originally remembered. "I dream about a pirate kidnapping me and having his wicked way with me."

Rand didn't laugh. "Rape fantasies," he whispered.

Yes, that's probably what it was, but she'd had them since she was a teenager and had read her first steamy romance novel. Pirates, barbarians, sheikhs, and yes, Vikings. A modern woman should deny that a fantasy rape was a turn-on. Rachel couldn't. Because it *was* fantasy; she'd never want it for real, but she loved imagining those steamy scenarios. "Or a handsome burglar breaking into the house." That was a good one, too.

"You hear something downstairs," he said, "but you're all alone and the electricity is out. You can't call anyone." He became a part of the fantasy.

"I can hear him enter the room." She slid the vibrator deep inside. Her body began to tremble. She closed her eyes, and there was only her fantasy and Rand's voice.

"He holds your hands and tears off your nightie."

"I'm so scared," she whispered. But she wasn't. She was wet, crazy with need.

"What does he do to you?"

"He fucks me, oh he fucks me, and he's so big."

The bed dipped as if her masked intruder were taking her. He pinched her nipple hard, and she cried out. "I don't want to like it, but I can't help it. My body just wants it."

"His cock is huge."

She felt his heat, smelled him, that hot, musky, aroused man scent. "He's so deep."

He circled her wrist, holding her arm high so that she couldn't bring it down. "You love the way he's fucking you."

"Yes, yes, it's terrible, but it's so much better than Gary. It's hot and hard and he wants me so bad. He forces me. I can't stop him."

"And you love it," he whispered in her ear.

"Yes, yes." She gasped with pleasure, the vibrator inside, on her G-spot, thrumming, making her mad. And him, Rand, close, watching her being taken, ridden, fucked. For a moment it was so real she could feel the pulse of a man inside her, the slickness of sweat between her legs, the wet sound of a cock slapping hard. Then she screamed, the world imploding around her, inside her, all over her, wet, sticky, hot, sweet, never ending.

9

SHE DIDN'T OPEN HER EYES FOR LONG MOMENTS. HER BLOND HAIR fanned out across the pillows, and the tips of her breasts were a dusky rose and still hard. His come bathed her stomach, glistening. He reached out slowly, rubbed it into her skin, up her abdomen, around her breasts, over her nipples, massaging the last vestiges of it into her chest so that she would smell him on her when she went home.

"Don't wash it off. I want you to sleep with it."

Rachel opened her eyes. Then she swallowed, and her gaze flitted away.

He held her chin, forced her to look at him. "That was perfect. Don't go embarrassed on me now."

She looked dazed. He put his hand to her cheek, his fingers still sticky with his own come, and took what he'd wanted when she'd first walked into his house tonight.

Her lips were sweet and plump beneath his. He slipped his tongue along the seam, then forced her to open. She moaned as if she'd been as desperate for the kiss as he. Desperation rose and waned. As he'd watched her hold the vibrator against herself, he'd wanted to be distant, to hold off. But as she'd spun her fantasy around them both, he'd needed to be there, right there. And now he had to have this kiss.

She wrapped her arms around his neck, anchoring him to her, until she was the one feasting on him. He steeped himself in her for long, sweet moments.

Then she fell back to the pillow and stared up at him. "I've never done or felt anything like that before."

He wanted to tell her that neither had he. He'd watched, he'd played, he'd *done* the same thing, but he'd never *felt* with the same intensity. Because he'd never before had a woman for whom all this was new. Her experience was more important than his own. "Tell me about that fantasy."

She blushed, something he would have thought was impossible to notice against her skin, already flushed with climax. "I'd never really want to be raped," she said, as if she had to justify herself.

"Neither would I." He smiled, petted her face, her neck, her shoulder, as if he were gentling a skittish animal. "But it's very hot to imagine waking to find myself tied to the bed by a sexy stranger who was just about to ride my cock. Completely against my will."

She snorted. "That's not the same."

He cupped her face, turning her to him. "No. It's not. But we can fantasize about anything we want."

"I used to read romance novels back in the days when the heroines were all kidnapped by pirates."

"It was a formative fantasy, then." She'd stopped reading them, he could tell, but she still trotted out that little female wet dream. He wondered how he could give it to her.

"You're like the fantasy," she whispered.

"An escape?"

She nodded. That wasn't a bad thing. Role-playing, fantasy, it was all a way to get her to drop her barriers.

Propped on his elbow next to her, their skin flush together, her heat reaching inside him, he played with the ends of her hair. "You did well tonight."

"Oh, did I?" She raised a brow saucily.

"Yes. I'm pleased with you, and I have to decide what we'll do tomorrow night."

"*Tomorrow* night?" She rose off the pillow.

"You'll have your sons back on Sunday, so I don't intend to miss a moment."

"I'll be exhausted."

"You mean you don't have an orgasm every day?"

She blushed again, a pretty pink hue. It was answer enough.

"Then we have to be sure you do," he said. "The more orgasms you have, the more you'll need."

"Isn't that the opposite of how it really works?" Her eyes flitted away as though she'd already found the answer for herself.

"No. A woman begins to crave orgasms. I want you to crave mine."

Yes, he wanted her to crave his orgasms, the ones he was responsible for, whether she gave them to herself while she fantasized about him or he gave them to her with his mouth, his hands, or his cock.

He leaned close, breathed in the scent of his come on her skin, then whispered against her hair, "Tomorrow night, I will do all the touching. And you will come more times than you can count."

RAND WAS RIGHT. HE WAS *ALWAYS* RIGHT. BY THE TIME SHE GOT home, she needed another orgasm. She smelled his come on her, and she came. She thought about his promise, how he'd execute it tomorrow night, and she came again. She thought about her fantasy burglar, and the orgasm simply dragged her under. She thought about all the nights in the week, all the things he could do to her, and she came again and again until she was so exhausted she couldn't move.

He was dirty and carnal. A voyeur and an exhibitionist. He was kinky.

Gary would never have watched her masturbate. He would never have come on her or rubbed his semen into her skin as if it were lotion. It had been so much more intimate than sex. Her definition of intimacy was changing. Intimacy was trusting a man enough to do things for him that you would never do for anyone else. The things your mother would have washed your mouth out with soap for mentioning.

Kinky wasn't bad; it was incredibly intimate. She would do just about anything he asked her to. What exciting thing would he want from her tomorrow night?

AFTER RETURNING FROM LUNCH THE NEXT DAY, RACHEL LOGGED into her personal email. She didn't make a habit of checking it at work, but if Rand had something special in mind for tonight, like a particular outfit or something he wanted her to bring, she might have to stop on the way home. Yeah, yeah, it was an excuse to get a kick out of talking to him, even if it was only email.

She'd given him her cell number, now her email address. Pretty soon, she'd tell him her last name and give him her home address. But Rachel didn't care. At the oddest moments, during her morning work routine, while she was getting ready for bed, she'd smell him, as if he were standing right behind her. He was intoxicating. He'd gotten into her head.

Her heart skipped a beat. There it was. His email handle was generic, as was hers, and the subject merely read "Tonight," but her pulse started to race anyway.

She opened the email.

Meet me at 8:30 on Skyline exactly 6.9 miles north of Highway 9, left-hand side.

He wanted her to go up to Skyline? Skyline Boulevard traversed the summit of the Santa Cruz Mountains. Six-point-nine miles north along Highway 9? There was nothing there that she could remember, although she wasn't sure whether that was past Woodside or not. Whatever. There was *something* there, and Rand had a plan.

"Yes, sir," she typed back, mentally saluting. It was fun, a game, not knowing what to expect. Hopefully tonight he would take her all the way. So far, they hadn't done much touching beyond that kiss. But what a kiss. Remembering, she melted all over again. He'd rubbed his semen all over her abdomen and breasts, but *he* hadn't made her come yet.

She was just logging out of her email when a scuffle out in the factory caught her attention.

"You idiot." Steve.

"It wasn't my fault." Matt.

"Then whose fault was it, kid?"

"I'm not a kid."

"No, you're a punk."

What the . . . ? With her office door facing the entry to manufacturing, Rachel could hear the yelling as if they were standing right in front of her.

Erin and Dominic were gone for two days, Yvonne was out for the afternoon, taking her daughter to the obstetrician, and Bree's door was closed. That left only Rachel, and Erin had told her to hold the fort while they were away. Of course, Yvonne hadn't liked that since she had seniority, but that didn't stop Rachel from taking her duty seriously.

"You shouldn't have—"

"I didn't—"

They were yelling over each other. Rachel marched out of her office and through the big arch into manufacturing. Steve was jabbing his finger at Matt's nose, and Matt's face was red enough to explode like an overripe melon.

The rest of the five-man manufacturing crew—though one of them was a woman—had made themselves scarce, either running down between the inventory shelves pretending they needed parts or out through the roll-up door at the back. Which was open, while the overhead heaters were blazing, wasting all that energy.

"What's going on?"

Neither of them listened to her. Honestly, they were like two big kids fighting on the playground, right in each other's faces. Matt was taller, but he was fifteen years younger and probably a hundred pounds lighter. Steve, whose bald head, stocky, muscled build, and tattoos screamed *motorcycle gang*, could have flattened Matt. Steve could flatten her, too.

But Erin had left her in charge. "Hey," she shouted over them. "If you two don't stop right this minute, I'm sending you to your rooms without dinner. Do you hear me?"

Matt pulled back, his lanky hair falling into his eyes, and looked at her. "What?"

"Do I need to repeat myself?"

Steve tilted his head, like a pit bull finally noticing the little pussycat. "Did you just tell me to go to my room?"

She stood taller. In her high heels, she was almost as tall as him. "Yes. Unless you both want to tell me what's going on." She glared at them. "Without yelling."

She thought she saw the wink of Steve's gold tooth before he cut off any hint of a smile. He stabbed a finger in Matt's direction. "This little asshole—"

"Language," she warned. If they wanted to be treated like kids, that's exactly what she'd do.

Steve's gold tooth flashed again, but this time he grimaced.

"This little miscreant put the wrong part numbers on all the transducers."

Rachel knew their products somewhat. Put simply, the way Erin had described it to her, the transducers were the probes used to make the ultrasonic measurements that the gauges recorded. "So put the right numbers on them."

Steve's jaw worked. He was their quality control technician, inspecting the parts before they were either shipped or put into inventory. Matt, she knew, had taken over the manufacturing of the transducers, which, until recently, had been outsourced.

"It is not my job to fix his mistakes."

"I didn't make a mistake," Matt jumped in. "We just had so many to get out today that I asked Fred"—their shipping and receiving clerk—"to put the part numbers on for me."

"So you're blaming Fred?" Steve got up in his face again.

Matt wasn't backing off like a sensible kid. "No, I—"

"I said stop." Rachel got right between them, pushing them apart with two hands like she was pressing weights. "Or I will put you in time-out."

That was enough to cool them down again.

"I gather the parts have the wrong number on them, but they have to go out today, and someone's got to fix it. You can worry about who's to blame later. For right now, let's figure out how to fix it."

They glared at each other, then at her.

"I'm waiting," she singsonged.

Steve huffed. "We have to stick the probes on a tester, figure out what they are, and re-mark everything. It's easy, but it will take time."

"How long?"

"All afternoon, but UPS is scheduled to pick up everything at four."

She glanced at her watch. They had two hours. "So let everyone take some."

"Susan and Tim have other orders to fill."

She growled low in her throat, like Marge Simpson. "Then let's put Matt, you, and Fred on it. I'll do some, too, if you show me how to use the tester."

They both stared at her.

"What?" she prompted.

"You're not a technician," Steve grumbled.

She narrowed her eyes. "Look, I can figure out exactly where to stick a probe." He wouldn't like where she put it if he didn't start cooperating. She stared him down.

He was silent a long moment, then his eyes began to twinkle. He let out a sharp bark of laughter. "Rachel, you're all right, you know."

She smiled back at him. He'd never really given her the time of day, as if she was *just* a receptionist.

"And, Matt, we're going to have to figure out what went wrong with Fred after we get the immediate problem fixed," she said.

"I—"

She held up a finger. "Later. Right now, get Fred, and Steve can show us how to use the tester."

"Yes, Rachel."

The two of them scurried off to do her bidding. Amazing. She allowed herself a small triumphant smile. See, she wasn't without skills useful in the workplace. Being a mom, she just happened to be great at conflict resolution.

10

DOWN IN THE TREES, IT WAS PITCH BLACK, BUT ABOVE, THE NIGHT along Skyline Boulevard was bright with stars and oddly warm, as if a storm was blowing in from the south. Warm was relative, though; it certainly wasn't summer weather. Rachel had dressed in a long wool skirt, matching sweater, and knee-high suede boots she'd had for years and worn only a handful of times.

She checked the trip odometer she'd set when she turned onto Skyline. Another couple of miles.

The trees bordering the road fell away into a landscape of rolling meadows, illuminated in her headlights for brief moments as she flashed by. As the tenths of the miles rolled over, she slowed. It would be a left turn. She didn't want to miss it.

Okay, six-point-nine. She pulled into a turnout and followed a dirt road as it sloped down to the left. Not far from the boulevard above, she saw Rand's parked car, just a dark shape against a darker night. He leaned against the hood, staring into the night.

Turning off the engine and killing the lights, she climbed out.

There was nothing but sky and stars and the dark blobs of the mountains.

"Come here." He held out his hand.

Rachel took it, and he pulled her down to lean on the hood beside him. The metal was still warm from his drive.

"Look at that," he said.

"I can't see anything."

He sighed. "All those people down on the flats, yet up here, there's nothing, no one, just us and an ocean of stars."

Behind them, a car whooshed by on the road, its headlights cutting the same path she'd made along the ridge. "Not quite alone," she answered. "Civilization still rears its ugly head."

He glanced back at the dying taillights. "Someone could see us if they looked for us."

With the car hood warming her bottom, it wasn't terribly cold, but soon she'd have to ask him to wrap his arms around her for heat. "So, what are we doing here?"

He looked once again at the hills that rolled down to the sea. "Car sex."

"Car sex?"

He smiled, and she thought she could see starlight twinkling in his eyes. "Yeah. Sex in a car. Didn't you ever do it in the back of your boyfriend's car?"

"No." She was the girl who'd wanted to wait. Then she'd dated boys who already had apartments. It was much harder to say no in an apartment. Then there'd been Gary.

"Well, I thought we'd kill two birds with one stone. Car sex and sex outdoors."

"You mean right here, right now?"

His teeth gleamed in his smile. "That's exactly what I mean."

"Isn't there supposed to be some romantic buildup?"

"You mean where we fumble around in the backseat like teenagers until finally you say yes after I have my hand up your skirt?"

She laughed. "That's not exactly romantic."

He pulled away from the hood and stood in front of her. Then, in a flash, he pushed her to her back against the warm metal, and fastened his lips on hers. It was so fast, so carnal, she opened her mouth to him and wrapped her arms around his neck to mold their bodies together. He tasted fresh, spicy, hot, and he was already hard for her.

When she was dizzy, he backed off a fraction, and whispered against her lips. "Changed my mind. We won't do the backseat. We'll do it right here on the hood."

"What if someone sees us?" No one would see them. But it made her hotter thinking that maybe, just maybe, someone on the road would glance down at the right moment, and see two writhing bodies on the hood of his car.

Sliding his hands down her flanks, he tugged her skirt until it was high enough for her to spread her legs and let him in. His jeans rubbed her bare inner thighs, his hard cock pressed to her center.

He cupped her butt in his big hands, pulling back a little farther. "Where are your panties?"

"At home."

"Slut." He dove in for a hard, hot kiss on her mouth. "Have you been thinking all day about fucking me?"

"No," she said, stroking his hair, so soft. "I've been thinking all day about"—she hesitated only a fraction of a second—"sucking your cock."

He pushed hard between her legs. God, she wanted to feel him without the jeans between them.

"You wanna suck me?" He slid a hand down between them and put his finger to her clit.

She simply sighed. It didn't feel like the first time he'd touched her intimately. It was more like he knew every inch of her body and what she needed.

"I think it would be better if I licked you"—he bent to nip her earlobe, his fingers like magic between her legs—"then fucked you."

She blew out a breath, mostly to cover her rising need. "I just don't know how I could turn down an offer like that."

He shoved his hands beneath her armpits and hauled her higher on the hood. Another car shot by on the road, but she didn't care as he eased down between her legs to blow warm breath on her.

For a moment, she saw herself, spread-eagled, a man between her legs. She'd only arrived five minutes ago. He moved so fast. There should have been a progression: kissing, petting, touching her breasts, then heading lower. Yet he overwhelmed her. He put his mouth to her pussy, and she cried out, loudly, her voice filling the night.

He spread her lips with his fingers and licked her clitoris, sucked it, circled it.

There'd never been anything like this, no one like *him*. He treated her as if he'd been put on earth to do this to her, as if it were the only thing that was important to him. She reveled in how he made her feel, the pure down-and-dirty physicality of stretching out under a canopy of stars and letting him do anything he wanted, everything she wanted.

"Oh God, oh God." She panted, twisting on the car hood still warm from the engine, or maybe from the heat her body generated, then she shoved her fingers through his hair and held him close. "Oh yes, oh yes." She didn't care that she wailed or moaned or chanted; there was just his tongue on her, his lips, his hot, wet mouth. Her husband had done it a few times in the beginning, but never like this, never like he *loved* licking her, like her pussy was ambrosia to him, her juice the sweetest of wines.

Then Rand put a finger inside her, taking her with his hands and his mouth, and Rachel shouted in total abandon. "Don't stop, oh God, yes, please, don't stop." The sound of her own voice shot her higher, the cries multiplying the sensations, magnifying them, until above her, all the stars burst in the night sky, showering down on her, burning her up.

SHE TASTED SO SWEET. SHE CAME SO HARD, CRYING HIS NAME INTO the darkness. Rand didn't want her to come down before he got inside her. He wanted her to climax again before the first orgasm ended. He made fast work of the condom, then rolled her to her stomach on the hood, pulled her down till her boots touched the ground, and shoved her skirt up over her shapely ass.

"Hold on, baby." He didn't need to test to know she was wet enough for him. He put his cock to her and pushed inside. She took him all the way. Then for a long moment, he rested on her, feeling the twitches of her body beneath him.

"Oh my Lord, that feels so good," she whispered with tears on the backs of her words. "Fuck me, Rand, please. I've dreamed about it so many times. Please, please."

Desperation. That's what he needed. He moved inside her. "Like this?"

"Yes, please, faster, harder."

A car flashed by on the highway, and he plunged deep. She stretched her arms out, curling her fingers around the edge of the hood along the windshield, and braced herself for him. An owl hooted, and he took her again. She moaned and pushed back, trying to force his penetration deeper. He held her hips and fucked her the way she wanted, buried himself in her heat. She smelled so sweet, and her moans were so fucking hot. The night rolled them in darkness and cool air, but their bodies created a fire to ward it off.

It didn't feel like the first time. It felt like they'd been doing this forever.

He levered himself up on his arms and took her, her breath panting out with each thrust. Then, on the inside, she clenched around him, worked him with her climax until he could no longer hold off his own. The orgasm was hard, blinding, excruciating, stealing his awareness of anything but the contraction of his balls and the heat of her body.

How long he lay prone atop her, Rand couldn't say. She didn't tell him to move. Finally, her cheek pressed to the metal, she whispered, "Wow." Then she pushed against him lightly and twisted her arm to see the glowing dial of her watch. "Fifteen minutes. I don't think I've ever come twice in fifteen minutes."

"I'm good."

She elbowed him. "You mean *I'm* good."

He wanted to gather her into his arms and cradle her in the backseat. But she was already pushing him off and trying to straighten her skirt. Bad man that he was, he littered, tossing the condom, then zipped his jeans. When he turned back, she put her hand to his cheek.

"No one's ever done that to me before."

"Fucked you on the hood of his car along the side of a road?"

"Wanted me, licked me, lifted my skirt, and taken me. Like you couldn't wait."

"I couldn't. I've imagined fucking you for weeks." He smoothed her hair. "Reality was better than fantasy."

"Sweet talker." She smiled. "You make me feel like a teenager." Then the laughter drained away. "I needed that."

He felt the *but* wanting to come out at the end of that sentence, yet she didn't add anything. "There are more surprises to come." He'd spent far too much time making plans. "They're going to be fucking hot. It'll be good for you that I have to keep topping myself."

"I'm sure it will." Then she stepped away from his touch. "I'd better go. It's late."

He wanted her to stay. "I promise not to make you drive so far tomorrow night."

"Tomorrow night?" she echoed.

"Every night that your boys are gone. An orgasm a day keeps the doctor away," he quipped.

She blinked. "I think it's an apple a day."

"You say apples, I say orgasms."

She didn't laugh the way he thought she would. "All right. Email me." There was something in her voice. He wasn't sure what exactly. Just that she was pulling away emotionally as well as physically.

He reached out to reel her back in. His hand on the nape of her neck, he held her close for a kiss, openmouthed, sweet, with a hint of the fire still burning inside him.

"I'll follow you to make sure you're safe." He felt her stiffen and added, "Just till we get into Saratoga."

In town, just at the bottom of Highway 9. "Right," she agreed softly.

But he lied. When they hit Saratoga, he put some distance and a couple of cars between them and saw her home safely.

GOD, IT HAD BEEN RISKY AND SEXY AND INTENSE, OVERWHELMING. Closing the front door, Rachel slid to her bottom on the entry floor. She hugged herself. Her breasts were still sensitive, her body still humming. She felt completely carnal, a different woman in her own skin. It had been so fast, yet so devastating. She'd screamed, she'd begged. She hadn't sounded or felt like herself out there, and it had been so good. He'd rocked her world in less than fifteen minutes. That wasn't merely devastating, it was terrifying.

The stars had been bright over her as he took her with his

tongue. Then his body had been hot and deep inside. She'd come so hard, her eyes were wet when he was done.

Yet it wasn't enough. She'd wanted to beg him to take her again in the backseat, to tell him once wasn't enough, that she didn't think she could ever get enough.

That's why she'd run. Because she couldn't *handle* more. This wasn't a relationship. It was supposed to be casual. Yet there was nothing casual about how much she dreamed of him, waking, sleeping, it didn't matter. But she did not have room in her life for more. She just simply didn't. She had to keep it on a purely physical level, no emotion.

She would see him again, of course. She'd see him tomorrow night. But by then, she'd have herself under control. She wouldn't be needy. It would be sex, really good sex, but *just* sex.

Except that sitting on the floor, her back to the door, she could still feel the imprint of his body on hers, still taste his kiss. He was so tall, so big, so male that she felt like a princess in his arms, cared for, adored, cherished.

She might very well be going back for *that*. It was the most frightening thought of all.

11

ON TUESDAY, THERE WERE NO MAJOR BLOWOUTS LIKE THE ONE
the day before. Even Yvonne hadn't groused about Rachel being
in charge. She was too busy showing everyone her daughter's new
ultrasound. Still, Rachel's day would have been a whole lot better
if Gary hadn't called.

"Can you take the boys tonight, Rachel?"

Tonight? Was he insane? She had a date with Rand. Her ears
started to roar like a Mack truck rushing by. No date with Rand?
No fast, hot, overwhelming intensely perfect sex with Rand? Obviously her little pep talk on the entry floor about *not* being obsessed
hadn't stuck.

What really pissed her off, though, was knowing Gary wanted
the night for a little Valentine's celebration with his twenty-five-
year-old girlfriend.

"Gary, you can't just call up at the last minute and change all
the plans." She thought she sounded exceptionally rational.

"Why? Have you got a hot date or something?" His voice was
sour.

As a matter of fact . . .

Of course, she wasn't going to say yes. She didn't want anyone to know about Rand, not the boys and especially not Gary. But she also couldn't turn it around on him. She only knew about his little nymphet through Justin, and she didn't want to drag her son into the middle of it like he was a tattletale. "No, Gary. I don't. I just expect a little courtesy."

"It can't be helped. I've got a business engagement that just came up, the auditors, and they want to discuss several audit issues over dinner."

It was a long, needless explanation. Sure, it was year-end, but he'd never had *dinner* with the auditors. But if he did, he'd have said just that, *I've got an audit meeting.* So he was lying.

Her blood boiled. She couldn't be with Rand if she didn't tell Gary she had a date she couldn't break, but that opened up a can of worms she had no wish to deal with. She wouldn't put it past him to tell the boys she was seeing someone. He'd do it just to be ornery.

She realized how resentful and angry her thoughts sounded in her own head. She couldn't remember ever feeling quite this bitchy before. "All right, Gary, I'll take them tonight. But you need to be more thoughtful in the future. I require at least a day's notification."

He laughed. "Since when?"

Since he'd started dating a much younger floozy, she wanted to shout. "Since I've decided to go back to school and get my AA degree."

"What the hell?"

There, that got him back.

"You heard me, back to school. I'm going to take some computer classes and work toward an AA degree in accounting."

"How the hell are you going to take care of the boys *and* go back to school?" he demanded.

"It requires good time management. Which means I won't be able to change plans for you at the last minute." She sounded so prim, so proper, so snooty.

"Fine. But don't expect me to take the boys so you can study for some exam."

"I won't."

"I don't know why you're doing this."

So she could have money to pay for all the things *Gary* decided the boys needed. "Because I want to, Gary. That's all you need to know. I don't have to ask your permission anymore to do what I want." She felt her blood pressure rising.

Across the roundhouse, Yvonne looked up from the copy machine, and Rachel realized she'd raised her voice. Dammit. She was letting Gary get to her. She pulled back, tried to sound reasonable. "It will help to pay for expenses, with the boys needing more things." Like team uniforms, school trips, iPods, MP3s, notebook computers, driving lessons, and cell phones. Justin would be a freshman next year, and before she knew it, he'd be wanting his driver's permit, too.

Gary snorted. "You make it sound like you bear the brunt of it. I'm the one that has to pay the mortgage."

"You're the one who left," she said sharply, then closed her eyes. Jesus, she didn't want to do this. She never should have told him about going back to school. It wasn't his business anyway. And she should have broken the news to the boys first. Whatever, it was done now.

"Fine, Rachel, if you want to be like that. Will you take the boys tonight or not?"

"I already said yes. You call and tell them to come home after school."

"Fine."

"And enjoy your dinner."

He hung up on her.

She sat for a long moment, her hands clenched so tightly her fingernails bit into her palms.

They hadn't fought during their marriage. They hadn't fought when it was over. There was a lot of seething resentment, sure, but now, for the first time, they were fighting about *not* taking the boys.

He'd started dating a floozy, she was having casual sex with Rand, and suddenly, everything was falling apart.

"I CAN'T MAKE IT TONIGHT. MY HUSBAND NEEDS ME TO TAKE THE boys."

Rand sensed a hesitancy in her voice. Did she expect him to get mad? "That's fine. Life happens. Tomorrow night, then."

"Look, I'm not sure we should do this *every* night. Maybe just once a week would be better."

So he hadn't imagined that subtle pulling away last night. "Is something wrong, Rachel?" Cell phone to his ear, he rose to close his office door.

"No. It's just that I'm not used to"—she hesitated, her breath sharp—"every night."

"Not used to *what* every night?" He needed to force her to spell it out, so they could talk about it and dispense with it.

She spelled it out. "S-E-X," she whispered, loud enough for him to hear.

"I'm sorry to hear that. But that's what I'm trying to change for you. A woman deserves to have her body worshipped *every* night."

She was silent, but he detected indistinguishable noises in the background so he knew she hadn't disconnected.

"I want to fuck you, Rachel. Every day, every night. Under the stars or on top of a bed. Last night was hot. But you promised to suck my cock, and you haven't done that yet."

Ah, there it was, her slight intake of breath. "Stop that," she murmured.

"I'm hard. If you were here right now, I'd fuck you on my desk. Have you ever done it on a desk at work, Rachel?"

"No." Her voice was breathy.

"Well, you need to. Perhaps I should come over there right now, close your office door, bend you over your desk, and fuck you from behind."

She gasped. "No."

He smiled to himself. "But you want it, don't you?"

"You're crazy," she murmured.

"Don't deny yourself."

Then she sighed. "Yes, I'm crazy, too. I'll see you tomorrow night."

He smiled to himself. "Shall I meet you in your office?"

She laughed. "I've got windows along the front of my office."

"Even better." Christ, he'd love to show up at her workplace late at night and take her over her desk. Or on the copy machine. Against the filing cabinet. He was hard, being taken in by his own fantasies, which wasn't a good thing right now since he had some appointments coming up. "All right, I relent on the questions. You can come to my house, and I'll do you on the kitchen counter."

"You're raunchy, you know."

"Yeah. And you like it."

She whispered something, and it wasn't until he'd hung up that he realized what she'd said. *I love it.*

RACHEL WAS SORE, BUT IN SUCH A DELICIOUS WAY. SHE'D BEEN TO his house three nights in a row, Wednesday, Thursday, and Friday. He'd taken her in every room of the house and in every position possible. He'd even done her on the backyard lawn. She'd tried to be quiet. He'd considered doing her on the deck outside his bedroom, but he admitted that he'd rather keep his exhibitionist tendencies under wraps in his own neighborhood. Unlike his neighbors.

God, she was in lust, completely and totally in ever-loving lust.

Sex wasn't the only good thing. Erin complimented her on how well she'd handled the shop while they were gone, especially the little tiff between Matt and Steve. Rachel took all the credit without saying it was like handling teenage boys. Yeah, things were looking up. More responsibility, then eventually more money.

On Saturday, she took a leisurely bath, thinking to herself how much she'd love a turn in Rand's claw-foot tub. They hadn't done that yet. One of these nights, she'd suggest it. Maybe tonight. She shaved her legs, then, without giving herself too much time to think, she trimmed her pubic hair. Opening a jar of homemade lavender-scented sea salt scrub her sister had sent for Christmas, she exfoliated until her skin was as soft as the proverbial baby's bottom. After the bath, she smoothed on buckets of lotion, then dressed without panties or bra, because Rand loved to simply lift her skirt and do her. She was almost forty years old, a few strands of silver starting to show at her temples, fine lines at the corners of her eyes, and this man still wanted to do her three times a night. Yes, *three* times one of those nights. Rachel smiled into the mirror as she applied her makeup.

She had a complete handle on it now. It was just sex. Really, really great sex, but honestly, she wasn't having any scary emotions about it. She wasn't even angry with Gary about his girlfriend, who was over at his apartment almost every evening, according to Justin, though she never spent the night. Rachel would have put her foot down on that.

If she wanted her privacy, she had to give Gary his, too.

She'd let her hair dry with the hairspray on it, to give it extra body, and now she fluffed it. Perfect.

The college had sent an email confirmation that she was registered to attend, and this morning, she'd signed up for the computer class covering basic spreadsheet and word processing. It started the first Tuesday in April, once a week, three hours. On the weeks she had the boys, Nathan would have to babysit Justin. Though God forbid she should use *that* term in front of Justin; he was *not* a baby. She'd discuss the whole thing with them tomorrow when they got home. She hoped to God Gary hadn't told them, but he'd probably want to win brownie points by making her look bad. Whatever. She'd think about that tomorrow. Tonight, she'd enjoy her last date with Rand for a week.

When she arrived at his house, he pulled her inside, pushed her against the wall, and slid his hands under her dress. She'd worn the leopard print again.

"No panties, you dirty bitch."

God, she loved it when he did that, called her names with that cheeky grin and dimples blossoming. She fought his hands away. "And you're a filthy man. You didn't even offer me a glass of wine before you attacked me."

They never ate dinner together. Sometimes he had cheese, crackers, fruit, snacks, but they didn't have dinner and they didn't go out. They just had sex. It was perfect.

"Upstairs." He grabbed her hand, hauled her up against him, and lifted her until she spread her legs around him and locked her ankles at the small of his back. He liked to carry her around like that, sort of he-man and all. He loved lifting her and doing her against the wall. Or on the counter. He just plain loved doing her.

Being wanted was power. She'd never felt so powerful.

"I've got big plans for you tonight," he declared.

One arm looped around his neck as he climbed the stairs, she put her hand between them to palm his cock. *Cock, pussy, dirty bitch, slut, fuck*; she'd started to love all those words. "Something certainly feels big down there," she teased.

"Oh yeah." He grinned and pulled her tight against him.

He was hard for her. She didn't have to work at exciting him. He saw her, he wanted her. He could stay hard for a long time before he came. The man had control with a capital C.

In the bedroom, he simply tossed her on the bed. She squealed, loving it. Sex with him was so easy. There was no baggage, no fear he might reject her. He required no special ritual, no perfect words. She'd realized that the marriage bed was a battlefield. Rand's bed was just something soft he could take her on over and over.

"So tonight we're going to have a special Olympic event."

She snorted. "What? Pole jumping?"

He grinned. "Olympic cocksucking."

He made sex such fun, another thing she'd never had, yet she couldn't imagine doing it any other way now. "And how many competitors do we have?"

"Just you."

She rolled to her stomach and propped herself on her elbows to look up at him. "Doesn't that mean I win by default?"

"No." He grabbed something from the table. "We're going to document your performance, then critique it. We both score you."

Document? Then she saw what he held in his hand. A camera. Her stomach plunged. "You're going to videotape me?"

"Yes." He tossed the video camera on the bed beside her. "I want to watch you suck my cock, every subtle nuance that I miss when you're actually doing it."

A chill skittered down her spine. She sat up. "I don't want to be taped." She'd sucked his cock. It wasn't such a terrible thing, kind of enjoyable in fact, but she hadn't swallowed, and she wasn't sure she'd done a great job at it. Rand was so much more eloquent when he was fucking her, using every dirty word in the book to tell her how much he loved sinking deep inside her.

She didn't want to critique herself, and she didn't want to see herself on video.

He looked at her a long moment. "I'll give you the SD card. You can preview the video yourself. Then, if you like it, we can watch it together the next time."

"But—" She didn't want to say the words. But really, what if someone *else* saw it?

"I'm not going to give it to anyone, Rachel. I'm not going to put it on the Internet."

She swallowed. "I didn't mean that."

"Yes, you did." He sat next to her, one leg bent at the knee, his other foot braced on the carpet, then he leaned into her, stroked her cheek. "I'm not going to hurt you, Rachel, not in any way. But I want this, to see the two of us. It's so different from doing it. But the video card is yours, not mine, and if you decide you want to erase it without showing it to me, you can do that. Just give it a chance first."

She flipped her hair over her shoulder, picked at the comforter. "I don't think I'll like myself on camera." Didn't they say it added ten pounds?

He trailed a finger along her jaw. "You will be so fucking beautiful with your mouth full of my cock."

He had such a way with words, the ability to take a filthy, dirty statement like that and make it an endearment.

"You're safe here, Rachel. I might push your limits, but I'll always keep you safe."

She sighed. "If I could just let go of all these fears." Then she immediately regretted admitting she had fears at all.

But Rand put his lips to hers, kissed her, then whispered, "So just let them go."

He made it sound so easy. He'd give her the card. She could watch it and if she hated it, she could erase it. It would never truly be in his possession. But what if she liked it? What if she enjoyed watching herself? What if they watched it together? How would that change their relationship?

Maybe another woman would try to figure out how he could screw her over, how he could download the video without her knowledge and share it with his disgusting buddies or post it on the Web for all the world to see.

Rachel didn't try to work out all the possibilities. She didn't believe he'd do anything like that. She'd known him less than a month, she'd fucked him a dozen times, if you counted multiple times in a night. She didn't *know* him really. Yet she didn't believe he'd harm her. She *wanted* to do as he said, let it all go.

"I'd like to see it," she whispered, then looked at him. "I want to perform." She put her hand on his thigh. "I want to suck your cock until you scream, then swallow every last drop." She licked her lips. His eyes followed. "Then I want to make you watch it all over and over."

"Done," he said. He pulled her off the bed. "Now take off your clothes, get on your knees, and suck me, baby."

Oh God, she'd completely lost her mind. Because she wanted it badly. And she did exactly what he told her to.

12

THE MOMENT SHE AGREED, RAND STRIPPED DOWN AND STARTED filming her.

On camera, she seemed almost shy unzipping her dress. Then she let it drop to the floor. She wore nothing beneath, her skin creamy white, her nipples already pearled with excitement, her pretty pussy freshly trimmed.

"You're fucking hot," he murmured, for her, for the camera.

She smiled hesitantly, her hands fluttering as if she wanted to cover herself.

"Leave the shoes, but kick the dress aside."

She did so with a flourish.

"Now get on your knees, baby." He watched her graceful fall on the small screen.

Her lips were lushly red, her eyes bright as she looked up at him. "Are you going to hold the camera the whole time?"

He laughed. "Part of the time. Then I'm going to put it on the tripod." He pointed to the setup next to the chair. In hopes that she'd say yes, he'd already placed the tripod in the best spot for the best shot.

As he stood above her next to the bed, she sat back on her haunches, her spine straight, her hands primly in her lap, strategically covering her pussy. "Now what?"

"Do what comes naturally."

She made a face that looked sexy and teasing for the camera. "None of this comes naturally." But she reached for his cock. He angled the lens to take in her fist wrapping around his hard flesh.

"That's it, stroke it, baby."

She caressed him slowly, almost leisurely, then ran her thumb over the tip, gathering a drop of pre-come to swirl over the head. "Mmm, you must like this."

"You know I love it."

She cupped his balls, squeezing him. Heat shot through his body.

"You're corrupting me," she said, then leaned into him before he could answer and sucked the crown of his cock.

"Christ." The top of his head felt like it would blow off. He could barely hold the camera steady as sensation rocketed through him. "I must be doing a damn good job of corrupting, then, because this is perfect."

"Mmm." Her mouth vibrated around him. She slid him deeper, her eyes closing, her lashes fanned against her cheeks, fingernails a flashy red around the base of his cock as she held him. That was new; she didn't normally paint her nails.

Then she opened her eyes and looked up at him.

"Jesus," he uttered with awe. She was so fucking beautiful, her lips and nails the same decadent red against his cock, her face flushed, her eyes a brilliant green where usually they were a gentle hazel. The soft lighting of the room bathed her body with golden hues, and her black pumps, the only thing she wore, were sexy as hell. When she saw the video, she would fall in love with her own image.

"Suck me, baby, please," he begged. His need would come through clearly. She would *feel* how badly he wanted her.

Closing her eyes once again, she slid her mouth over him until she left lipstick prints on her hand. Then she pulled all the way back to work the slit of his crown with her tongue.

"Fuck," he whispered. He wanted to close his eyes and revel in the sensation, but he didn't want to miss the sight either.

She swirled her tongue down the length of him, blew his mind on the suck back up. She did him fast, she did him slow, she worshiped the tip, then dragged her teeth down him. And all the time, she squeezed and stroked his balls. Had he taught her that? She'd said she'd rarely done this for other men, but for him, she'd become an expert.

"Baby, baby, baby, that's so good."

Up, down, inside out, and around, she took him, until his legs started to tremble and his guts churned with need. His balls were tight, he was so close, just another moment of heaven.

"Wait. Stop."

She opened her eyes, his cock filling her mouth. Beautiful. Perfect.

"It's time to put the camera on the tripod."

She didn't resist one last hard suck that left him almost mindless. His legs felt like rubber, and his hands shook as he affixed the camera to the tripod. He collapsed in his reading chair, spread his legs, and patted his thighs. "Come here."

She crawled across the carpet on her knees, and he wished to God he'd had that on video, too. Next time.

When she was between his legs, he hit Record on the remote connected to the camera, which also gave him zoom capability at the push of a button. With the view he'd angled it at, his cock sliding in and out of her mouth would be fully visible.

"Take me again, baby, I'm all yours."

"You're right," she murmured, wholly aware of her power over him in that moment.

She took him in her mouth and sucked in earnest. Rand simply laid his head back against the chair and closed his eyes. His hips rose involuntarily, fucking her mouth as she sucked him.

"Jesus, baby, you're so goddamn good at that," he praised. "You're killing me." His legs began to tremble, and his nuts were hard with need.

Then she took her hand away and deep-throated him. He almost cried, it was so fucking sublime. He punched zoom on the remote, held it that way for long moments, then zoomed out again.

"God, you're a quick study."

She hummed her pleasure at his compliments, and he felt it thrum through his cock. She was the perfect student, learning exactly what he liked by the sounds he made. She circled her tongue just under the ridge of his cock, he groaned, and she knew to come back to that. She teased his slit, he gasped, and she remembered, returning again and again to the spot to drive him crazy.

His balls were so tight, they were ready to explode.

"Not yet, baby." He pulled free of her luscious mouth. "Get on my lap facing the camera." He grabbed a condom he'd laid on the side table, tore the package, and rolled it on, then shifted for the best camera angle.

"I thought you were just going to videotape me sucking you."

"This'll be better." He guided her, helped her spread her legs over him, his sheathed cock rising up. Putting a finger to her clit, he tested her. Her body jerked, and she sighed. It was the first time he'd touched her tonight, yet moisture bathed his fingers. "You're so fucking wet. Put me inside you. I want you to see me taking you on camera." He prayed to God she'd let him watch, too.

"Yes," she murmured, her hair falling forward as she took his cock in hand and rubbed herself with the tip.

He would die to see the perfect look of concentration cross her face. She would forget about the camera. There would be just his cock inside her, just her body riding him.

"Fuck me," he murmured. "I need you to fuck me so bad."

She rose, her thighs taut as she balanced herself, fit him in, dipped, taking just his crown. Then, God help him, she contracted her muscles around him.

"Fuck." He almost came. "Where'd you learn that?"

"When you did me on the kitchen table the other night."

He remembered. It had been good, but this, the angle, maybe even the camera, made it so much hotter.

She began to ride him, taking him deeper with every downstroke.

He held her hips. "Perfect, baby."

Hands on the armrests, shoes braced on the carpet, she took him. Before, it had always been the other way around, him taking her, but now, he was all hers. She had all the control, her body squeezing him, milking him. He groaned, filling the room with the sound of his need and the erotic slap of their bodies, hot, wet, sweaty skin to skin.

"Yes, yes, yes," she chanted.

He reached up to pinch her nipples, and she cried out. Her body gushed around him, climaxing hard, but she didn't stop fucking him. She rode the wave, panting, moaning, writhing, clenching until he thought he'd either come or die.

In some small part of his tiny reptilian brain, he knew he'd never had it like this, never found a partner quite like her, a sweet and potent mixture of lady and whore, of student and teacher, of slave and master.

Then she killed him by pulling away.

* * *

"JESUS CHRIST, DON'T STOP."

She loved the crazy need in his voice, the vein throbbing at his temple, the wildness in his eyes. She rolled off the condom and tossed it on the empty package in the trash.

"You want a perfect video," she said, stroking him, squeezing him. "And I'm going to give it to you."

Her body still quaked with the aftershock of orgasm, the sensation of him inside her, the taste of his pre-come on her tongue. He was salty, yet slightly sweet, unexpectedly delicious, but it was also the way his body trembled for her, how badly he needed her mouth on him.

She licked the crown of his cock, running her tongue around the ridge, then along the slit. He groaned, laid his head back, his body arching deeper into her mouth. He made her love doing this, tasting him, the texture of his cock against her tongue and lips.

She slipped him free long enough to talk to the camera. "I'm going to make you come so hard, your eyes will roll." She squeezed his balls, and he jerked, opened his eyes a mere slit, but said nothing, as if he were no longer capable of speech.

She sucked him hard and fast, pumping her fist around him, then pulled back, playing him. "You're going to come in my mouth. You're dying for it."

"Jesus, yes."

"You're mine," she said to his cock and loved the power of his groan.

Sucking just his crown, she stroked him with a tight grip, her thumb and finger just below the ridge of his cock in a spot she'd quickly learned that he loved. She knew his body, what he liked, what made him rise fast, what kept him from coming before she was ready. But until this moment, she hadn't thought to use any of it. Not until the camera. Not until she wanted to prove how good she was. She wanted him powerless, crazy, all hers. *This* was what made cocksucking perfect, what made her love it beyond the sweetness of his taste and the scent of him in her nostrils. Because he loved what *she* did to him.

He shoved his fingers through her hair and held her close, his body arching, falling. His muscles tensed and bulged. The scent of come and sexy male sweat rose off him like perfume. He filled her mouth with salty sweetness, not his full essence, but the precursor. He called her filthy names in a guttural voice.

Then he said *her* name, almost with reverence. "God, Rachel, yes, Rachel, perfect, Rachel. Rachel, fuck, Rachel."

She melted somewhere deep inside. The sound of her name on his lips right along with that dirty word was the sweetest endearment she had ever heard.

Then he jerked, held her fast, his cock throbbing, his taste filling her. She drank him in, but he kept coming. At the last moment, still feeling the spurt of him, she pulled off and took him on her cheek, her lips. She wanted that for the camera.

She wanted him to see that she owned him in that moment. That she'd fucked him, swallowed him, and taken him on her face.

If she decided to show him the video, of course.

He was still breathing hard, the vein at his temple thick and pulsing, but he opened his eyes, reached down and hauled her onto his lap.

"Fuck," he whispered.

She could never have imagined that word sounding so beautiful. Like a testament.

"You have come all over your face."

She laughed. "You were supposed to say something romantic."

"My come on your face is totally romantic." He wiped it

away, then circled her nipples with it, rubbed it in like it was scented lotion.

She licked the last of it from her lips and thought she would never forget the taste of him. Not ever. How could she not have liked doing this? Only because before it hadn't been Rand. That was disloyal to Gary, but she didn't give a damn.

He wrapped his arms around her, and she snuggled deeper into his chest, pulling her knees up. She'd lost the shoes somewhere along the way, not really remembering when.

"Fuck," he said again, then pulled back to look at her from beneath half-closed lids. "I knew it was going to be good, but you still managed to amaze me."

She petted his face, then burrowed into his neck and kissed the salty skin of his throat. "I bet you say that to all your women."

"No one's ever amazed me like you."

She felt pleased yet shy. "It was the camera. It got your motor running."

He kissed the top of her head. "It was your cocksucking."

She laughed. "You're so genteel."

He lifted her chin. "You're perfect." Then he kissed her.

She forgot everything and simply reveled in his mouth, his lips, his tongue against hers, his taste mingling with hers.

"I smell my come on you. It's so fucking hot." He licked her cheek.

"You're a dirty man." But she liked that he relished everything about the experience. He was so sensual, so uninhibited.

She wondered if she'd appear as uninhibited on the video.

He picked up the little remote attached to the camera tripod and pushed a button. "Shall we watch it?" he asked, as if he'd read her mind.

"No. Not yet." Suddenly she was self-conscious. What if she looked fat or flabby or horrible? She didn't want him to see.

Except that he would have already noticed her flaws over the past week. Whatever. "I'm not ready yet."

"Take it home with you. It's yours." He waggled his eyebrows. "But if you want to bring it back later, I would certainly be willing to fuck you while we watch it."

"Wouldn't that be like having sex to a porn video?"

"Yes. But it's hotter when you're the star."

Good God, she'd just made a porno. "How many other porn videos have you made?" Suddenly it bothered her that he might have done this with other women.

"I have never made a video like that. I've had sex in front of a camera, but it was never like that."

"You haven't seen it yet."

He held her gaze, a finger along her chin. "I don't have to see it. I felt it. I've never been so into a woman that I forgot the camera was there."

She was terrified he was mouthing platitudes and horrified that it should matter. This was supposed to be just sex.

Closing her eyes, she felt his skin, smelled him. Oh God, it was such *good* sex, and his platitudes were *so* perfect.

"I better go," she whispered, climbing off his lap.

His fingers left a trail of warmth. "Will you watch it tonight?"

"Maybe tomorrow." Suddenly it was going to take courage.

"Call me after you've seen it."

She pulled on her dress. He rose and zipped it for her, then reached for the camera. He removed the SD card as she slipped into her shoes.

God, he was beautiful. So lacking in self-consciousness, just simply, magnificently naked.

He laid the small card in her hand and curled her fingers around it. "Tell me if it makes you hot all over again."

She was afraid of what it would make her feel, suddenly sure it wouldn't be good.

13

BETWEEN LOADS OF LAUNDRY, RACHEL CLEANED THE BATHROOMS, scoured the kitchen, mopped the floors, dusted, and vacuumed. All the while, the SD card, which she'd hidden in her lingerie drawer with the vibrator, called to her.

She'd had untold fantasies last night, about Rand, about masseurs, having sex in a crowded room with everyone stopping to watch them. She'd heard about sex parties; she imagined going to one, watching and being watched. She imagined a ménage à trois with Rand and a handsome stranger. Over and over she replayed the fantasy about a burglar breaking into the house and forcing himself on her. Her thoughts were getting downright kinky, but that fantasy made her the wettest because it was the one to which she'd masturbated for him. Because she could still hear his voice.

Even as she'd cleaned today, the fantasies had assailed her. Her panties were wet, and her shirt teased her nipples with every swish of the mop, every push on the vacuum. That was the thing about cleaning; you could think about anything while you were doing it. By the time the house was spotless, the laundry folded and put away, all she wanted to do was throw herself across the bed, spread her legs, and go to town with her vibrator, accompanied by Rand's special brand of phone sex. Her own touch wasn't enough now unless she had Rand's voice, too.

In all her life, she'd never felt like this. She was a different person, a new woman. It was Rand. It was multiple orgasms. It was amazing, tantalizing. The effect was physical as well as emotional. Every touch while she showered felt sensual. Her nipples were perpetually hard. Sometimes she could feel her clitoris throb. Her skin was hot, her pulse racing. Everything she did or thought led right back to sex, to orgasms, to Rand.

She wanted to watch that video. She wanted to see Rand's cock in her hand, her mouth, her pussy, and his come on her face. She wanted to watch herself in the throes of ecstasy.

She'd half expected him to call. If he had, she would have succumbed to the lure of his voice and that video.

"You're crazy," she told herself as she rolled the vacuum back into the closet. But she was sweaty, achy, needy, and wet. And suddenly standing in front of her bureau, a hand on the lingerie drawer. She'd buried the video card beneath her panties and bras and some bright scarves she hadn't worn in ages, right there with her vibrator.

"Okay, you can watch the beginning, just to make sure you don't look horrible and fat," she told herself.

Geez, what was the big deal about watching it anyway? For God's sake, she'd made it, and that was infinitely worse, if you were comparing morals and all that stuff. Besides, it was private, just for her and Rand. Or just for herself, if she chose. What was the moral issue in that?

It was just that she was doing things she would have been horrified at if a friend confessed them to her.

Yet it was so sexy. He made her feel special, desirable. A woman again.

"Screw it. I'm watching it, and I don't care." Maybe she was talking to Gary. Or her mother. All those disapproving voices.

She locked the front door, threw the deadbolt, lowered the blinds, and closed the curtains. She could have played it on the computer, but she'd fought tooth and nail to keep the new forty-two-inch flat screen they'd purchased shortly before Gary's divorce announcement. Not for herself—or to spite Gary—she'd wanted it for the boys, and she sure couldn't afford to replace it. The nifty TV had an SD-card slot.

She put in the video card, hit the right buttons on the remote—an amazing feat—and curled into the corner of the family room sofa.

Oh God. There she was in forty-two inches of living color.

"You're fucking hot," Rand said as her dress fluttered to the carpet. She was naked but for the shoes. And she wasn't fat.

Rachel felt herself go warm inside. Oh no, she wasn't fat; in fact, with no one around to hear her think it, she could honestly say she was beautiful. And shy. Rand's voice made her gooey all over again. That's how she'd felt when he said those words. Absolutely gooey. Her own voice surprised her, too. She had a very sexy voice.

They talked; he told her what he wanted. His cock, wrapped in her hand, was magnificent on the big screen.

"That's it, stroke it, baby."

Watching, listening, she could *feel* him in her hand again, the smooth, warm flesh, how hard he was, the slight unsteadiness of his voice. A tiny drop of pre-come rose from the slit of his cock. It had felt like silk as she smoothed it over him. She caressed him, talked to his cock, cupped his balls, then suddenly she swooped down and sucked him into her mouth. She remembered that first taste of him, salty yet sweet.

She took him deep, her eyes closed, and God, she looked like a woman sipping Dom Perignon and eating chocolate. Her red lipstick and fingernails were decadent on his flesh.

She glanced at her nails now, some of the polish already

chipped off after cleaning. Up on the screen, she was Cinderella at the ball; down on the couch, she was just a scullery maid.

On-screen, she opened her eyes and looked at him.

"Jesus," he murmured. "Suck me, baby, please."

She drowned in the sound of his voice, his desire. He'd made her beautiful to the camera, the lens loving on her face. She didn't feel disgusting or perverted. She was perfect. His gorgeous cock in her mouth was delicious. She could taste him even now, feel the silkiness of his flesh between her lips. She'd loved sucking him, adored it, wanted so much more of it.

She was good. God, she was good. She could hear it in his voice. But she wanted to see his face, see how she affected him.

The moment came. With an abrupt scene change—the point at which he'd stopped the camera to put it on the tripod—she was suddenly between his legs as he sat in the chair.

Oh. My. God. She had never seen a more perfect man. Every muscle bulged with perfection, not an ounce of fat. The planes of his face were taut with desire, his skin flushed with need. For her, for what she could do to him.

He talked to her, praised her, as his body rose and fell to meet her mouth.

"Jesus, baby, you're so goddamn good at that. You're killing me."

His legs started to shake, and she removed her hand, sucking him deep, all the way. The camera suddenly zoomed, and she could actually see the pulse of blood through his cock.

For long moments, there was just the delicious slurp of her mouth on his cock, as if she were sucking candy, his throaty purr of pleasure, and her own moans. She hadn't realized she'd made any sound at all. But there, on the screen, was the evidence of how much she'd loved it.

This wasn't filthy or raunchy or disgusting. It wasn't porn. It was art. She was wet watching herself, watching him.

Then he stopped her, rolled on a condom, and pulled her astride him.

"I thought you were just going to videotape me sucking you." She heard the nerves in her voice. It had been the first time since she'd dropped her dress on the floor that she'd started to feel uncomfortable.

Rand stroked her clit. "You're so fucking wet. Put me inside you. I want you to see me taking you on camera."

With that one touch, she'd wanted it all. The sight of his cock filling her made her heart flutter. All the sounds, the movement, their hot breath, her moans and cries—Rachel was flushed and wanting all over again. Even as she watched, she couldn't resist spreading her legs and slipping her hand inside her sweats. She was so wet, so hot, dazed, drugged.

She watched as she orgasmed on-screen, as she squeezed her eyes shut, moaned, threw her head back, and slammed down on him, taking him deep, holding him in, her body shaking, her breasts bouncing. While she watched, she drenched her fingers with her orgasm. Then she was sucking him again, and when Rand splashed her face with come, she climaxed once again in the here and now. It was beautiful, perfect. She wanted that, what he'd done to her up there on the screen, she wanted it again and again.

Finally, he was just holding her. She hadn't realized he'd still had the camera going then.

They were lush and loving in each other's arms. They whispered, smiled, and he rubbed his come all over her breasts. Then he kissed her. God, she remembered that kiss, the taste of his come still in her mouth, the scent of it all over them.

She remembered being afraid to watch the video. Now she knew why. It wasn't her fear of looking disgusting or slutty.

It was *this*.

On her TV screen, Rachel kissed him like a woman in love.

* * *

"IT WAS SO COOL, MOM." NATHAN, EXCITED AS ALL GET-OUT ABOUT his first driving lesson. "I took the online classes every night, so on Saturday I could get behind the wheel." Gary had taken him down to get his driver's permit. "Mr. Filpot"—the instructor— "said that's the fastest anyone's ever done it."

"That's wonderful, honey." Rachel didn't want to say anything to bring him down. She hadn't seen him this animated since Gary had left her.

Gary had dropped the boys off early, before dinner. He probably wanted to get started on screwing his girlfriend every night before he got his sons back in a week.

Gosh, that sounded bitter, especially since she'd dropped the boys on him an hour early last Sunday to do the same thing with Rand. She'd rushed around the house this afternoon, erasing any evidence of her debauchery with the video, stowing the SD card and her vibrator safely beneath her panties and scarves. She'd wanted to call Rand, hear his voice one more time, tell him how much she'd loved their movie, but it was too late.

"What do you guys want for dinner?"

"Hamburgers and sweet potato fries," Justin jumped in, probably feeling like he'd been ignored while Nathan went on and on about his driving lesson.

"The hamburger's frozen."

"We can go to the store, Mom," Justin insisted.

"And I can drive." Nathan glowed with his excitement.

Oh God. She should have known that was coming. "You need a little more practice with the instructor before we go out."

"I only get six hours of driving with him, and to get my license, I need fifty hours of practice. Dad let me drive."

Rachel resisted rolling her eyes like Justin. This was the ever-increasing habit, pitting her against Gary. Honestly, now that she'd agreed to his driver's permit, it was bad policy to deny him the practice. That was passive-aggressive, to say yes to the lessons, then nitpick about his behind-the-wheel time.

"All right. Let's do it."

"Yes." Nathan punched the air.

By the time they arrived back home, Rachel had a tension headache, her teeth hurt from clenching them, and she'd worn a hole in the passenger side floorboard slamming on brakes she didn't have.

"You did great, Nathan," she said as she sliced the sweet potatoes.

"Except when he almost ran down that old lady and her shopping cart in the parking lot," Justin added.

"Did not," Nathan shot back.

"Did, too."

"Boys. Is your homework done?"

"Yes, Mom."

She gave them both a look.

"Almost," Justin muttered.

Nathan didn't look at her; obviously his wasn't done either. "Finish it up while I'm making dinner," she said.

It was a pleasant evening, the burgers were good, and they watched an action movie the title of which she couldn't even remember and didn't care about. Curled into the corner of the sofa, she marveled at how nice the last three hours had been. No fighting or sniping, no sullenness. All she'd had to do was agree to let Nathan drive. She should have given in months ago. After all, she'd lost the battle anyway.

Over dinner, she'd told them about her going back to school. Neither had put up a fuss. Nathan had graciously said he'd have no problem babysitting Justin, at which point Justin elbowed him. The timing had been just right, another boon out of letting him start his driving lessons. Things were definitely looking up in the Delaney household.

As things exploded on the screen, she thought of her own explosions of a very different kind. The things Rand had done to her, what she'd done to him. Oh, it was bad to be thinking about it when the boys were in the same room, but she couldn't stop since she wasn't the least bit interested in the movie.

Really, what could be the harm? Neither Justin nor Nathan would ever know. She didn't sigh or moan. She just . . . imagined. And wondered how she would survive a whole week. Rand had pegged it. Once you started getting it, you wanted more. Desire didn't wane; it grew exponentially. Like you'd gotten hooked on a drug.

She was barely aware of the exciting finale in which someone jumped onto a moving gasoline truck and saved the day by blowing it up without singeing a single hair.

Then it was an hour after bedtime, the house quiet around her. Rachel couldn't sleep. She tossed and turned, her body on fire like the exploding gasoline tanker, and when she glanced at the clock, she'd been lying there an hour and a half. She was wet, her nipples aching, her skin sensitized to every shift of the covers across her skin.

She needed an orgasm. She wouldn't be able to sleep without one. She should never have watched that damn video this afternoon. It played over and over in her mind. She could taste Rand, smell him, feel his hard flesh beneath her fingers. She needed relief, just a small one. She knew she shouldn't do it with the boys home. Bad, bad, bad. But she couldn't sleep. It was crazy. She wanted Rand, his voice in her ear. She needed it, had to have it. She couldn't stop herself.

Rachel reached for her cell phone, turned on the Bluetooth, and dialed Rand's number.

14

HE'D WAITED TWENTY-FOUR HOURS FOR HER TO CALL. BY SUNDAY
night, he'd figured it would be the following week since she'd
been so adamant she wouldn't do anything with the boys in the
house.

"I have to be very quiet," she whispered when he answered.

"Does that mean you can't have an orgasm?"

He could hear the beat of silence ring through his bedroom,
then she said, "You're a dirty man for getting me to do this."

"I'm a very good man or you wouldn't have called. Did you
like your movie?"

"It was filthy."

"So you loved it."

She laughed softly, and his balls tightened. She had such a
sexy voice. He was sure she didn't have a clue about that, and if
he told her, she wouldn't believe him.

"Let's just say it was interesting."

"How many orgasms did you have while you were watching it?"

Again, that beat of silence.

"Come on," he urged. "I won't tell anyone."

"Two." Pause. "At least."

Christ, she got him going. She was demure, yet when she let herself go, she was amazing. "Which part did you like best?"

"Well, uh . . ." She hesitated. "I don't know."

"Yes, you do." He wanted her to admit what it was. He liked learning about her needs, storing them up, using them to make the experience better the next time. "Was it when I fucked you? When you could see how beautiful you are, how perfect my cock looks inside you?"

"That was good," she whispered, then added the crowning touch, "but I loved sucking you and watching you come on me."

Holy hell. "Touch yourself for me."

A long, lovely sigh fluttered across the airwaves. "I've been touching myself since you picked up."

"Dirty woman." Jesus. She'd actually called him for phone sex while the kids were home. He didn't want to compromise her personal code, but he also didn't see anything wrong with it. Her kids had no clue what went on in their mother's bedroom, but they couldn't expect a gorgeous woman to put herself on the shelf until they were out of the house. "I want you to come."

This time she moaned, softly. "I needed to hear your voice."

He liked the fact that she *needed* him, that it wasn't enough on her own.

"I watched that movie"—her breath hitched—"and it made me crazy for you. It was so naughty, Rand. I couldn't help watching it." She talked, her voice rising, falling, her breath a pant, then a moan. He stroked his cock to her sounds. "You were so big, Rand . . . and I could taste your cock . . . as if I were doing it all over again." Her voice stopped and started. He wished to God he'd been to her house, so he could picture her on her bed touching herself for him. She groaned, then grunted softly, as if she was trying to hold it all in, but she was coming for him, creaming, his name barely on her lips, but there.

Then her voice again. "Oh God, I really shouldn't have done that. But it was so good."

And she was gone. He hadn't come, but Rand didn't care. He stroked leisurely, keeping himself hard, and imagined her spread-eagled before him.

He imagined stealing into her room to give her a fantasy.

Christ, it was good awakening Rachel from the deep slumber of a seventeen-year marriage.

RACHEL COULDN'T BELIEVE SHE'D CALLED RAND. FOUR NIGHTS IN a row, she'd succumbed. By last night, Wednesday night, she'd called him the moment she was sure the boys were asleep, giving up resistance completely. Where the Borg and Rand were concerned, resistance was definitely futile. As she put together lunches for the boys, she couldn't stop thinking about Rand, about the way he made her come with just words. God, she needed him. How the mighty fall when they're horny. He'd figured out how much she loved the burglar and pirate fantasies, and he embellished, sometimes giving her to the whole darn crew, who were, of course, well bathed and freshly shaved before they had at her, as befitted a fantasy. Rand made sex so much fun. *Especially* over the phone.

Life was good everywhere. Nathan was human again. Justin was a perfect little eighth grader. They did their homework and even helped with the dishes. *What's* up with that? She knew she shouldn't look a gift horse in the mouth, but honestly, she'd started to worry that her sons had been taken over by pod people.

The high school and middle school were across the street from each other, and though they could have walked, she'd been driving them this week. Or rather, she'd been letting Nathan drive to get his practice hours in. The lessons were improving his sense of responsibility. And what Nathan did rubbed off on Justin; it always had.

Hot sex and well-behaved children did wonders for a woman.

Rachel breezed through the morning, marveling at her efficiency. Bree was closeted in her office with the IRS auditor. The guy was wide-shouldered and tall, like the watchdog he was supposed to be. Rachel was proud of Bree. She'd been nervous about firing Marbury and conducting the audit herself, but she was in there doing her thing. Rachel gave her a thumbs-up behind the auditor's back before Bree closed the door.

When Rachel delivered Dominic's mail, he was in his office rather than his testing lab. "Hey, Rach." He smiled.

Dominic was a hottie at six-one, with dark hair and a sexy smile that made a girl melt. Of course, he only had eyes for Erin, which was amazing after fifteen years of marriage and the tragedy they'd been through.

Rachel liked the nickname he used for her. Funny thing, she hadn't noticed his smile until Rand walked into her life. Then, all of a sudden, she'd started seeing all men in a sexual light. Like a woman in heat.

She laid his mail on his desk. "It's mostly junk." But Dominic liked to pick through his own junk.

"You have a few minutes to review a sales brochure for me? I've got Atul and Cam working on something else right now."

Dominic did all the marketing, in addition to engineering their products. Atul handled the website and documentation, and Cam was their software engineer.

"I don't know enough about the products, Dominic."

"It's not rocket science. Check it for typos and stuff that doesn't make sense. It should be in layman's terms anyway. Give me your opinion on whether it catches the eye."

She felt a rush of pleasure, just as she had when Erin complimented her on how she'd handled Matt and Steve. "Sure, I'll read it right away."

He slid the brochure across the desk. "Take your time. Tomorrow is fine." Then he started leafing through the mail.

Back in her office, Rachel got out her red pen and began marking up the brochure. It was fun. She wondered if Erin had said something to Dominic about giving her more to do. When she'd started at DKG almost five months ago, she'd answered phones and sorted the mail. She didn't have any job skills, but thank God Erin had taken pity on her and given her a chance. Now she did everyone's filing, matched payables and receivables, and entered purchase orders, too. She was learning a bit more about each of the systems, becoming more valuable.

She returned the corrected brochure to Dominic after lunch and told him she'd help out anytime. At one-thirty, the phone rang, and Rachel was shocked that the caller wanted her. No one ever wanted to talk to the receptionist.

"Hello, Mrs. Delaney, this is Miss Watson from Principal Torvik's office over at the high school."

Rachel's heart started to race, and spots swam before her eyes. "Is Nathan okay?"

"He's not injured. Don't worry. Principal Torvik would like to meet with you today at four-thirty."

"Meet with *me*?" She felt like an idiot, echoing the woman. Principal Torvik the dickhead wanted to see her. "Did Nathan use his cell phone in class again? Because I told him not to after the last incident."

"No, Mrs. Delaney. Principal Torvik simply wants to discuss some behavioral symptoms Nathan is exhibiting."

That sounded ominous. "What does that mean?"

"Please, Mrs. Delaney. That's what the principal would like to discuss with you. At four-thirty."

Dammit, why wouldn't the woman tell her? Maybe Miss Watson didn't know. "Yes. All right. I can be there."

"Thank you, Mrs. Delaney."

She stared at the phone for fifteen seconds. Just when she thought things were improving, what had Nathan done? Rachel left a terse message for him to call her at his next break. She'd barely pushed End when her cell rang.

It was Gary, not Nathan. "What the hell is going on, Rachel? The principal's office just called and ordered me down there for a meeting this afternoon."

It would have been nice if Miss Watson had said she'd informed Gary, too. "She didn't give me any information."

"Well, he's been with *you* the last four days. What the hell have you let him get up to?"

"I haven't *let* him get up to anything. He's been fine, doing his homework, just fine."

"Right." Gary growled under his breath, as if she was the *only* problem Nathan had. "I don't have time for this, Rachel."

Yes, well, when they were married, she'd have attended the meeting on her own, but now they had two separate households. She held her tongue about who was responsible for the divorce in the first place. "We need to show Nathan a united front."

"This Torvik guy sounds like some ass who's into power trips. It's probably not Nathan's fault at all."

She didn't disagree with him, especially since Nathan had been so good this week. "Let's hear the man out, Gary."

He grumbled and said what she'd known was eventually coming. "Can't you handle this, Rachel?"

"He's with you half the time, Gary. We both need to hear what's going on and come to a mutual understanding about how we're going to deal with it."

"Fine," he spat into the phone, then she heard dead air.

He hadn't always been like this. Yes, he'd been depressed, but even after he'd said he wanted a divorce, he still hadn't been such . . . an asshole. There wasn't another word for it.

Nathan didn't return her calls. This is why they had the phones, for emergencies, not for texting their buddies. At four, she called Justin, told him they had an appointment at the school, and she'd be home right after.

So far, Justin was pretty easy. He hadn't taken up Nathan's habit of pitting her and Gary against each other, but then, he hadn't wanted anything badly enough yet. *Note to self: Start saving for Justin's driving lessons and insurance.* She hadn't realized how it could affect their self-esteem.

When she arrived at the school administration offices, the principal's door—bearing only a black nameplate that read PRINCIPAL'S OFFICE, as though the principals changed too often to get a real nameplate—was closed. Nathan was already seated in a waiting-room chair. Everyone who passed stared at him through the glass windows, the kid that had gotten sent to the principal's office. He kept his head down.

Before speaking to her son, Rachel approached the desk. "I'm Nathan Delaney's mother."

Miss Watson was at least sixty, with a long nose, steel hair, and huge glasses that had been popular back in the seventies. She glanced up at Rachel. "Principal Torvik is running a bit behind." She held her thumb and finger apart to indicate how far behind. "Since Nathan's father isn't here yet"—she raised a brow and left it at that—"please have a seat."

As Miss Watson turned back to her computer, Rachel sat down next to Nathan. "You didn't return my calls," she said quietly.

"I'm not supposed to use my cell phone in class," he said, the sullenness back in his voice.

"I asked you to call me back *between* classes."

"I didn't have time." He glanced outside the office window, his eyes following a pretty blonde in a cheerleader uniform.

Rachel pressed her lips together. Dammit, things had been going so well. "What happened?"

"Nothing," he said, his lips in a petulant frown.

"Nathan, why does the principal want to talk to us?"

"Ask him."

She put her hands on the chair arms and let out a sigh. "All right. That means we'll hear his version first."

"It won't make any difference. You'll still take his side."

"Nathan," she started, but just then Gary burst through the door.

He didn't look at Nathan, but spoke instead to Rachel. "Do you know what it's like trying to get across town at this time of day?" As if it were her fault.

"Mr. and Mrs. Delaney," Miss Watson said. "I'll let the principal know you're both here." She punched a button on her phone console, then murmured into the receiver.

Moments later, the office door opened and a young man backed out, his eyes downcast. He was older than Nathan, probably a senior judging by the slight shadow of manly beard on his chin. "Thanks, thanks, thanks," he said in triplicate.

His jeans rode too high on his waist and were therefore too short, and he wore a white button-down shirt beneath a dark blue Windbreaker that was too tight. He bobbed his head at the low rumble of a voice from within the office. Then the boy turned. His eyes flitted over Nathan's polo jacket, and his body stiffened. Gaze on the carpet, he turned sideways, hugging the edge of Miss Watson's desk, as if to keep as much distance between himself and Nathan as possible. Once past, he almost tripped over his own feet in a rush to get out.

Then the principal himself was at the door. "Mr. and Mrs. Delaney, sorry to keep you waiting."

Rachel didn't hear anything else. There was just a roar in her ears, like she was standing between two freight trains fighting to drag her under their wheels.

One of the trains was Gary.

The other was Principal *Rand* Torvik.

15

HE MIGHT HAVE BEEN SILENT ONE OVERLONG SECOND, BUT THAT was Rand's only reaction. Then he extended his hand. Gary was there first, shaking it, smiling like a glad-hander at one of his National Society of Accountants meetings.

Oh my God, oh my God. That's all Rachel could think. For God's sake, she'd been having nasty sex with her son's principal. They'd made a *movie.* Wasn't there some school rule against that kind of thing?

Rand was holding his hand out. Did he expect her to shake it like everything was fine and dandy? Yes, obviously he did.

His grip was warm, firm. His gaze didn't reflect a thing. "I'd like to talk with you both, then we'll invite Nathan in."

Neither she nor Gary disagreed.

He wore a white shirt, red tie, and dark suit. It might have been the same one he'd worn that day in front of the vibrator shop.

"Please, have a seat." Ever so polite, he ushered them into two chairs opposite his desk. Afternoon sun fell on his blond hair as he sat down in his commanding leather chair.

Framed diplomas and certificates hung on the walls, the print so small, Rachel couldn't read them. Books filled shelves and topped filing cabinets, and binders were stacked neatly on a conference table. He had a computer, a phone, pens in a holder. His inbox wasn't empty, but it wasn't full either. He kept on top of things, and his office looked normal. *He* looked normal.

Good God, he was a teacher, a principal, he worked with kids. And he was *kinky*. He watched his neighbors have sex. He videotaped her.

Rachel couldn't wrap her mind around it all.

Yet she was a mother, a receptionist, and she had boys over to her house for tent nights in the backyard. And she'd gotten kinky *with* Rand. She took off her panties while his neighbors had sex. She masturbated for him over the phone.

Heat flushed her skin.

"Is that all right with you, Mrs. Delaney?"

She hadn't heard a word he'd said. This was about Nathan, and she wasn't even listening.

Rand rescued her. "I want to review the details before we bring Nathan in."

"Yes, yes, of course."

"First of all, he's a good kid, very smart. I'm sure on some level, he realizes his behavior is inappropriate."

"Just cut to the chase, Principal Torvik," Gary said. "We can take it."

She sliced a glance at Gary. Was she imagining it, or had he deepened his voice? She had a horrible moment of comparing them. Rand had six inches and thirty pounds of muscle on Gary. Gary had five years on Rand, but he wore them like ten, with dark puffy pouches beneath his eyes and his hair thinning where Rand's was thick. She cut off that train of thought.

Rand eyed them both. Did she imagine that his gaze softened when he glanced at her? "Nathan has been involved in some instances of bullying."

Gary puffed his chest up and scowled. "My son doesn't bully."

For once Rachel had to agree with him. "Nathan would never pick on anyone. We've taught him better than that."

"Nevertheless, he's been reported in some incidents of name-calling and other forms of bullying."

Gary drummed his fingers on the arm of his chair. "I'm sure he didn't mean anything by it."

Rand ignored him. "Specifically, we have a class of developmentally challenged students. Nathan has been overhead using slurs, especially against one boy in particular."

Rachel remembered the young man leaving Rand's office. There had been something a bit different about him, and he'd given Nathan a wide berth. "The boy who was just in here with you?"

Rand nodded, then spoke directly to her. "Wally. He's autistic, but quite high-functioning. He's also verbal. Some autistics are not." Then he included them both in his gaze. "I don't want this bullying to cause any setbacks for him."

Gary thinned his lips. "Well, we'll have a talk with Nathan. I'm glad to hear it isn't something more serious, like cutting class or fighting."

Rand leaned forward, spearing Gary with a look. "It's extremely serious. Today at lunch"—his voice was deadly—"after running into Wally and knocking his tray to the floor, Nathan called him a stupid little retard who had his head up his ass."

Rachel felt the blood drain out of her head. She heard the echo of Nathan in their kitchen, calling Principal Torvik a dickhead, and on the heels of it, she could actually hear her son saying those words in the same tone to that boy.

"I don't believe it," Gary said. "He would never do something like that. Whoever told you that was exaggerating."

Rand stared him down a long moment. Then he said, ever so politely, "Please don't be one of those parents who is part of the problem rather than the solution."

Rachel jumped in, aghast that Gary was making things worse. "We *are* part of the solution, Principal Torvik. Have there been any other incidents?"

"Yes. He's become involved with some sophomores on the JV basketball team."

"He plays water polo," Gary said.

"He wants to play basketball," Rachel said. And he'd been hanging out with boys he thought could help him make the team.

"He's gotten tight with them over the past few months. Picking on other students is some sort of test with them. Name-calling, shoving, pushing, vandalizing lockers, graffiti. I've had to discipline several of them."

"Can't you put a stop to *them*?" Gary asked. "They're a bad influence on him. Maybe he's not actually doing it, just standing there watching. An innocent bystander."

"Nathan has been seen in the group, has done nothing to stop the behaviors, and though students have reported that he's been involved before, this is the first time it was verifiable."

Gary blustered, his face red, then asked, "Who heard him?"

"I did."

Gary slapped his mouth shut. Rachel wanted to cry. How could Nathan say that to anyone, let alone a handicapped boy?

She thought about the kids Nathan was running with, some of whom already had their driver's licenses, and probably cool cars, too. No wonder he'd wanted his permit. He was competing. She hated the way he was doing it, but she was sure this was all about looking big around his friends. Since starting back at work, she'd felt the pinch of being out of touch, of not knowing his friends, their families. That lack of involvement was coming home to roost.

"What do you suggest we do at this point"—she cut herself

off before calling him Rand—"Principal Torvik?" *Please, have all the answers for me.*

"We need to address the root cause, Mrs. Delaney. You can ground him, try to keep him away from these so-called friends of his, but he already knows what he did was wrong. We need to know why, what's going on in his head."

She knew what was going on. It was the divorce, his dad dating a bimbo, a mother who wasn't home anymore—out screwing the principal he despised, no less—his whole life changing, insecurity. And, to top it off, being a teenager.

"Shall we call Nathan in now?" Rand asked.

Rachel nodded. Gary grunted.

God, how was she supposed to fix it all?

HE'D EXPERIENCED THE MOMENTARY SHOCK OF RECOGNITION, the initial *Oh shit*, then, just as quickly, it was over. Rand had wanted to smile. The law of attraction. Everything was part of a circle, and there were no coincidences. He'd found her in one area of his life, and she was bound to turn up in another. It was actually no surprise that she was Nathan's mother. There was always more than one connection.

Nathan looked like her. Yes, his hair was brown, hers blond, but they had the same face, the same eyes, the same smile. At least when Nathan smiled, which he didn't often do around Rand.

He felt her pain. There was nothing worse than not knowing what to do for your kid. Except not understanding why it had happened. He might not have children of his own, but he'd been an educator for close to twenty years, first as a science teacher, then moving into administration. He knew kids. Nathan's problem was the divorce and not feeling like he fit in anywhere.

Rachel's problem was the asshole ex-husband.

Gary Delaney was a small-minded man who couldn't see beyond his own needs. He didn't deserve a woman like Rachel. Thus, he'd lost her.

"I didn't do it on purpose," Nathan said with that same militant stare. Except that he focused on the edge of Rand's desk, not meeting his mother's eyes, not meeting Rand's.

"We had this discussion earlier, Nathan," Rand said. "We're not having it again. This is a different discussion. I'm not going to suspend you. I'm going to let your parents handle the issue as they see fit this time."

"Thank you. You can rest assured we'll take care of it, Principal Torvik," Rachel said.

Wrong time, wrong place, but later, he wanted to hear her say that in the bedroom when she was down on her knees. Or he was on his. He'd think about that when she called him tonight. Right now, he had other things to deal with. Like the ex.

Delaney clenched and unclenched his fists. "We'll talk to him and draw our own conclusions."

He'd expected that kind of reaction. Delaney wasn't merely small-minded, he was a small man. If he admitted Nathan had a problem, he'd have to admit he'd fucked up by divorcing his gorgeous wife. Rachel hadn't talked much about her marriage, but he'd read between the lines and realized the ex was at fault.

"Your parents understand that if I have to call them again, the measures I'll be forced to take will be greater."

Nathan merely stared sullenly at the same spot on the desk. Rand had explained Wally's disability. But all most kids saw was that his jeans were too short and his clothes too tight as if he'd outgrown them, he never looked anyone in the eyes, he abhorred being touched, and he talked in threes, short sharp sentences, sometimes only one word, but always repeated three times. Something about the number three made him feel safe. The clothes did, too, like a child holding on to a security blanket. What kids noticed was his strangeness. Nathan *still* didn't understand, no matter how Rand described autism.

"If you want to come in and talk to me, Nathan, my door is always open," Rand said.

The boy snorted.

"I can make an appointment with the school counselor, if you'd prefer."

Nathan's face reddened. "I don't need a counselor."

Rand didn't practice magic. He couldn't perform miracles. He'd had his eye on Nathan. He was a good kid; Rand felt that in his gut. Long ago, when he was Nathan's age, he'd fallen in with a bad crowd. They'd smoked pot—and inhaled. Things may have gone from bad to worse if not for Mr. Lumberger, his math teacher. All it took was one adult who gave a damn about him. Rand strove to do the same thing for his students. When he saw a good kid on the brink, like Nathan, he didn't let him fall over into the abyss without reaching out a hand to grab him. Mr. Lumberger was why he'd become a teacher; kids like Nathan and Wally were why his job had become his vocation.

He had, however, made some mistakes with Nathan, but he would keep offering his hand until he figured out what the boy really needed.

In the meantime, Nathan had Rachel. Even without his help, Rand believed she'd be enough to bring Nathan around. Unless the asshole ex-husband got in the way.

"I WANT TO TALK TO YOU." GARY PARKED HIS CAR IN THE DRIVE AND followed her into the garage. Nathan was already inside.

It had taken three tries on the remote to open the garage door. She'd changed the batteries, but something else was wrong, maybe the reader. Gary had still done nothing about it.

"I have to make dinner, Gary. What do you want?"

Hands jammed at his hips, legs spread, he blocked her way into the kitchen. "That guy's got it out for Nathan for some reason."

Gary wanted to take Nathan's word that it was an accident, but Rachel believed Rand. Rephrase, she believed the principal. But would she have been so adamant if she wasn't having sex with him? Who knew? "He has no reason to make up the story."

"So you believe your son would pick on some retarded kid?" Gary said the word with a sneer.

"They're mentally challenged, not *retarded*, and if Nathan felt backed into a corner by these new friends of his, he might take the line of least resistance and do what they tell him to."

"That's bullshit, Rachel. Have you even met these kids?"

"No, I haven't. Have you?" she threw back at him, but guilt made her face flush.

"I have a mortgage to cover, Rachel, and I don't get paid for the overtime I have to work." Oh yeah, he just had to grind in that he'd gotten the short end of the settlement stick.

She covered her mouth. They weren't fighting about helping Nathan. They'd turned this whole thing into being about *them*. "Gary, let me talk to Nathan. When we're not with the principal, he might be more willing to open up."

"Fine, talk to him. Let me know how *that* goes." His tone was snide as he turned away.

She couldn't let him go. "Has he been acting differently when he's with you?"

"What do you mean? He's perfectly normal."

"I mean, like he's upset or something. You know, about the divorce." They'd talked about the effect of the divorce on the boys in the beginning, but since finalizing, that discussion was over.

"He's fine when he's at *my* place, Rachel." He pointed a finger at her. "*This* is why you shouldn't be out during the evenings, doing schoolwork or anything else. The boys need your undivided attention."

"At least I'm not pushing off some twenty-five-year-old bimbo on them."

He narrowed his eyes. "That's what this is all about, isn't it? That I'm seeing someone."

"What this is about is your son being called into the principal's office, and we're damn lucky he didn't get suspended. It's not about whether I go back to school." Or who she was fucking, for that matter. God forbid Gary should ever learn that. "Just go home to your girlfriend, Gary." Shit, she shouldn't have said that, but he made her mad. She tried to push a little calm into her voice. "I'll talk to Nathan, and I'll call you in the morning."

"This isn't about Sherry. They like Sherry."

It even sounded like a bimbo name, but Rachel didn't say anything negative. "They think she's nice," she said reasonably.

He sneered. "Don't you try turning them against her."

"I'm not." But she wanted to smack him for the snide attitude. He was the one who'd left. Maybe it was his own guilty conscience talking. "Now, I'm going in to make dinner."

Gary grunted and stomped back to his car.

Why had everyone started fighting? They should be settling into their new lives now. Instead, they'd all started sniping at one another, her, Gary, the boys.

But the worst? Her son's principal was also her lover.

16

"WHAT HAPPENED, NATHAN?"

"Oh, so now you ask me. But not in front of *him*," he groused.

Nathan was being contrary; she *had* asked him before they even went into the principal's office. Fighting over it, however, wasn't productive. "I didn't ask when the principal was present because I didn't want to embarrass you by sounding like I was giving you the third degree." Actually, at the time, she'd been incapable of saying anything for fear of saying the *wrong* thing. *Especially* in front of Rand. She didn't want to look stupid or inadequate.

Dinner had been a silent affair. Even Justin had eventually stopped chattering. Afterward, Rachel did the dishes, left Justin to the remainder of his homework, and followed Nathan's tracks to his room. She heard his voice on the phone when she knocked, but when she entered, he'd already hung up and was hunched at the computer.

Rachel sat on the end of his bed. "Would you please look at me while we talk?"

He toed his feet on the carpet to swivel around to her. "I didn't see that kid. I knocked into him, and he dropped his tray. That's all." He glared at her.

She knew he'd rehearsed that lie. "Principal Torvik says you called the boy a name." There was something about giving Rand the title that made her pulse flutter. Then again, it could simply be that he was her secret vice.

Nathan looked away. "I don't remember what I said."

She wouldn't call him a liar. All she said was, "Nathan."

He shrugged, strongly enough to toss his short hair. "I might have said *something*. Because I was pissed that he got right in front of me like that."

"What did you say?"

His shoulders went up, down. He pressed his lips together, scowled. "I don't know, it might not have been too nice, but it was in the heat of the moment, not a deliberate thing like that dickhead Torvik said."

"You're already in trouble for using demeaning names, so don't make it worse." She was sure he'd said what Rand claimed he had. "Calling people names is unacceptable. Especially people who are less fortunate."

He made a face, hung his head. "I won't do it again, Mom."

Now he was simply placating her. "There have to be consequences, Nathan. You're grounded this weekend. No going out with your friends."

"But, Mom, there's a game Friday night."

"What game?"

"Basketball." He cleared his throat. "You gotta watch the guys play and figure out how they work together and everything to get on the team."

"Have I met any of these *guys*?" She knew she hadn't; she'd been remiss. They were the bad influences Rand had mentioned.

Nathan made a noise in his throat. "No," he said, his voice sullen again. "You're working. You can't even come to after-school stuff. How are you supposed to meet anyone I know anymore?"

His freshman year, she'd gone to all his polo matches, but now she was working. And Nathan was playing the blame game with her. Rachel wanted to bury her face in her hands. What was the right thing to do, the right thing to say?

"Your father and I will make it to a game and meet everyone." Nathan opened his mouth. She cut him off with a frown. "But you aren't going out this weekend."

"Mom," he whined, "I have to go to *every* game or I won't make it onto the team next year."

Part of her wanted to say he could go just so she could tag along and evaluate these new friends of his, see if Rand was right about their negative influence, but actions had to have consequences. "You should have thought of that before you got angry that someone else was in your way."

She was almost through the door when he called out. "Mom. I have my driving lesson on Saturday at ten. Do I get to do that?"

Right thing, wrong thing. Was the lesson a class or a privilege? God, she didn't know anymore, but they'd already paid for it. "You can take it."

He made a noise. She thought it was triumph.

In the family room, she turned on the TV just to have sound while the boys finished their homework. What was she supposed to do about Rand? Of course, she'd have to stop seeing him. She definitely couldn't be caught at his house watching his neighbors have sex. What a scandal. It was dangerous. He could lose his job. The whole thing was crazy.

But oh God, she was going to miss him.

* * *

RAND SUSPECTED THERE WAS AN ISSUE WHEN SHE DIDN'T CALL Thursday night, followed by no call Friday or Saturday. When she showed up at his house at seven-thirty on Sunday wearing jeans and a jacket she wouldn't take off, he knew she was cutting him loose. He was only surprised she didn't send a *Dear John* email.

"I'm sure you'll agree," she said, her voice as stiff as her back, "it's for the best under the circumstances."

"I don't agree."

Her mouth actually dropped open. "What do you mean?" She was cute when she gaped.

"We'll have a glass of wine and talk about it."

She snorted. "I can't be *seen* here."

"There's no one to see us, Rachel."

"Your neighbors. People talk. It could get around."

He took her arm, steered her toward the kitchen. Like a child, she let him lead her.

"What will get around?" he asked as he took down glasses from the cupboard. "That we've been keeping company?"

She looked at him like he'd just been released from Bedlam. "That we watched your neighbors have sex. That we had sex on the hood of your car up on Skyline. And we made a *movie*."

He wasn't sure which to tackle first, so he did them all at once as he poured her wine. "We gave my neighbors the audience they wanted, we had sex on my car in the *dark* when no one was around, and we didn't put out a *YouTube* video. We made a private movie for ourselves." He smiled. "Did you bring the video card?"

She snorted. "No, I didn't bring it. And I don't need any wine. I told you I can't stay." She glared at him.

He'd seen her overcome with desire. He'd seen her dreamy.

He'd seen her in orgasm, and he'd seen her unsure and lost in his office. By far, however, the glare was the best. It made him hot. Better not tell her that, though. She didn't appear to have her sense of humor about her at the moment.

Besides, he was minimizing her concerns. "Come into the living room. We can talk about Nathan, too."

She scowled. "I don't know what I'm going to do about him. If he knew I was seeing you . . ." She puffed her cheeks out in imitation of a major explosion.

"I know, he hates my guts." He carried the two wineglasses through the kitchen into the living room.

She followed, took the wine, sat next to him on the sofa, then downed a long swallow. "I wouldn't put it that strongly."

"I would." He hadn't handled Nathan well. He'd heard what the boy said and blown a gasket, effectively humiliating Nathan in front of his peers. Teenagers were pretty damn unforgiving about that. But Wally was a tender soul, and Rand couldn't hack the way Nathan spoke to him.

"I'll handle Nathan," she said. "He's not why I'm here."

Right. So they'd talk about Nathan later. "Okay. You're here to say we can't see each other anymore. And I'm telling you there's no reason we shouldn't."

She shook her head at him. "You could get fired."

"No one's going to fire me for having sex, Rachel."

"But I'm a mother."

She was so serious, he couldn't laugh. "You are not the first single parent to date a single teacher."

"We're not dating," she rushed to answer, her voice rising. "We're fucking, and watching other people fuck, and doing it on the hood of your car."

He smiled. "I love it when you say *fuck*."

"Stop that." But she laughed, then covered her mouth. "This isn't funny."

He pulled her hand down, tipped her chin with his finger. "We haven't done anything I'm ashamed of. Just because I'm your son's principal doesn't mean you should suddenly be ashamed either. While being a mother is the most important job a woman could have, that doesn't mean you're not also a beautiful, sexy lady who deserves more than a vibrator."

She looked away, took up her wine again, drank, then curled her fingers around the stem. "I can't explain it except to say that we're kinky. If we weren't kinky, it wouldn't be so bad."

"So, if we were just having missionary sex in a bed, it would be okay to tell your son you're seeing me."

"No." She gave him a look. "I don't want my sons to think casual sex is fine."

"I agree. Nathan is fifteen years old, and casual sex isn't a good idea at his age. But I'm forty years old and—"

"And I'll be forty in August." She pressed her lips together. Nathan often did exactly the same thing. "But that's not the point. Kids don't differentiate."

"So it's better to just lie to them about what adults do."

"You're twisting my words."

"There are differences between adults and teenagers, Rachel. They've got to learn that, too."

She growled, set aside her wine, stood, walked away, then turned. "You're college-educated, a teacher *and* a principal, for God's sake, so I don't expect to win any debates with you. It's just fact that we can't see each other anymore. Period."

She waited for him to say something. He'd never begged a woman to stay. The end of his relationships were always mutual. Sometimes nothing needed to be said. But he didn't want Rachel to leave. He hadn't explored everything he wanted to with her. He liked her, admired her, wanted her. It wasn't love. He wasn't sure he believed in love. But he believed in the law of attraction. He was a teacher, and she was the student in whom he saw immense potential. He couldn't bear letting that potential go to waste. He couldn't bear letting *her* go.

"Nathan never has to know about us, Rachel. No one does. We're consenting adults. What we do is our business." He rose. She let him approach without bolting, allowed him to take her hand. "I don't want you to leave yet. We aren't done. There's so much more to come." He dropped his voice to little more than a whisper. "You need it as much as I do."

Her skin flushed. Against his palm, her hand heated. She smelled like freshly picked flowers and hot, needy woman. If he put his hand between her legs, he knew she'd be wet.

"I don't know," she whispered.

She did know, but she wasn't ready yet.

"Think about it," he urged.

"I've *been* thinking about it."

"Think about it tonight. Then call me tomorrow."

He imagined taking her sweet, lush lips, but he didn't. Unfair advantage.

She stepped back. He let her go. She looked at him over her shoulder as she left the room. He'd hoped she'd decide right then. Giving her more time might be the death knell.

Then again, tonight she would be alone in her house, alone in her bed. She wouldn't be able to stop thinking about him. Just as he wouldn't be able to stop thinking about her.

17

IT WASN'T FAIR. WHEN SHE SHOULDN'T HAVE BEEN THINKING about Rand at all, Rachel was consumed with wanting to know everything about him, why he'd become an educator, if he loved his job, what his triumphs had been, what he'd regretted, why he'd never married or had kids of his own when obviously he had to love kids. The fervency with which she wanted to know these things was somehow more intimate than merely wanting sex.

Monday night, it took five tries to get the damn garage door opener to work. She focused on her anger rather than on Rand. Tuesday, the remote worked. With nothing to grouse about, thoughts of Rand came back full force. God, she missed sex with him, missed his voice late at night. She wanted to cry on his shoulder about Nathan, confide that she didn't know what to do. It was awful, weak.

She couldn't talk to him, of course. The two parts of her life had to remain separate. She couldn't mix them, or the boundaries would get skewed.

She suddenly realized she was thinking like Rand, that their sex life was their business. Not her sons'. Not Gary's. Not the school board's or the teachers' or the students'. She picked up her phone and punched in his number. Like she wanted to show *them* that she wasn't going to let anyone run her life or tell her what to do.

Rand answered, and his voice was so good, her heart hurt just to hear it. She hung up because it was insane to want him this badly.

By Wednesday, she was so crazy for an orgasm, for *him*, that she didn't care anymore.

"You called last night," he said, not allowing her the first word.

"Here are the rules," she told him. There had to be guidelines to keep herself in check. "You talk dirty to me and make me come. We don't talk about Nathan or anything that has to do with the other parts of our lives. Agreed?"

"So this is just a phone thing."

She wasn't sure. She couldn't commit. She just needed him now. "Tonight is tonight. We'll talk about what's going to happen later"—she paused—"later." She was being needy and sounding bitchy. If he'd said that to her, she'd have slammed the phone down.

"Agreed," he finally said.

Oh, thank you, thank you. "Tell me a fantasy."

She was naked on the bed, her skin warmed, her body wet, her nipples peaked.

"I've been watching you for weeks," he said. "I want you, but I have to figure out how to get to you."

Her flesh hummed to the rhythm of his voice, the deep tones. For now, she simply ran her fingers lightly over her body, her breasts, abdomen, thighs. "Mmm" was all she said to keep him going.

"You're in the penthouse, and it's a fortress up there. I imagine storming it, and taking you, holding you down, forcing my cock inside you. I'm crazy with thinking about it."

He had so many variations on the theme. A stranger wanting her from afar. Then not so far, and finally taking her, forcing her. "I've noticed a man watching me," she told him fretfully. "I come home and bolt all the doors."

He went with it. "But I'll get to you," he murmured, then dropped his voice. "I have a plan."

She hadn't known a man could love fantasy like this. She'd thought the male psyche was mostly visual, needing pictures, but Rand loved talking, loved hearing her spin a fantasy as she touched herself, then cried out her pleasure. "I'm so afraid. I sense you out there sometimes."

"And you dream that I'll breach your walls."

God, yes, she wanted him right here in her bedroom. She wanted him to breach *her*. She spread her legs, caressed her inner thighs. He made her love the slow build. "I do dream about it, but it's just a fantasy. You can't reach me."

"You think you're so safe that you leave the balcony doors open, never dreaming anyone could scale your walls."

She imagined the penthouse, the dark night, a light breeze ruffling the curtains, the air currents blowing across her body, caressing her as she lay naked in her bed. Her fingers became the breeze, wafting through her pubic curls, teasing her breasts. "I imagine I can see someone on the balcony, but I know it's only my imagination."

"I've climbed that wall, and I'm watching you through the French doors. You're on the bed touching yourself. You have no idea I can see everything, how wanton you are, how you touch your pretty pussy, the one I've been dreaming of."

She moaned, rolling her finger over her clit. "I'm safe in here, but I'm so wet imagining a stranger is watching." She played into his potent words. With her eyes closed and only his voice in her ear, the scenario was almost real in her mind.

"You're not even aware of me when I part the curtains. You're on the bed, touching yourself, caressing, moaning, and Christ, it makes me as hard as iron." His voice dipped down to a whisper. "I watch you."

In her mind's eye, he was standing over her, salivating. Her clit was hard beneath her fingers, heat radiating out, rushing along the surface of her skin, tingling in her toes.

"I put my hand over your mouth and fall on top of you."

She could actually feel his weight pinning her to the bed.

"You can't move. You can't scream. You can only look up at me in the darkness."

She moaned, because she couldn't speak, couldn't make any other sound.

"I put my hand over yours on your hot little cunt."

That word. It was filthy, and God, it made her so wet. She uttered soft terrified noises for him.

"I hold your wrists together in one hand and tug your arms over your head. Then I see the pretty scarf sitting on the bedside table, and I bind you to your headboard with it."

"It's red," she whispered, thinking of one she had in her lingerie drawer. Overcome with the images, she needed more, so much more.

"Slut red," he agreed. "You're at my mercy, and now my fingers are the ones rubbing that throbbing little clit, and inside you, stroking."

She could feel him touching her, and she mewled like a frightened animal. She didn't want to like what he did, but he'd caught her when her blood was high, when she was horny.

"You're so wet and your skin is so hot. I fuck you with my fingers. You struggle, but it's only token. You love this."

Oh yeah, she did. "Please, don't hurt me."

"I'm going to fuck you like you've never been fucked in your life."

"No, no." She writhed on the bed as if she were trying to buck him off. But his fingers were in her; she couldn't stop him. He was too strong.

"I spread your thighs and nudge you with my cock."

"Oh no, please, you're too big."

He gave an evil laugh. "The bigger the better."

"Please don't fuck me." She whimpered. It felt so good, his voice, his fantasy, her hands on her own body. She grabbed the vibrator off the bedside table. "Please don't put your cock in me." She sounded like Nell begging Snidely not to do her, but secretly Nell had always wanted him over the insipid Dudley.

"Fuck. I thrust deep in you."

The vibrator slid all the way in, thrumming inside like the pulse of his cock. "Oh no, oh no," she chanted, because God, it was so good.

"You can't stop me. You're so tight, so fucking ready. You don't want to stop me. You've teased me on the street, pretended you don't see me, but you've wanted my cock in you all along."

"Oh God." The sensations were immense, almost as if he were there, inside her, fucking her, forcing his cock into her.

"Fuck, fuck, fuck," he chanted. "This pussy is mine. I'm going to keep you locked away forever, tied to this bed with all your pretty scarves, where you'll always be mine."

She rocked and rolled on her bed, both hands between her legs, one working the vibrator inside, the other putting pressure on her clit, rubbing, stroking, circling, his voice in her ear the whole time, never letting her down, pushing her higher. She bit her lip, cried out. "No, no, please, no." Then she screamed, long and low, a wail, totally alien to her, from deep in her chest, deep

in her need, deep in him and the fantasies he made her believe
were real.

"JESUS," HE WHISPERED. THEN HE SMILED AS IF SHE COULD SEE HIM.
"That was hot."

She laughed softly, a sexy, dreamy, satisfied sound. "How do
you do that?"

"I have a vivid imagination." But he wanted reality, her in his
bed. They'd never spent the night together, but he'd have loved to
wrap his body around her now and fall asleep. "Was it as good
for you?" He wanted to keep her talking.

"It was embarrassing. I wailed."

"Yes, you did. It was fucking sexy. That's when I came." He'd
shot high up his belly. He rubbed it in. He wasn't ashamed or
afraid of his own come.

"We can only do this over the phone."

Her words threatened to kill the mood, but they were in the
right direction. First, she'd cut him off completely, but he'd
known she'd change her mind. She needed him. He needed her.
Neither of them was done yet.

"We've proven the hypothesis that phone sex is almost as
good as real sex," he said, the operative word being *almost*. He
figured that within a week, she'd realize phone sex wasn't enough.
She was too much woman to go without a man's touch now that
she'd had a taste of it.

"So you agree to the ground rules?"

Her ground rules. They'd made him hot. Talk dirty to her and
make her come. No talking about Nathan. That was okay, too;
he'd be talking with her in that other compartment of their lives.
They now had a foot planted firmly in each part, and there, he'd
help her with Nathan. The boy was definitely salvageable.

"I will agree to the ground rules if," he bargained, "you come like that every time we talk."

"And you won't push to meet face-to-face?"

"That wasn't one of the ground rules."

"I just thought of it."

"Rachel, you know how I feel. You know what I want. Don't expect me not to ask for it."

He couldn't remember a woman affecting him with this intensity before. It had to be the mentoring thing. He'd been born to mentor, and she'd fulfilled him in yet another way.

She sighed. "All right. But I'm a mom, and I know how to say no in the face of wheedling."

He laughed. Her sense of humor was back. With every phone call, he'd be a step closer to her return to his house and his bed. Or his deck. Or the hood of his car.

18

NATHAN SAT IN THE CHAIR OPPOSITE RAND, WITH A TACITURN face that would have been handsome if he smiled. He was taller than his father, and Rand didn't think he was done growing.

Rand opened the conversation. "How's the week been?" He'd given Nathan a week to consider things.

"Fine." Nathan's lip curled slightly.

He decided not to beat about the bush. "We didn't finish our conversation regarding Wally."

Nathan raised his eyes, glowered. "I told you it was an accident. You don't believe me. There's nothing to add."

Rand had seen. It was no accident. What he wanted to know about was the three minutes before, when Nathan had been in the huddle with Tom Molcini, Rick Franchetti, and a couple of other JV basketball players. The boy had looked nervous and uncertain.

"Do you dislike Wally for some reason?"

Nathan blew out a breath. "I don't even *think* about him."

"Then why would a student"—a freshman who would remain

nameless for purposes of this discussion—"say that yesterday you and some other students were seen hassling him again?" He'd received several versions of the latest incident, and none of them matched, just that a few of the basketball players, including Tom Molcini and Rick Franchetti, plus Nathan, were on scene. Rand didn't mind stretching the truth to see if he could get a reaction.

"What do you mean by hassling?"

"The contents of his backpack were tossed onto the floor."

Nathan lowered his gaze to the desk. "He probably dropped it," he muttered. "I don't remember that happening."

Wally lacked even the most basic social skills, but he was intelligent. Over the six months Rand had been principal, the boy had made improvements. Until a few students, who should know better, had started picking on him. Now he was in decline.

"Wally's a good kid, and we both know he doesn't deserve this. Let's talk about who's really responsible."

"I'm not a rat," Nathan said through gritted teeth, then added, "and I don't know anyway. What happened with Wally in the cafeteria was an accident."

"So no one put you up to it."

Nathan flushed. "Why would anyone do that?"

More aptly, why would Nathan defend them? Rand wasn't sure when the problems had started. With a student body of more than fifteen hundred, he hadn't learned all the names and faces yet. First you began to recognize the overachievers, the under-achievers, the special kids, the popular kids; it was only natural. Nathan hadn't come to his attention until a couple of months ago when his name started cropping up in reports involving others who had a reputation for bullying. There'd been no proof until Rand himself had witnessed the incident in the cafeteria, but Nathan was a follower, not a ringleader. He wanted to join the *in* crowd or get on the basketball team, and the price of admission was giving a bad time to kids lower on the totem pole. It was probably as much a hazing for Nathan as it was bullying for Wally. But Rand wasn't tolerating bullies at his school, especially when a special-needs kid like Wally was involved.

"Nathan, I need your help on this." His biggest mistake was that he hadn't noticed Nathan until the trouble started. He'd established no rapport with the boy before he'd questioned him about the incidents. It had all been downhill from there.

"I *don't* know anything, and I *can't* help you."

"I know you don't approve of this kind of activity."

Nathan pursed his lips into a militant scowl. "I don't have time to worry about Wally. I've got enough to do to take care of myself." He grabbed his backpack off the floor, yanked it onto his lap, and sat forward, waiting.

Rand heard the unspoken plea in Nathan's words with no clue how to interpret it. "You're free to go. But I'll be here if there's anything you can think of that will help Wally. He needs you, Nathan."

Nathan didn't answer. He jumped to his feet, yanked open the door as if he'd like to break the handle.

That had gone exceptionally well, hadn't it. Rand shook his head. Dammit.

For the most part, he loved his job, but being unable to solve problems for a boy like Wally, even one like Nathan, sat heavily on his shoulders.

The fact that this was Rachel's son turned it into complete failure.

"I'D LIKE TO COME TO THE BASKETBALL GAME WITH YOU TOMORrow night," Rachel said to Nathan over the phone on Thursday.

"You can't." His voice was surly. "Dad's coming."

Her heart lurched at his dismissive tone. "That's fine. We can both attend."

"It's bad enough that *he's* there. I don't need the other kids thinking my parents are checking up on me."

Rachel rolled her lips together. It was ridiculous that his words should hurt because Gary got to go instead of her. "All right. Next week then."

"Yeah, sure, whatever," Nathan said caustically. "JV games are over for the season, and there's only one varsity game left after this one. It's on Tuesday."

He was so contrary. Last week, he'd made it sound like she'd committed a crime because she'd never gone to a basketball game. He wasn't even playing, for God's sake. "I'd like to come anyway."

"Fine," he spat out. "But if Principal Tor-Vik"—he uttered the name with disgust—"is there, I'm leaving."

Rachel sighed. *Please, not again.* "Did something happen with Principal Torvik?"

"He called me into his office to ream me out again over Wally, and what I *didn't* do to him. Every minute of every day, watching what I do, *hounding* me. I'm not a criminal, Mom. Can I sue for harassment?"

She closed her eyes, shaking her head wearily. "We aren't suing for harassment. Just keep your head down. I'm sure nothing else will happen." Damn, wasn't *that* a wishy-washy answer.

Nathan obviously thought so, too. "Right. I have to finish my homework, Mom."

She didn't want to let him go, but what else was there to say that wouldn't make it all worse? "Okay, honey. Love you."

She cut the connection. She and Gary had discussed this. They would go to the basketball games, though Rachel hadn't realized there were only two left. Whatever, they'd both agreed to make an effort to be more involved. It had actually been a civil conversation, and Gary was holding up his end. She'd ask Erin if she could leave a little early on Tuesday. Justin could join them, and they'd all go out for hamburgers afterward, make a fun evening of it.

With her goodnight calls done, she still wasn't tired.

And Rachel gave in to the desire to hear Rand's voice.

"Horny already?" he asked. "It's not even ten."

Busted. Yet for some inexplicable reason, his assumption irritated her. "Actually, I called about Nathan."

"I thought we weren't supposed to talk about Nathan," he said levelly, his tone overly reasonable. As if suddenly he were talking to an irate mom he had to soothe.

"I'm wearing my *mother* hat now." God, she sounded like a bitch again. She'd already been irritated when she called. It wasn't Rand's fault. Still, shouldn't they discuss his conversation with Nathan? "He said you had him in your office again. I wish you'd let me know these things up front."

"I don't call parents whenever I bring a student into my office for a discussion. I only call if there's an issue."

She felt like a chastened child. So she rebelled like one. "Why did you bring him in if there wasn't an *issue*?"

"This was a follow-up. I do that. It's my job. To keep abreast of student situations." He sounded cold. She could imagine him using that tone with Nathan.

"I wish you'd told me about it last night. I would have been prepared."

"Our evening activities are separate from our daytime activities. Wasn't that your ground rule?"

It pissed her off that he was throwing it back in her face. "Let me rephrase. If you're having an issue with Nathan, I would appreciate a heads-up."

"For you, Rachel, I'll call ahead of time. Then I'll report the discussion to you afterward."

"You don't need to be sarcastic."

She was able to count to ten before he answered. "I didn't intend to come across as sarcastic. I apologize."

She pursed her lips. She was simply incapable of coping with Rand in two distinct parts of her life. Her initial reaction had been the right one. She couldn't have both. "This isn't going to work, Rand. I just can't do it."

"Rachel, we can work it out. I didn't realize it would bother you that I talked to Nathan without your knowledge."

She noticed he didn't say it wouldn't happen again. "I have to handle my family situation first. This thing between us is not helping." She had to think of what was best for Nathan. Phone sex with his principal wasn't going to cut it. "Let's take some time apart, okay?"

"Rachel—"

She pushed the End button and cut him off. She was pathetic. She hadn't even told him she couldn't see him anymore; she'd simply been wishy-washy, just like she had with Nathan.

RAND STARED AT THE PHONE. IF HE'D APOLOGIZED AND SAID IT would never happen again, perhaps she'd have listened. But he'd have been lying. It would happen again. He and Nathan weren't finished, and this issue hadn't been laid to rest. The bullying was ongoing. No matter how much he wanted Rachel back in his bed, he wouldn't compromise his principles, no pun intended.

But he wouldn't let Rachel walk away without a fight. He'd come up with another plan for her, something very special.

19

THEY NEEDED TO TALK, FACE-TO-FACE, SCREW DITCHING HIM OVER the phone. Since she hadn't returned any of his calls, her statement now had much more meaning. *Take some time apart*—that was tantamount to saying they were through. They were so far from through, and Rand was going to prove it to her.

On Saturday night, he drove past Rachel's house. It was dark. If she was out, she hadn't even left the front porch light on; he'd have to give her a lecture on safety issues. He wasn't about to give up, though, and parked several houses down due to her hypersensitivity about anyone guessing they had a relationship. The street was full of cars; his wouldn't be noticed.

The lawn sloped up sharply from the road, the house on the rise of a hill, the main floor a level higher than the garage. From the driveway, he climbed the path, wide concrete steps bordered by overgrown bushes that had lost their shape. He was hidden from the street as the walkway turned and the steps narrowed, becoming steeper as they led to the porch. A large juniper obscured the view of the front porch from the road. It needed trimming, too. Another safety issue. Anyone could be hiding up here, ready to jump her when she went for the front door. He glanced at the lighted dial of his watch. He wondered where she'd gone and how long she'd be, but he'd wait as long as necessary.

In only a few minutes, headlights flashed across the front lawn, then the bushes. She was home, yet nothing happened for long moments. Finally the minivan's door slammed, and soft-soled shoes scuffed the concrete path.

She was exceptionally sexy in the tight jeans he liked and a fitted top beneath a short-waisted sweater. Rummaging in her purse for her keys, she didn't notice him in the shadow of the juniper. Finally pulling the key ring out, she opened the screen, holding it with her foot as she unlocked the front door.

She still hadn't seen him. She was completely vulnerable to anyone hiding on the porch. Didn't she even sense the danger around her?

His heart began to race; a plan formed, so quickly he didn't have time to analyze the judiciousness of it. He saw only how perfect the opportunity was to make the fantasy they'd shared become reality. And an object lesson in personal safety.

He waited until she'd shoved open the door, then followed her, pushing her into the house and kicking the door shut behind him. He heard the screen slam.

"Don't move," he whispered. "Don't turn. And I won't hurt you."

"DON'T MOVE. DON'T TURN."

Rachel froze, her heart stopped, her skin chilled. She hadn't even heard him behind her, but now he was in her house.

"And I won't hurt you."

She caught her breath. Oh God. That voice. She should have

been terrified. She should have turned and slapped him for scaring the crap out of her.

Instead, she held her purse out to the side. "You can have my money. Just leave me alone."

Her pulse beat loudly in her eardrums, yet she could hear him breathe, make out the rustle of his clothing as he reached for the bag.

He took it, dropped it. "Money's not what I want."

She swallowed. "Please don't hurt me."

He stepped up close behind her, touching her with nothing but his body heat. "This won't hurt. You're going to like it."

She knew it was him, but she let it be real, let her heart pound with fright. "What are you going to do?" Even her voice trembled.

She still had her arm out, as if she were to afraid to put it down once he'd taken her purse. He reached under her sweater, trailed his fingers up her torso to the underside of her breast.

"I'm just going to touch you," he murmured. His breath was sweet with a mint, warm against her cheek.

"My husband will be home soon."

"Don't lie," he said. "I've been watching you. Your *ex*," he emphasized, "doesn't live here anymore." He pinched her nipple hard, perhaps in punishment for the lie.

She felt her knees go weak with desire. "Please, just take the money and go."

He moved up flush against her, his cock hard along the base of her spine. "I'll take the money later. First, we're going to play a little game."

Her breath hitched as she inhaled. "What game?"

"It's like strip poker, except we don't use cards, and you always lose and have to take off another piece of clothing for me."

"Please," she whimpered, but her panties were damp.

"First your shoes."

"I—"

He put his hand over her mouth. "Just do it."

She wriggled and wobbled, toeing off both tennis shoes.

"Now the sweater." His mouth at her ear, he licked her.

She shivered, trapped the sensual moan inside, and instead sniffed as if she were terrified. Then she pulled the sweater down her arms. He grabbed it before she was done, yanked it off and threw it to the entry floor.

"The T-shirt," he ordered.

She pulled it over her head, and the chill of the house did nothing to cool her flesh.

"Look at that pretty bra," he murmured, reaching across her to trace the lace over the swell of her breast. Beneath the cup, her nipple pearled.

Then he finger-walked down her bare belly to her belt buckle and pulled it free. His fingers rested a moment at her waistband. "Unzip the jeans."

She sniffed again, whimpered, and moved slightly away from him as if she were getting ready to unzip and peel off her pants. He let her. In the next instant, she elbowed him hard in the ribs.

He hadn't said the game couldn't work against him.

Grunting, he stumbled back, and Rachel took off. If she could get to her bedroom, she could lock the door and grab the phone on the nightstand.

"Bitch," he growled, and he wasn't as far behind her as she'd thought.

She made it to her room, slammed the door.

His foot was in the way.

He sent her flying as he shoved it open. She landed on her ass by the foot of the bed. Rolling, she crawled toward the nightstand and the phone, but then he was on her, pinning her to the carpet.

"That wasn't nice. I was going to be gentle, but now you've pissed me off."

He grabbed her beneath the armpits, hauled her up, and tossed her across the bed as if she weighed nothing. In a flash, he flattened her against the mattress, then yanked her arms over her head and imprisoned her wrists in one big hand.

It was dark, his face in shadow, but she could smell him, that unique scent that was him and only him. Her body reacted, heating, liquefying.

"I'm going to fuck you," he said, low and lethal. "You can't stop me. All you can do is take it and make it easier on yourself by not fighting me." He insinuated a hand between their bellies and yanked on her zipper.

"Never," she said between clenched teeth.

She bucked and rolled against him, trying to throw him off. It didn't do a thing. One-handed, he tugged on her jeans, first one side, then the other, until they were over her hips, her panties coming off with them. Pulling up and off her, still holding her wrists, he shimmied the jeans down her thighs until they were loose and he could push them down the rest of the way with his foot. One sock stayed on, the other came off. She wore only her bra now as he flopped back down on her.

"Now, isn't that better?" he whispered. Nuzzling her neck, he nipped her, then said, "You smell sweet. I'm going to make you feel so good." Then he pushed his leg between hers, parting her thighs.

"No." She struggled, kicked at his calves with her heels. It didn't faze him one bit.

His hand touched her pussy, then his finger slipped between the folds. "Christ, look at that. You're wet. I knew you wanted this."

"Get off me," she said, but God, how she wanted to arch into his touch, rub herself against him.

He pinned her to the bed with his upper body, raising his hips just enough to keep his finger on her clit, circling it, rubbing in all her moisture, driving her mad. "Feel how hard that little clit is. You want this. You want to come."

He held her legs immobile with his own, and she tossed her head on the bed because it was the only part of her body she could move. "Stop it, stop it," she chanted at him.

He reared back, shoving a hand in his pocket. "I'm going to fuck you now."

She could see his face, the taut lines, his eyes blazing. He'd have to put the condom on. He'd have to let her go. Yet still holding her wrists together, the foil packet in his teeth, he unzipped his jeans, pushed them down, and took out his cock.

The sight stole her breath. He was hard, the vein pulsing, his balls tight, the crown almost purple in the dim light from the outside streetlamps falling through the bedroom window. She wanted that cock. Her mouth watered for it. She wanted to beg. But there was the game to be played.

Though he was straddling her, he had to release her hands to tear open the condom and roll it on. Just as he was concentrating on the task, she bucked her hips and pushed. It was enough to pitch him to the side, and she was free. Up and running, she made it through the bedroom door.

He threw himself on her in the hall, slamming her face-first to the carpet. She lost her breath, and in the next moment, she felt him spread her legs, coming down between them.

"So this is how you want it," he snarled. "Like a bitch under me."

She thrust up, trying to throw him off. "Get away from me."

But he put an arm beneath her, hauled her up to her hands and knees, then he was there, his cock hard, right at her pussy. His arm still tight across her belly, his shirt pressed to her back, his breath at her ear, he entered her fast and hard.

It was so good, she screamed with the pleasure of him inside after so many long days without him.

He covered her mouth with his hand. "Don't make a sound, bitch, just take my cock."

She fought not to match his rhythm, not to rock back into him, not to moan. Instead she whimpered and cried and begged him to stop.

"Don't lie, you love it, you little slut."

God help her, she did. She knew it was Rand, a game, a role play, but he was also the handsome stranger breaking into her home, setting her sexually free.

"Fuck, I love your pretty little cunt. I love how it feels, how it milks me, works me. Fuck, fuck."

The dirty words, the compliments, his body, his voice, the game, it all turned her inside out. "Yes," she whimpered.

"You love it, tell me." He panted between the words.

She couldn't resist him anymore. "Yes, yes, I love it. Fuck me, fuck me harder. Please, oh yes." She closed her eyes, went blind with the pleasure. His cock, like steel, his body pounding. She clenched her fingers in the carpet and held on, pushed back, fucked him as hard as he fucked her. "Fuck, fuck," she cried, loving the word, loving everything about this moment.

Then her orgasm ripped through her, and she screamed for him.

THEY LAY IN A HEAP ON THE HALL CARPET. RAND WAS SPENT, LOST in the sensations that still pulsed through his body, in the feel of her against him. He caressed her breast with one hand, stroked her hard nipple.

She sighed.

Should they talk? Should he continue the game? He went for the role play, sliding his hand over her mouth.

"I'm going to leave now. Don't call the police. Don't tell anyone." Then he lowered his lips to her ear, realizing he hadn't even kissed her. "And remember that I can show up again at any time.

I can break in here and fuck the hell of your sweet little cunt whenever I want."

She whimpered.

"You're a fucking hot little number. Oh yeah, I'll be back. Now, don't move, don't look, not until you hear the front door close."

He pulled back, leaving her huddled on the carpet, naked and gorgeous in nothing but her lacy bra. He stole into the bathroom, wrapped the condom in a tissue and shoved it into the wastebasket.

She lay still where he'd left her, except that now she'd curled into a ball. He hoped he hadn't given her knees rug burn.

Christ, it had been so fucking hot. He hoped she felt the same. At the end, she'd gone wild for him; she *had* to feel the same as he had.

After closing the front door softly behind him, he took the steps two at a time until he reached the turn down to the drive. He passed her minivan, then jogged along the street to his car.

He belted in, then sat for a long moment with the urge to rush back, ring her bell, beg her to let him back in, let him sleep with her in his arms. He waited until he'd stuffed the need back down, then started the car.

They'd just played a hot little sex game. The next move was hers.

20

HE SHOULDN'T HAVE SHOWN UP AT HER HOUSE. IT WAS A VIOLATION of all the rules they'd made.

That's what made it so damn hot. Rand was a rule breaker, even as Principal Torvik set his own rules. Rand said yes when she said no. He reeled her back in when she tried to swim away.

She was still wet. Her body still hummed. She lay on the carpet reliving each sensation, every word he'd said. Finally, her skin began to cool. She hadn't even had a chance to turn on the heater, and the groceries were still out in the minivan. In the bedroom, she pulled on a pair of soft old sweats, then padded back down the hall. She emptied the trash in the main bathroom, just in case anyone accidentally saw the evidence of what *Mom* had been doing. She found her purse and keys in the front hall. Oh yes, she'd loved that momentary fright, the one that got her going before she knew it was him. In the kitchen, she went straight to the garage door and punched the opener attached to the wall. The remote hadn't worked again, thank God for that. She'd intended on coming inside to open the door, then pulling the minivan into the garage to retrieve the groceries.

As she did that now, she pondered the possibilities. How could he have planned it to such perfection? Or was it coincidence that he'd been there, an opportunity he'd jumped on? Maybe he'd been coming to see her, to beg her not to cut him off completely. Or maybe he was a stalker.

She put away the groceries. She'd planned to prepare some meals tomorrow to freeze for the week ahead. She wandered into the family room, stood for a moment, then went back to the kitchen, where she'd set her purse and cell phone on the table.

No, she shouldn't.

In the end, she couldn't resist and punched in his number. When he answered, she started crying. "Oh my God, Rand, oh my God."

"Baby, what's wrong? Tell me."

"A man broke into the house and raped me. It was awful. It was terrible. I was so scared."

"Jesus," he said.

She smiled.

CHRIST. HER TEARS TURNED HIS HEART OVER. SHE HAD KNOWN IT was him, hadn't she? Hell. Yes. She must have. He wasn't wearing a mask. She'd seen his face.

Except that he'd made her keep her back to him. Until he was on top of her on the bed. She'd seen him then. But it was fairly dark, only streetlight illuminating the room. Dammit, she should have at least known his voice.

"Did he hurt you, cut you, hit you?" Of course, that's what he'd ask first. But this couldn't be real.

"Just because he didn't hit me or cut me doesn't mean he

didn't hurt me," she said harshly, sniffing. "He made me have sex with him. He *raped* me, Rand." She sobbed.

"Did you call the police?" That would be the second thing he'd want to know. If this were real.

"No. I can't let anyone else know about this."

"But he could come back."

She sniffed again. "I know."

There was something in her voice, a sly note of seduction. She was playing him, probably paying him back for that first moment when she thought it was all real. Hell, he was going to play right back at her.

"Tell me what happened, everything. I have to know if he hurt you."

"I went out for groceries, and when I got back, he was hiding on the porch, and after I unlocked the door, he pushed me inside."

"Oh, baby, I'm so sorry."

"He closed the door, then he made me take off my shirt and my shoes. That's when I elbowed him in the stomach and tried to run away."

Yeah, she'd given him a hell of a jab. But it was deserved. "Did you run for the back door?"

"No. I wouldn't have made it. I tried to lock myself in the bedroom, but I couldn't get the door closed before he shoved his foot in." Her speech was fast, her voice breathy, and she was making him hot all over again. He gave her a comforting sound, urging her to go on. "Then he was all over me on the bed, Rand. He tore off my clothes, squeezed my breasts, then touched me between my legs." She stopped, waited.

She wanted something from him. What? Funnily enough, he couldn't remember the exact details as to when he'd done what. "Did he hurt you then?"

"Rand, you're going to be mad," she whispered.

"I promise not to be. Just tell me. It'll be all right."

"I was very wet, Rand."

He was suddenly marble hard in his jeans. She had such a sweet, sexy voice, low, seductive. "You naughty girl. Don't tell me you actually liked it."

"I didn't want to, Rand. But he was so big and manly, so powerful. I couldn't help it. There he was between my legs, and I just got so wet."

"You are bad. So you let him fuck you."

"No. I didn't. Honestly. I still fought him. He was holding my arms over my head, and he had his fingers between my legs, and he told me he was going to fuck me."

He slouched back in his chair. Oh yeah, he remembered. She'd made him so fucking hard with her struggles. Her skin was like silk, her pussy wet, her clit plump and begging for it.

"He took his cock out of his jeans." There was a note of reverence in her voice. "He was so big. I actually salivated, Rand. I couldn't help it."

"You wanted that cock bad, didn't you?"

"Yes. You just can't know how much I wanted to reach out, touch him, then suck him."

"Oh, you need to be punished for that."

"But I didn't do it, Rand. I swear it."

God, he wished she had. Though what had happened was just as fucking good.

"Then, when he tried to put on the condom, that's when I rammed him again and ran out."

"Thank God, baby, you got away."

"He caught me in the hallway." She stopped for two beats. "He fucked me doggy style right there in my own hallway."

"Jesus." He could still feel her pussy gripping him, taking him even as he took her, the cool darkness of the hallway around them.

"I liked it, Rand," she whispered. "I loved it. He fucked me, and I screamed with how good it was."

"You dirty bitch." He could barely breathe. She'd turned him inside out.

"He called me names, and I loved it."

"You are so fucking bad."

"You know what else, Rand?" she said on a mere breath.

"No, tell me."

"I'm going to fuck him again."

Then she was gone, only blank space left on his cell.

Jesus. She had him. He was hers. He jerked off in the dark of his bedroom and came almost as hard as he had inside her house, inside her.

TUESDAY MORNING, NATHAN HAD GROWLED AT HER WHEN SHE'D reminded him she'd be leaving work early to make it to the basketball game at four. This Tuesday game was the last of the season. She absolutely would not miss it.

Of course Erin didn't have a problem with her cutting out early occasionally, and she met Justin outside the middle school. She'd wanted to include him in the outing, too. They crossed the street to Nathan's high school, heading back through the maze of hallways to the gymnasium. It was an open campus, shaped like a wheel, the quad in the center, the gym on the far side, and all the classroom buildings fanning out like the spokes of a wheel. Students still mingled in small groups, others dashing past. Music from band practice floated out through an open door as they passed. The musicians were pretty darn good.

Everywhere, Rachel kept an eye out for Rand. She'd worn butt-hugging jeans to work this morning, with a red T-shirt tight over her breasts and a short black blazer. Bree had smiled knowingly, Erin hadn't said anything, but Yvonne had given her a long up-and-down perusal. Whatever. If she saw Rand, Rachel wanted to look sexy and hip, not like some dowdy old mom.

She was still reeling from Saturday night. The sex was hot, the phone sex afterward exciting. They'd crossed another line. He'd been in her house. He was the principal; he'd probably looked up her address. She wouldn't put it past him to figure out where she worked, too. But she for damn sure knew he'd be in her house again. He'd turned her inside out and all around. She wasn't giving him up. If she could have gotten away with it, she'd have unlatched the bedroom screen and let him sneak in to ravish her while the boys slept. She wanted it that bad. She couldn't risk them catching her at it, though. How would she explain? She needed to keep Rand her secret, with no one to judge her. This wasn't like the masseur; she knew what Gary would say. She wasn't going to listen.

Rand had called her Monday night. She hadn't answered. Part of it was feminine wiles. Keep him guessing as to what was going on in her mind. The other part was Nathan. She had to think of him, to put the boys first and her own needs second.

But the minute she dropped them off at Gary's on Sunday, Rand Torvik better watch out.

Justin was talking. She suddenly tuned back in. "He thinks it's embarrassing you're coming to games he's not even playing in," Justin said. "Like you're checking up on him."

Her youngest son could be a fountain of information. He wasn't a tattletale so much as a talker. She wanted to say she *was* checking up on Nathan, but communication was two-way, and she didn't think Nathan needed to hear that.

"You're not going to pull that crap with me, are you, Mom?"

She stopped on the edge of the quad. "First, I am not checking up on Nathan, and second, I will make a concerted effort to attend as many of your soccer games as I can. I was remiss this year. It's not *checking up*, it's being involved."

Justin shrugged. "I don't care whether you're involved. I'd rather know I've got meat loaf to come home to for dinner."

Rachel laughed. "You and your stomach, that's all that counts."

She ruffled his hair. He didn't pull away. He was so different from Nathan. She wouldn't say more mature, just less sensitive. He didn't seem to care what other kids thought of him. Or maybe it was safer to say that he was picky about whose opinion he valued. He didn't choose friends based on their popularity at school. She didn't know why he was that way. Her mother claimed that children's personalities were determined in the womb and the first few months after birth, affected by the mood of their mother at the time. With Nathan, Rachel had been nervous, all the new-mother things a woman worried about. Would he be healthy, would he love her, was he gaining enough weight, was that cough something she needed to call the doctor about, yadda, yadda. When Justin came along, she'd been through it all and was much more mellow. She didn't put a lot of stock in her mother's old wives' tales, but she had to admit Nathan was a worrier like she'd been, and Justin was pretty darn laid-back.

A low rumble of voices, feet, clapping, shouts, and cheers drifted on the breeze, getting louder as they crossed the quad to the steps leading up to the gym's open doors.

Inside, it was chaos. She hadn't expected the game to be so well attended, but the school had spirit. The bleachers had been pulled out from the walls on all sides, and most of the seats were full. Cheerleaders in blue and yellow outfits punched their pom-poms in the air, chanting out cheers the audience yelled along with. There were two male cheerleaders, which they certainly hadn't had in Rachel's day.

The two teams were out on the court warming up. The referees were checking their whistles, and the coaches were shouting last-minute instructions.

Scanning the crowd, she couldn't find Nathan.

"There they are," Justin shouted, grabbing her hand and pointing. Her youngest son didn't mind touching her. She followed the line of his finger, and there was Nathan, three-quarters of the way up on the far bleachers. His expression was glum, even put-upon. Next to him sat Gary, leaning down to shout something in his ear. She hadn't expected Gary. He'd done his duty on Friday.

On Nathan's other side sat a pretty brunette, midtwenties, slender features, and big red lips. She put those big red lips forward, leaning across Nathan to say something to Gary. He turned as she spoke. They smiled together. Even Nathan smiled.

Dear God. The bastard had brought his girlfriend.

21

RACHEL FROZE, HER HAND PUNISHINGLY TIGHT AROUND JUSTIN'S. "What's *she* doing here?" She regretted her tone immediately, wanting nothing in her voice to communicate any emotion, but the words were out before she could stop them.

"She said she had fun on Friday night and wanted to come again sometime." Justin rolled his eyes. "It reminded her of when she was a cheerleader."

Which wasn't that long ago. Rachel's fingers felt numb, but no way was she running out. "What's her name again?"

"Sherry."

"How often is she over?" she asked as they made their way around to the opposite bleachers, past the flouncing cheerleaders, behind the athletes' benches.

"Not *every* night."

That's illuminating, she wanted to say, but refrained.

"She doesn't spend the night, if that's what you mean."

Thank God. "I didn't mean that." It was exactly what she meant. "I was just curious how—" Rachel stopped herself. She wanted to know how hot and heavy they were, how long they'd been dating, how they'd met, if they'd known each other before the divorce—way too many questions to pump her son for answers to.

Nathan saw her as they started to climb the bleachers and scowled. Then he looked at Sherry, who was practically bouncing on her seat like she wanted to join in the cheers. She was young, God, so young.

Rachel stuffed down her emotions. She would not be bitchy in front of the boys. She would not sound like a jealous woman who'd gotten dumped by her husband for a younger woman. Because really, life was better without Gary. Okay, it would be better when Nathan was no longer angry about everything.

God help her, she wished Rand was here, right here, so she could cling to his arm and beam up at him, and watch Gary's face pale because he was so much less of a man.

Stop the madness!

Her head ached with all the noise.

Then Justin was sidling past Sherry, Nathan, and Gary, and sitting down in a vacant spot. Rachel had two choices, push past all of them, too, or sit on the end next to Sherry.

"Hi," the girl said brightly, holding out her hand. "You must be Rachel."

Duh. She was looking at Sherry's hand like it was a bug to be squashed. How terribly embarrassing the whole situation was. Why the hell hadn't Gary said something? They'd talked civilly on Sunday, and he hadn't said a thing about leaving work early on Tuesday to attend the game. He'd done it for *Sherry*, because she'd had *fun.* Yet he'd groused when he'd had to take time off to go to the principal's office with his ex-wife. Rachel gave a mental groan. She needed to stop her runaway thoughts.

She was forced to sit next to the girl. "You must be Sherry," she said, her voice sounding sickeningly sweet even to her. "It's nice to meet you." She was going to throw up.

Sherry's T-shirt was tighter, the neckline lower cut, and though she was slimmer, her breasts were much larger. They were disgustingly pert, the breasts of a young woman who'd never had children. Her dark hair cascaded luxuriously over her shoulders. She wore sandals despite the fact that it was still winter, with a toe ring on each foot, a diamond glittering in one.

"I hope you don't mind that I asked Gary to bring me again. We just had so much fun on Friday." Sherry tapped Nathan's knee. "Didn't we?"

He nodded.

"Hi, sweetie," Rachel said over the din.

Nathan nodded again but didn't say anything. Well, at least she and Sherry got the same reaction: silence.

"Nathan's going to try out for the team next year," Sherry said, as if Rachel wasn't his mother and didn't know. "He's watching all the teams and the strong players and all that stuff, so he's really prepared this time."

Nathan had told all that to Sherry? This was mortifying. Then all the announcements started, the cheerleaders stopped cheering, the coaches got up, the players were introduced over the loudspeaker, then the game was on.

"He likes water polo," Rachel said.

"Oh yeah. Water polo's great." Then Sherry was punching her fist in the air because one of the boys had dribbled. It was such an odd term.

Rachel wished she was sitting next to Nathan so she could ask him about the players and secure all the information Sherry had obviously gotten, probably without even prying it out of him. But it was too late to change seats. He watched the game deliberately, as if he was making mental notes. She wondered where his so-called friends were.

The girl prattled on, like she was making small talk, stuff about the plays, everything innocuous. If Rachel didn't know she was sitting next to Gary's girlfriend, it would have been like talking to a chatty teenager at her son's basketball game. Sherry was actually nice.

"How did you and Gary meet?" Rachel allowed herself the question.

"Oh, I'm the Purchasing AA. I started there about six months ago."

An admin. Which was just about what Rachel was at DKG. Except that she was fifteen years older. "That's nice," Rachel said noncommittally.

"He was just such a funny guy, always making me laugh."

Gary? Funny?

"So I asked him out." Sherry laughed. "I'm kind of forward that way."

Rachel didn't know how she felt about all this. Sherry was sweet, and certainly friendly. She included Nathan in some of the things she said about the game, and he responded, smiling. Then she'd lean over and shout something at Justin. He'd shout back. It was unnerving, almost threatening. Rachel didn't like that about herself. She didn't want to wish her boys would hate this pretty, fresh-faced girl their father was dating.

"Do you want a soda?" Sherry asked.

"I . . . well, yes, thanks. A Coke would be great."

"Gary, I'm getting drinks," she called out. "Who wants what?" She noted the list, then Gary reached into his wallet and handed her a twenty.

Rachel watched her bounce down the bleachers. Glancing at Nathan, she saw his face turn pink and followed the line of his gaze. Three boys seated a few rows below were nudging, laughing, staring at Sherry's butt, and one of them shot Nathan a thumbs-up. He surreptitiously raised a thumb in return, then quickly covered it when he saw Rachel looking at him. Hmm, so those were his friends. And they were checking out Sherry's butt. All right, definitely not the influence Rachel wanted for Nathan.

Down on the gym floor, one of the school clubs sold the cans out of two huge coolers behind a table they sat at. Sherry leaned over, affording the Peeping-Tom boys a nice view as she pointed into the cooler. One of the kids put all the cans in a cardboard holder for her.

Rachel slid over into the now-vacant seat beside Nathan. "Good game?" she asked, feeling oddly tongue-tied.

"Yeah" was all he said.

She wanted to ask how he felt having both his mom and his father's girlfriend here. She wanted to ask if those boys checking out Sherry were his good friends. Instead she kept her mouth shut for fear of saying the wrong thing.

Then Sherry was back, handing out the cans, passing Gary the change. Nathan said, "Mom, you took Sherry's seat."

In a daze, Rachel moved over and let Sherry sit down.

Suddenly, she was the odd man out.

RAND DIDN'T GO TO ALL THE GAMES. BETWEEN FOOTBALL, BASKET-ball, and baseball, not to mention wrestling, soccer, water polo, and track, he couldn't possibly attend everything.

This, however, was the last varsity basketball game of the season, and Rachel had said she was coming with her sons. He hadn't met the younger boy, but Justin would be a freshman in the fall. That was all Rand knew. The nights they had together weren't spent talking, unless it was about sex, but he'd gleaned a little.

He'd experienced the strangest urge to attend the game, see her, talk to her, get her to introduce him to her sons. Maybe Nathan wouldn't glower. When Rand dreamed, he dreamed big.

He entered the gym during the last quarter, watching from the end of the bleachers. A few students noticed him, said hi. A young English teacher fluttered her lashes at him. As for the rest, all eyes focused on the gym floor. The acoustics in the big auditorium were deafening, and every time a boy pivoted on the court, his gym shoes squeaked loudly. But damn if the kids didn't get into the spirit of team sports, hooting and hollering, cheering the players on.

He scanned the crowd for Rachel. Beyond teachers, coaches, and the players' parents seated behind their sons' benches, there were few adults. He found her on the opposite side of the court, about halfway up, seated on the end next to a dark-haired young woman, a student he didn't recognize. No, not a student, this one was probably in her midtwenties. To her right sat Nathan, then the ex, and, Rand assumed, the younger son on his right. Rand imagined he could see a bit of Rachel in the boy's face. The whole family. Was the girl Rachel's sister or . . .

Rand tipped his head, watching the ex, or more specifically, watching the ex glancing back and forth between Rachel and the girl. There was something in his expression, fearful, even a little frantic. Then Rand got it. This was a new girlfriend. Gary the asshole ex had brought his girlfriend, probably to tweak Rachel's nose. The girl was at least fifteen years younger than Rachel, and pretty. Rachel, however, was prettier, her smile sweeter.

He couldn't believe the asshole would put her through the humiliation. He had the urge to march up there and deck the guy. Better yet, he should climb the bleachers, sit down next to Rachel, put his arm around her, and lay one hot, sexy tongue kiss on her.

Of course, he wouldn't. She'd freak because of Nathan and Justin. And while Rand liked his kink, he didn't mix school and sex. He'd never dated a teacher, not even anyone in administration. Schools were communities. What you thought was private soon became gossip in school hallways.

The clock was ticking down. His team wasn't going to win

this one, unfortunately. Neither was he. Approaching Rachel after the game wasn't a good idea.

Instead he watched her until the final buzzer went off. En masse, the crowd rose out of the bleachers and swamped the players down on the court. There was the downer of losing, but you couldn't tell from the cheering, backslapping, and ruckus going on.

After surveying the rowdy crowd a few moments longer, Rand melted out into the night before everyone else exited, beating the throng. It would be full-on dark soon, and he took the steps down to the quad, turning back as the gymnasium's doors began to disgorge its occupants. He hoped to catch a glimpse of her.

On the opposite side of the quad, a tall male figure dashed out of the music wing, heading for the stairs outside the gym. He didn't make it up before becoming engulfed in the game's exiting crowd.

Was that Wally? What was he doing here? Wally didn't like crowds, but his locker was down the wing adjacent to the gym. Rand lost sight of the boy as the quad filled up.

There was the usual jostling and horseplaying. He searched the crowd for Rachel and her family, trying to cover both sets of double doors, but the game had been well attended, and he had trouble spotting any of them.

A small crowd seemed to be gathering at the top of the stairs, then he heard a shout. Rand got a feeling, a bad one. Wally had disappeared somewhere over there. In another moment, Rand began to run, pushing through gaps in the students and parents now dotting the quad.

Then the crowd at the far end parted, and a body tumbled down the stairs.

Jesus. They needed more lighting out here for night games. He couldn't see anything as he elbowed his way through the knot of onlookers.

Wally lay on the ground at the foot of the stairs, his hands over his face, shoulders shaking. Rand squatted down. The boy's sleeve was torn, his elbow scraped. Rand reached out, but didn't touch him. Wally had an aversion to touching.

"You okay, Wally? Talk to me."

"Fine, fine, fine," Wally chanted in his usual set of three.

"What happened?"

"Trip, trip, trip." Wally's voice was high, almost singsongy.

"Take your hands away, Wally. I need to see if your face is bleeding."

First Wally spread his hands, gazing up at Rand through the bars of his fingers.

"That's not good enough, Wally."

The boy slowly slid his hands down. "Okay, okay, okay."

Rand didn't see any blood beyond the scrape on his elbow. "You look okay, Wally, but I want to take you in to see Coach Milford. He's got a first-aid kit, and he can clean up that scrape."

"Good, good, good," the boy chirped, but Rand noted moisture beneath his eyes. He'd been crying. Maybe from the fall, maybe from before.

Rand looked up, studying each and every face staring down at them. Tracking the path of Wally's fall, he locked gazes with the young man hovering at the top of the stairs.

Nathan Delaney.

22

WHEN THE GAME ENDED, NATHAN HAD PUSHED PAST THEM AND shot down the bleachers as soon as Rachel and Sherry stepped into the aisle. Something about seeing his friends, he'd said, as if he was too embarrassed to let his mother meet them. She'd wanted to shout after him to be careful on the steps, but he'd melted into the courtside crowd.

"Are we going for burgers, Mom?" Justin asked.

That's what she'd told him, but if they did, there was no way to avoid inviting Gary and Sherry. Gary and Sherry. She wanted to laugh at the rhyme but was afraid it would sound hysterical. "I thought we'd pick up some takeout," she answered as they hit the gym floor.

She followed the flow in the direction she thought she'd seen Nathan go. She *would* meet his friends, no matter how he tried to dodge it.

"But, Mom," Justin whined, "I thought we were going to Clancy's."

She'd mentioned that somewhere along the way. Clancy's had

the juiciest burgers in the Santa Clara Valley. Even now, her mouth watered thinking of a teriyaki burger drenched in sauce and mushrooms. You had to eat it with a knife and fork, but it was delicious.

Oddly, salivating made her think of Rand. Okay, not so odd. He was that kind of man. She'd scanned the crowd, but hadn't spotted him. He probably didn't attend many of the games, not wanting to show favoritism to any one sport.

"Clancy's sounds great," Gary said, meeting her gaze. "My treat." Sherry hung on his arm, smiling, looking around, as if she enjoyed all the sights one could see shuffling through a slow crowd.

Rachel very nearly cringed. Now she was supposed to have dinner with his girlfriend? That was going too far. Of course, he had to come off as magnanimous, too, by offering to pay.

"Well," she started.

"Come on, Mom," Justin said, bouncing on his shoes. "Dad's even gonna pay."

She felt like a cheapskate. Didn't anyone else see how awkward this was?

"Let's get Nathan," she said. Maybe she should let Gary and his girlfriend take the boys to dinner.

Dark had descended when they hit the concrete outside the gym, and the lights above the doors inadequately illuminated the stairs. A crowd had formed, stopping their progress. Rachel pushed up on her toes, bracing her hand on Justin's shoulder.

She saw Nathan at the top of the stairs in the midst of a group. "This way." She headed in that direction, pushing through, feeling Justin behind her.

Nathan had lost his friends along the way and stood at the head of the quad steps, a cluster of students, all two steps back, surrounding him. A young man lay at the bottom. Beside him, Rand squatted, his gaze on Nathan.

She felt strangely queasy observing the look that passed between them. "Nathan," she said. "What's going on?"

"Nothing," he snapped, without turning his head.

Rand's eyes flashed to her, saying something she couldn't read in the relative darkness. Then he spoke quietly to the boy on the ground. It was Wally, the same young man she'd seen in Rand's office the day they'd met to discuss Nathan.

Together they rose, Rand with his hand up as if he wanted to take the boy's elbow. "Clear a path," he said sternly, holding his arm out to guide his charge up the stairs without actually touching him. "We need to talk again," he murmured softly as he passed Nathan, once again glancing at Rachel as if the words were meant for her, too. Then they disappeared around the corner of the gym.

"Nathan, what was that all about?" she demanded.

"Nothing." He shook his head, dropping his gaze to the concrete. Around him, the other students moved on, for the most part making a beeline for the parking lot.

"Is that the boy you had the altercation with the other week?" she prodded, trying to get him to talk.

He turned on her. "I didn't have an *altercation*. We accidentally bumped into each other, and he dropped his tray."

That wasn't what happened, but Rachel decided not to tackle the issue now. "What just went on here?"

"I didn't touch him tonight either," Nathan growled. "He just fell." He bunched his hands at his sides.

Rachel felt his anger roll over her, and she stepped back, knocking into Sherry.

"We're going for burgers, son, coming along?" Either Gary didn't get that something was wrong or he was attempting to defuse the situation. "Clancy's."

"Dad's buying," Justin added, as if Nathan needed additional incentive.

"Can I drive?" Nathan asked.

"Sure."

"Gary, it's dark," Rachel said quickly.

He shrugged. "He's got to have ten hours of night driving to get his license. You take Justin with you."

"Oh, fun," Sherry said, playfully slapping Nathan's shoulder. "You're gonna do great. It's a piece of cake."

Rachel wanted to smack her. "Nathan can drive with me. Justin, you go with your father, and we'll meet you there." She wanted a few minutes alone with her son to figure out what had happened on the stairs.

Gary opened his mouth. She shut him up with a glare. It was her week with the boys, and Nathan would do the driving with her. "Okay, we'll meet you there," Gary had the brains to answer. He put a hand on Justin's head and steered him toward the parking lot.

She was getting used to driving with Nathan, no longer feeling it necessary to slam her foot to the floorboards. She let him get out of the parking lot and onto the main road before she started in on him. "All right, tell me what that was all about."

"Mom, I'm driving. I can't talk." He looked in his mirror, then remembered the blind spot and glanced over his shoulder to change lanes. Good boy. He was actually doing quite well with his driving these days.

"It can't be distracting to state simply what happened to that boy. Wally, right?"

He grunted. "Yes, it was Wally."

She didn't accuse him. "Did you see what happened?"

"No." But there was that telltale sullen note in his voice.

"Then why did Principal Torvik say he'd talk to you later?" And why did Rand always manage to see her son at his worst?

"Because he has it in for me," he said with a sharp edge. "He sees me and decides everything is my fault." This time he moved back into the right lane without looking over his shoulder. A car honked.

"You didn't look, Nathan." It was her fault; she *was* distracting him. In her need to know, she'd chosen an inappropriate time for this discussion.

"Mom," he said, almost a wail.

She had to admit she'd attacked as soon as they got in the car and put him on the defensive. Not the right way or the right time to start this conversation. She let it drop.

Until later.

LATER DIDN'T COME. CLANCY'S WAS CROWDED FOR A TUESDAY night. The food was ordered at one window, then picked up at another, and the eating was family style at long lacquered picnic tables. The huge hall was ringed by old-fashioned pinball machines that were constantly ringing and clanging.

Dinner was an hour of listening to Sherry laugh. She laughed at everything. She was so happy, it was sort of manic. Okay, that was Rachel's bad mood, but the girl was the antithesis of Gary. Except that she noticed Gary smiled more, even talked more. He'd never liked Clancy's because you didn't have your own table or booth. Everyone shared. Even the huge platter of fries in the middle got shared. Well, not with everyone around them, but within their group. The fries were as good as the teriyaki burger, and she ate more than she should.

"Gary says you're going back to school. That's exciting." Sherry was seated opposite between Nathan and Gary.

Rachel gaped at Gary. Did he tell the girl everything? "Yes."

"What are you going to major in?" Sherry's puppy-dog brown eyes were bright, as if she was actually interested.

"I don't know yet. I'll just take some computer classes to start."

"I can help you do your homework, Mom." Justin beamed at her.

The little smart aleck was giving her a bad time. It was kind of sweet. "Thank you, dear."

"Well, if you ever need to leave Nathan and Justin with me and Gary, you know we'd love it." Sherry gave her an ever-so-bright, white-toothed smile.

Rachel was speechless. This girl wanted her sons? Rachel looked at Gary. His burger had suddenly become fascinating.

Okay, find your tongue, woman. "Well, uh, that's nice. But I'm sure I can handle classes and homework. Nathan and Justin are old enough to be alone for a couple of hours in the evening." There, they'd both go for that, grown-ups, their mom trusting them to be by themselves for an evening. When she was fourteen, she used to babysit until midnight for several different neighbors.

"It would be easier if they were with us," Gary finally said, his eyes narrowed.

Us. She didn't like the way that sounded. *Us* against *you.* If she started giving them inroads, they'd try to take over. Yet when she'd first broached the subject, he'd pounced on her, saying he wasn't going to take care of the boys all the time just to convenience her.

"It's not an issue right now," she said. "It's one of those late-start classes and doesn't begin until April."

In the intervening weeks, she'd think up a way to make sure Sherry didn't somehow steal her boys away.

RAND HAD WAITED IN VAIN FOR RACHEL TO CALL. MAYBE SHE hadn't needed sex, hadn't needed him. Though he liked to think it was as hard for her to hold off as it was for him.

Then he'd seen her tonight, on the stairs beside Nathan. Why the fuck did it happen again? Why did circumstance keep getting in their way? There was some reason, something that needed to be accomplished. Nothing was coincidence. He just didn't know what that *something* was. It definitely involved Nathan, and probably Wally, too.

Rand fully intended to pull Nathan into his office tomorrow. He'd talked with Wally tonight as the coach cleaned his scrapes. The boy had no explanation for what happened. Rand noted some of the faces surrounding them, and he'd call those kids in, too. Someone would give him the story, but Nathan was uppermost on his list to have a hard discussion with. And Rand didn't want any blowups with Rachel about it.

She always saved her calls for him until after ten-thirty. He was usually in bed, naked, waiting. Tonight, he sat in the big leather chair in his office. He'd often imagined having her in this chair, bending her over it and taking her from behind. Tonight, though, was about something different.

He took the offensive and phoned her. On the fourth ring, he wondered if she might refuse to answer. Then her voice was simply there, and his heart rate spiked.

"What happened?" she said. She was usually soft, seductive, dreamy. Tonight, her voice was cold.

Well, hell, he hadn't expected anything else. She was Mama Bear protecting her young. "I don't know. I didn't see." He'd been too busy looking for her. "Tomorrow I'll interview some of the kids present."

"Didn't the boy tell you what happened?"

The boy. "Wally," he supplied. "He didn't say much. He's not a big talker." Wally had repeated various iterations, in his usual threes, that he was fine. He liked to listen to band practice, and apparently his mother had been late picking him. Rand made a mental note. There was sometimes a key that helped unlock an autistic child's mind. Perhaps music was Wally's.

"Is he all right?"

It seemed three questions too late. "Fine, fine, fine," he said softly, imitating Wally.

"Maybe he just fell." Her voice held a helpful note.

"I'll learn more tomorrow." Then he got to the reason he'd called. "I will be talking to Nathan."

"He said he didn't have anything to do with it."

He waited a beat. "I'd like to hear his version."

She sighed. Christ, he'd so wanted to hear her sigh, but not like this. "What time do you want me to be there?"

"I don't want you there, Rachel."

"I'm his mother."

"I'm not going to railroad him. I'm not even going to accuse him."

"Then what are you planning to do?" She was suddenly snappish.

"I'll let him tell you about it tomorrow."

"Tell me now," she insisted.

"Rachel, I've been doing this a long time. Parents are not always helpful in these situations. There are resentments."

"He resents *you*, Principal Torvik, not me."

He accepted the verbal slap. She was worried and pissed. He could understand that. "I'm going to offer him some after-school activity. Two hours a week."

"Doing what?" Wariness made her voice harsh.

Trust me. He didn't say it. "I want him to tell you, Rachel. If you're there, he'll feel ganged up on. We already did that. Now it's time for something different." He was actually curious if Nathan would tell her about his plan at all. "Will you give me that latitude?"

"If I were the parent of another child in your school, would you consult me first?"

He had to ask himself if Nathan was the special case. Or she was? With another parent, he might handle it differently. The fact that she'd been having sex with him distracted her. She worried what Nathan would figure out. She worried about siding with him against her son. He wasn't sure she could view the situation without their extracurricular activities getting in the way. God forbid he should say that, though.

So he lied. "I'd write them a letter."

"But you don't know that he actually did anything."

As of right now, he didn't have any evidence to accuse Nathan. He had only suspicion. Nathan might not have done anything, but he did know what had happened. Rand wasn't sure he'd ever get it out of him. "Let's put it this way. He doesn't have any sports in the spring, so he'll have extra time and we'll put it to good use."

The phone was silent for long moments. The grandfather clock in the hall chimed once for the quarter hour. "All right," she huffed out. "Don't make me regret this."

"I've already told you that you're never going to regret anything we do."

"This is *you*, not we."

She was right. So he finally said it, "Trust me, Rachel."

"Famous last words," she whispered.

23

FOR THE THIRD TIME IN AS MANY WEEKS, RAND HAD NATHAN IN his office. "Wally could have been seriously injured, a broken arm, a broken leg. You saw what happened, Nathan. I need to know."

Nathan sat mute in the chair opposite.

Earlier this morning, Rand had summoned the four kids he'd seen in the circle around Nathan. Molcini and Franchetti had not been among them. Very suspicious. Those two had simply vanished from the scene, but Rand had noticed them inside the gymnasium earlier. The kids he interviewed, a boy and three girls, claimed they'd seen Wally at the bottom of the stairs, but not how he got there. Wally's mom had tried asking as well, but he hadn't changed his mantra of "fine, fine, fine."

Nathan was the only one Rand could possibly get anything out of. Yet the boy had been a nonverbal specimen in his damn chair for the past five minutes.

"All right. You leave me no choice." Rand almost laughed at his own dramatic words. *Yeah, blame the kid when you feel help-*

less. "I've decided you need something to occupy you after school. I'm assigning you to two hours per week in the special education lab."

Nathan jerked his head up. "What?"

"The special ed lab. You will provide an hour of tutoring after your last class. Tuesdays and Thursdays should work."

"You can't make me do that." He gaped at Rand. "I haven't done anything wrong."

"Think of it as community service. We're short on tutors. They need you." Rand thought it was a perfect solution. He'd found that you couldn't continue to bully someone once they became humanized in your eyes. As he got to know the kids in special ed, Nathan would learn a little compassion.

"I don't know how to tutor." Nathan shook his head, spread his hands.

"There are teachers in the lab. They'll help you while you help the kids."

"But—but—" Nathan stammered.

"But what?"

"Everyone will make fun of me," he blurted out, his eyes almost wild, as if he were a cornered animal.

Nathan's fear was the crux of the matter. "Then you'll know how it feels and have some empathy for Wally."

"Principal Torvik"—a whine crept into Nathan's voice—"you don't understand."

"Then explain it to me."

Nathan's mouth gaped like a fish. Then he shut it, and shut down. "Nothing." What he'd been about to say was gone.

"What, Nathan?" Rand knew the opportunity had already passed.

"Fine," he said morosely. "Tuesdays and Thursdays for one hour." Then he glared at Rand. "One hour and that's it."

"That's all I ask." Though Rand could sure as hell hope for a lot more.

And part of the *more* was Nathan's mother.

RACHEL HAD PROMISED TO TAKE NATHAN DRIVING FOR AN HOUR after dark. Justin wanted to stay home to finish his homework. She had her cell phone. He had his. He was thirteen. He could handle being home alone for an hour. She was not going to be overprotective. She did not need Sherry to look after the boys.

It had also given her an hour alone with Nathan. But, dammit, during that entire hour, he hadn't said one word about his meeting with Rand earlier in the day. She couldn't ask because she wasn't supposed to know.

Damn Rand for putting her in this position. She should be able to talk to her own son. What was she supposed to do if Nathan never mentioned the meeting or the after-school activity Rand had assigned him?

A piece of her just wanted to cry. She felt helpless. The worst part was that if Rand weren't Principal Torvik, she would have started talking to *him* about her issues with Nathan. And Gary. And Sherry.

Trust me. That's what Rand had said. Yet while she trusted him with her sexuality, trusted him not to put her video on the Internet or expose her affair to her son, to give her a hot rape fantasy without ever hurting her, she didn't trust him emotionally. She couldn't tell him about Gary and Sherry, or that she was terrified of losing the boys. She couldn't expose all her fears. Hell, she hadn't even told him about the massage. That said something important, the fact that she was incapable of sharing her most humiliating moment with him.

By the end of the driving lesson, she was utterly exhausted. She pushed the remote as Nathan pulled into the driveway. Thank goodness it worked without an issue, otherwise she might actually have screamed. "All right, you can take the minivan into the garage."

So far, she'd always had Nathan get out, then driven the minivan in herself, but he had to learn sometime. She kept her mouth shut as he maneuvered the vehicle into the garage. It was big enough for two cars, but there was a support beam in the middle. She breathed a sigh of relief as he made it past with plenty of room, not cutting too close on either the passenger's or driver's side.

"Good job," she said, her hand on the door.

"Mom."

She felt something, a mother's sixth sense. This was important. "Yes, honey?"

"Principal Torvik sentenced me to two hours a week of detention in the special ed lab for what happened to that kid last night." He paused, then tentatively asked, "Can he do that without any proof?"

"What do you mean, two hours of *detention* in special ed?"

He grimaced, the expression clear in the overhead garage light falling through the windshield. "I have to tutor those kids. I don't see why. They've got teachers in there."

"You mean the developmentally challenged kids like Wally?"

He snorted. "Yeah."

That's what Rand had done. It wasn't detention. It was brilliant. Whatever was between Nathan and that boy, Rand was forcing them to work it out in a supervised environment.

"He doesn't have any right because I didn't do anything."

She realized what she said could alienate Nathan, yet at the same time, he still wasn't taking the responsibility she felt he should. He was trying to finagle a way out. "It's not detention, Nathan. Those kids need help. You don't have any sports in the spring, and it will be a worthwhile thing for you to do."

"But, Mom," Nathan whined.

"This will help your situation with Principal Torvik. I'd like you to help out in that lab. It will look good on your college applications, too." She wasn't sure but didn't care.

He tightened his hands on the wheel, his knuckles whitening. "You people just don't get it."

"Don't get what?" she said gently.

His lips worked into a compressed frown. "You just don't know how everyone's going to ride me about this." Then he shoved the door open and was stomping up the garage steps before she'd even gotten out of the minivan. The keys were still in the ignition.

Rachel sighed. She'd made another wrong move. But she liked what Rand had done. It was actually a stroke of genius.

She hoped Nathan could eventually see that, too. Maybe then, if he ever found out about her affair with his principal, he wouldn't go completely ballistic.

SUNDAY NIGHT ON THE ROAD TO NOWHERE, AND RAND'S HAND between her legs. Rachel couldn't think when he touched her like that, let alone drive. But he'd insisted she do the driving so he could do all the playing. They were like teenagers, getting sex anywhere they could. Maybe that was because Rand was around teens day in and day out; his brain had been infected by all those raging hormones. But God, it was good, and a very good thing, too, that she'd worn a skirt instead of jeans.

Highway 280 was as empty as a ghost town as they passed through the back hills between Stanford University and the Linear Accelerator. On this moonless Sunday night, it was dark, not even the lights of houses or businesses to break the blackness. All the land around here was owned by Stanford, so civilization hadn't taken over and ruined it all.

"Oh," she moaned, rocking gently against his hand.

Slut that she was, she'd gotten to his house in under ten minutes after dropping the boys off with Gary. She'd been in such a rush, she hadn't cared that Sherry was baking fresh chocolate chip cookies. No, she'd been in a rush to get *here*, which was wherever Rand wanted to take her.

And take her he did, with his fingers all over her, dipping inside her. "You're going to make me crash," she said in a breathy sigh. Yes, they might crash and burn eventually, but she didn't care about that anymore. No matter what else was going on in her life, she needed these interludes to keep herself sane.

"Not a problem," he said. "My insurance covers the car no matter who's driving."

She groaned. "You're so bad. I'll lose control." She wanted to lose control with him, just not here on the freeway. But Rand loved making her crazy.

"You can do two things at once," he muttered. "But have no fear, I won't make you come until we stop."

True, right now he was teasing, keeping her on the edge, her senses heightened, her body dying for more.

Then he licked his fingers. "Christ, you taste good, and you're so damn wet."

"It's been more than a week," she said dryly. She'd been going crazy.

"I'm going to make you feel so good tonight," he murmured as he went back to playing, circling her clitoris a couple of times, then backing off when she started to squirm.

It was thrilling to be driving through the dark night with his hand on her, his breath at her nape. She wasn't going to have an accident, but she loved the way he made her body feel, all creamy and needy. She'd jump him the moment they stopped.

His finger now inside her, rocking gently to the movement of the car, he seduced her. "I'm going to lay you down in the middle of the living room carpet, and put my mouth to your pussy." He loved words, and using them was as much a part of sex as using his body. "I'll circle your clit with my tongue, tasting you." He mimicked his description with his touch. "Then I'll fit two fingers inside you, right on your G-spot, and lick until you scream."

Oh God, she could imagine it. If she'd been able to close her eyes, she would have been right there in his living room.

She laid her hand on top of his. "Are you going to fuck me?" she asked, giving him the naughty word he liked.

He laughed. "I'm going to wash your mouth out with soap."

Just like her mother had. "Sorry, it won't do any good." She lowered her voice. "I'm already a slut. You've corrupted me."

He nuzzled her ear. "Just the way I like it."

They raced along the highway between rolling hills. Rand jutted his chin. "Get off at the next exit."

His touch was steady and constant on her clitoris now, and she fought the quaking in her legs, putting both hands on the wheel to keep the car straight. She didn't care what he said about insurance; she was not going to wreck his car.

"Turn left," he instructed when she rolled to a stop at the bottom of the ramp. The light changed, she followed his directions, then just after they'd passed under the freeway, he pointed to the Park and Ride. "In there."

The lot was half full of cars, people using the convenience of the place to meet for a trip up to the city or into the mountains, but no one was here now.

He was on her the moment she shut off the engine, stealing her breath with a bone-melting, openmouthed kiss. His fingers drove her higher. She gave herself up to him, his kiss, full-bodied, not sloppy, his taste sweet and flavored with the hot male scent of him. And his touch, Lord. He used just the right tension on her clitoris, his fingers slippery with her juice. She was at the peak two seconds after they'd parked, moaning into his mouth, grinding her hips against his hand, holding him right there. Her body seemed to vibrate, every muscle tensing, needing. She groaned deeply against his lips, took his tongue, devoured him. Then suddenly she couldn't breathe, and she shoved him away, her eyes closed, needing only his finger on her. Until finally she imploded, fire radiating out, her body bucking. Her hand around the nape of his neck, she rode the wave holding his face against her throat, then collapsed into the seat.

For long moments, they simply breathed together. Then she opened her eyes, focusing on him. "You are a very bad man."

He grinned, a cheeky dimple deepening at the side of his mouth. "But I have very good fingers."

She nodded, sighing. "I have to admit that's true." His hand was still warm between her legs. She didn't remove it. He didn't stroke, simply cupped her as if he wanted to hold the sensations inside for her to enjoy a little longer.

"I thought it was the woman who was supposed to give the man a blow job while he was driving."

This time when he smiled, both dimples came out. "We still have to drive all the way home."

She turned his wrist and glanced at his watch. "Thirty minutes," she said, her voice bearing a note of wonder. "I can't believe you did that to me for half an hour."

He winked. "Mind-blowing, huh?"

Yes, it had been. Just wait till she got her chance. Honestly, though, it was crazy. They could have had an accident. Or a cop might have pulled up alongside them. Adults just didn't do things like that. Yet with Rand, she took all kinds of risks.

And she'd take the next one, sucking him on the way home. But first: "Thank you for what you did for Nathan."

"It was my pleasure. He's a good kid."

She should have expressed more, but Rand stroked the hair back from her face and said, "I've got a surprise for you."

"Mmm," she murmured. She'd had too many surprises this week, but she hadn't gotten one from Rand. His would be better.

"We're going on a trip."

24

RACHEL PULLED AWAY, FORCING RAND TO STRAIGHTEN INTO THE passenger seat. She eyed him warily. "I can't do that, Rand."

"Yes, you can, Rachel," he mimicked her.

He never tried to cajole or mollify. He simply stated. *This is what will happen and you will comply.* "I can't leave the boys, plus I've got work."

"It's one night," he said, his eyes sparkling. There was no moon, so where did that sparkle come from? "We fly out Saturday morning and return Sunday in plenty of time for you to be home when the boys get there. They'll never know you're gone."

"But—"

He put a finger to her lips. "No buts. We're doing this. The flight is short. And I've got plans." Now his eyes seemed to glow. Where on earth did the light come from? There was something in him that always seemed to be lit up.

"Where are we going?"

"You'll find out when we start boarding the plane."

She shook her head. "I don't know. This kind of thing makes me nervous." She didn't have the money to pay for a trip, yet it felt wrong to let a man do the paying. Because they weren't dating. They were just having sex.

"You analyze too much. I want this. I will have it." He leaned in, lowered his voice. "And you will love it."

Maybe it was that she didn't like having no control. That all he had to do was tell her to get in the car, drive, spread her legs, and she did. Worse, she loved doing it.

He waited silently as if he knew all the thoughts running around in her head.

Really, what was so bad about flying away with him? What was so bad about him making her come wherever and whenever he could? She'd never before experienced the things he made her feel; it was like constantly jumping off a cliff, each one higher than the last. Rand was one big thrill ride. She wasn't compromising herself; she was adding joy to her life. Gary had apparently found that with Sherry, and Rachel deserved no less.

"All right," she said. "You win. What should I pack?"

He grinned, triumphant. "Just the toiletries you want. I'll provide all the clothing."

She rolled her eyes. "God help me."

He chucked her under the chin. "Oh yeah, God help you. 'Cause I'm going to drive you crazy."

"Believe me, you already do."

He opened the car door. "You ain't seen nothing yet," he said as he climbed out, rounding the hood.

Rachel scooted over the console into the passenger seat. Rand belted in and started the engine. "All right, your turn to make me pay for what I just did to you."

"Oh, you'll pay, buddy boy." Then she leaned over and unzipped his jeans.

* * *

CHRIST, DID SHE MAKE HIM PAY. HE WAS A RISK TAKER, AND Rachel's mouth on him was worth any risk, but he'd chosen 280 for a drive because at this time of night there was little traffic on this particular highway.

He stroked her hair with one hand as she took him to heaven. Fuck, it was good, but he'd been hard and ready from the moment he put his hand between her legs.

She sucked him gently, the same way he'd caressed her, taking him on a slow, steady climb. She cupped his balls, and he tightened in response. A car passed them going twenty miles faster, the occupants oblivious to Rachel's bobbing head. If there was a cop around, he'd be following that car, not worrying about Rand, who'd managed to stay on the straight and narrow despite Rachel's delicious mouth.

"That's it, baby," he murmured.

She drew hard all the way to the tip, teased the slit of his cock, nearly blew his head off, then slid back down.

Life was perfect. Wally was fine, Nathan had made it through his first tutoring class, if grudgingly, and now this. Rachel. In his car, his cock in her mouth. She'd taken to cocksucking like a duck to water. Next, he'd have her all weekend. A full night. He'd take advantage of every moment.

A surge of sensation rocketed through his body as she suddenly deep-throated him. His hips drove up, he held her head down a moment, and Christ, he almost came. She sucked harder and faster in reaction. Rand exited the freeway, made a couple of turns, then pulled into a vacant parking lot, coming to a stop beneath some trees in a corner bordered by a hedge.

"Fuck," he whispered to her. "Suck me. Make me come."

She drove him right over the edge. He shouted her name as he filled her mouth with his essence, his being. Even when he was done, drained, she didn't let him go, sucking softly, shooting tremors through his body.

After long, exquisite minutes, his body finally calmed. He pulled her up, kissed her, tasting his come on her lips.

"I didn't know men kissed after that," she murmured against his mouth, as though, after all they'd done, she continued to marvel at it.

"I like it. Same as I like kissing you after I've made you come with my tongue." Sharing was perfection.

She settled against him, soft and pliable in his arms.

Then he looked out the side window. Shit. He'd parked in front of a church.

Yeah, he was a risk taker. And she was worth any risk.

IT WAS MONDAY. SHE HAD A WHOLE WEEK TO DO ANYTHING AND everything with Rand. He was good for her. He made her feel sexy and alive. She was *not* giving up the hottest thing she'd ever had in her life. Nathan and Justin never had to know.

Between answering calls, inputting invoices for Bree, and running the cash receipts to the bank, she thought of all the nasty, filthy, delicious things she and Rand could do. They could watch his neighbors again. This time, he could do her on the deck, providing their own show in return. Or maybe they could invite themselves over.

"Rachel."

She jumped as if Erin could see all those dirty thoughts like a cartoon bubble over her head. "Oh, oh, sorry. I just couldn't figure out this invoice for a minute." She rustled the paper on her desk; she wasn't even sure it was an invoice.

"Want me to look at it?"

"I've got it now." Rachel smiled so widely her cheeks hurt.

"There's something I'd like to talk about." Erin pulled out the extra chair in Rachel's office. Her work space wasn't much bigger than a closet. She had room for her desk, a two-drawer filing cabinet, and a bookshelf; that was it. She didn't have a window, but one wall of the office was all glass, including the door, so she could see anyone entering through the front, in addition to viewing the common area. She had no privacy at all. But then, she was a receptionist and wasn't supposed to need it. She didn't resent that either.

Erin crossed her legs. "Yvonne wants to take eight weeks off when her daughter's baby is born, to help out."

"That sounds good," Rachel said. Yvonne would be a grandmother in early July.

"I'd like you to train to take over her work while she's gone." Erin regarded her with a wary eye. "Are you interested?"

Rachel felt her heart climb up her throat. Erin was really asking if she was up to the task. Yvonne did inside sales. That meant she talked to customers and suppliers. She knew the distributors, the products, the parts, how everything fit together. She advised customers on what transducer went with which instrument, and on and on. If Rachel did Yvonne's job, she'd have to know all that, too.

"I'm not sure, Erin. I don't have any idea about that stuff."

"I'm asking you now so that Yvonne can give you a few months of training."

She swallowed. *Yes, but*—Rachel heard the thought in her head and was appalled. What a defeatist attitude.

"I'll be here to answer any questions, too." Erin uncrossed her legs and leaned forward, propping an elbow on her knee. "Rather than hire someone from outside, I'd like to give you the opportunity. Of course, we'll pay you for any overtime."

Overtime. She could use the money. But would that mean less time for the boys? More time for Sherry to try to take over?

Screw it. She was acting like a weenie. "I'll give it a try." She took a deep breath. "But as I learn more and become more valuable to the company beyond just being a receptionist—"

Erin put up a hand. "We'll need to think about your salary and your position. I agree. Let's get through the next three months and evaluate. Deal?"

"Deal."

"Good. Why don't you spend an hour with Yvonne today?"

"Sure." She'd have to get her act in gear and stop daydreaming about Rand all the time.

Things were actually looking pretty darn good. She'd be gaining more skills and would probably get a raise when Yvonne returned, because Erin was a woman of her word. Nathan was helping special-needs kids. Having Sherry take the boys when she had class wasn't *such* a bad thing. This new relationship of Gary's might actually turn out to be a benefit.

And tonight, there was Rand and so many delicious possibilities.

"NO," YVONNE SAID, HER VOICE RISING. "THAT'S NOT THE RIGHT probe for that instrument."

Rachel wanted to tell Yvonne exactly what she could do with that probe.

They'd been at it for an hour and a half in Yvonne's office. The task: fill two distributor orders, which were for different instruments, extra transducers, et cetera, et cetera. The issue was that the order called for gauges of different types and *accessories*. Well, you had to figure out what the damned accessories were. Yvonne had been doing it so long, it was a no-brainer for her.

But she wasn't exactly the best at imparting how Rachel was supposed to figure it out when she had no brain, so to speak.

"But you said," Rachel started.

Yvonne cut her off. "You're not *listening* to what I say."

Rachel looked at her notes. She'd written it down correctly. Yvonne had simply changed what she'd said, at least Rachel thought she had. But she could be wrong, too.

Able to see directly into Bree's office, she made a face when Yvonne wasn't looking. Bree smiled and shook her head.

Yvonne was a sweet person. She cared about everyone. She was born to be a mother, and she mothered them all just the way she mothered her own daughter. Somewhere in her midfifties, she was a tall, dark-skinned woman who, as much as she mothered, could also be exacting. Right now, Rachel wasn't measuring up.

"Is there a product manual I could read for the different gauges?" Rachel asked. She knew there was. In fact, the manual was one of the *accessories*.

"You'd never understand those manuals. They're for the people who use the product and they wouldn't mean a thing."

"But the manual should list all the components."

Yvonne snorted, her skin creasing around her lips. "You can't read a manual every time you have to fill an order. You'd never get anything done."

"I just meant as a reference."

Yvonne stabbed a finger at the screen. "It's all right there. The part number tells you everything you need to know."

They were going in circles. Either Yvonne wasn't a good teacher or Rachel wasn't a good student. For the life of her, she couldn't find in her notes where Yvonne had explained how the part number told her anything. Rachel learned best by doing things herself, but Yvonne did the entry for an entire order, then pushed the keyboard over and said, "You try the next one."

Rachel realized her notes didn't make enough sense.

Bree crossed the roundhouse, heading outside. A little while later, she returned. By that time, Yvonne's voice had given Rachel an extra-strength headache.

Yvonne stomped over to retrieve a folder from one of her filing cabinets and Bree, back in her office, pointed to a bag on her desk, flapped her hand back and forth between Rachel and herself, then touched her fingers to her lips.

The sign language could have meant Rachel should shut up. Then again, it could mean food.

"Let's break for lunch. I'm getting a hunger headache."

"Okay," Yvonne answered, her face practically buried in the filing cabinet as if she couldn't quite read whatever she was looking at.

Bree made some more hand signals that Rachel interpreted as *Let's eat outside at the picnic table where it's sunny. I can see you're ready to murder Yvonne.*

Which would be exactly right. Yvonne was a dead woman if Rachel didn't get a handle on herself.

25

RACHEL SLUMPED DOWN ON THE SEAT. CURRENTLY UNOCCUPIED, the picnic bench was on a knoll a few steps from the parking lot. A haven for smokers, it was far enough away from the building entrances to be within legal limits. The sun warm on her head, she could go to sleep right here. Yvonne had tired her out.

"I'm not a good student," she confessed to Bree. "How am I going to make it through a computer class if I can't make it through Yvonne?"

Bree opened the bag. "I got you ham and cheese." She fished out a wrapped sandwich.

"Thanks." Bree was as thrifty as Rachel and usually brown-bagged it. But today, Bree had been reading her mind. Rachel needed something extra. She opened her purse, dug around in the pocket for a five-dollar bill.

Bree waved her off. "It's my treat."

"You don't have to do that."

"I know." She smiled. Bree was so pretty when she smiled, but she lacked the laugh lines that would indicate she did it often. "You can do the same when you see someone driving me crazy."

Rachel rolled her eyes, then sagged. "She just goes so fast, I can't follow what she says." She unwrapped her sandwich, and really, after three bites, she did feel better. Maybe it was only a hunger headache. "It's all the accessories."

"Look at the bill of material. There are upper level part numbers that include all the accessories. You drill down from the top. The problem on orders and invoicing is that customers don't always need all the accessories and sometimes they want to switch something out. But learning how to use the bill of material is a start."

"How do you know all that?"

Bree shrugged, minimizing her knowledge. "I have to know how the bills of material work in order to do the standard costs. And I've worked with the invoices, too."

Rachel grimaced. "I'm never going to pick it up." Matching invoices hadn't prepared her for inside sales; neither had entering Erin's purchase orders.

Bree ate her egg salad delicately, like a bird. "If I can figure it out, you can."

Rachel realized she was sounding defeatist again. She couldn't let Yvonne's attitude beat her down, but most of all, she wouldn't do it to herself. "You're right. I have to manage Yvonne better, make her slow down."

Bree put on her sunglasses against the bright day. "Yvonne's threatened by your learning her job."

"But she wants the time off to help out her daughter when the baby comes."

"She thought Erin would get a temp. A temp is less threatening."

"I'm not going to try to take her job."

"I know that and you know that, but Yvonne's very territorial."

Bree was being unusually talkative, Rachel noticed, just as

she'd been the night they went out for drinks. In fact, she talked a lot more in general these days. Well, more for Bree, at any rate. After confronting Marbury, she'd changed, as if that one incident had been a threshold for her. Then there was her success with the IRS audit—DKG was going to get a refund—which had further boosted her confidence.

Rachel told herself she could do the same thing, boost her own confidence. "The best thing I can do is reassure her in a very diplomatic and nonthreatening way that I'm not after her job."

"Excellent." Bree pulled the crust off the rest of her sandwich. "So, I've been waiting more than a month to hear about your man. I can't stand the suspense anymore."

Behind the sunglasses, Rachel couldn't tell whether Bree was concentrating on the egg salad or looking at her. Yeah, she was definitely different. Before, Bree never would have asked. She also wouldn't have used that sarcastic drawl. Rachel liked the new Bree.

"He's taking me away for the weekend, and he won't tell me where. It's a surprise." It felt good to confide about Rand.

"A dictatorial man." Bree raised a brow above the rim of her glasses.

"Not exactly." But it gave Rachel cause to think. "Well, maybe a bit. He wants what he wants."

"When he wants it," Bree finished for her.

"I like that, though." She wondered if she should tell Bree he was her son's principal.

Bree smiled. "I enjoy an authoritative man, too."

She waited to hear more about Bree's boyfriend, but that's all she said. So Rachel went on with her confession. "He told me not to bring any clothes, that he'd provide everything."

"Kinda scary, huh?"

Bree actually understood her. The clothes thing made Rachel the most nervous. "If he makes me wear short-shorts so my butt hangs out, or he gets it wrong on my size"—Rachel narrowed her eyes—"I'm not stepping out of the room." Men didn't seem to have a concept of what made a woman feel fat or unattractive.

"Then he'll just have to take you shopping once you're there."

Rachel nodded. "That would be a bonus." She wouldn't feel bad making him buy clothes for her if he stranded her with nothing to wear.

Bree wrapped up the unfinished half of her sandwich. She'd probably save it for tomorrow. No wonder she was rail thin. After stowing it in the bag, she leaned her elbows on the picnic table. "Being dictatorial is a two-way street."

"What do you mean?"

"You should take a surprise for him."

"Like what?"

"Ropes."

Rachel just gaped at her.

"Tie him up. Do bad things to him."

Really, Bree never ceased to amaze her. First there was the condom in her purse, now a little bondage. "That's interesting."

Bree smiled again, a cat-that-ate-the-cream smile. Good Lord, just what had Bree been up to?

Hmm, tying Rand up. Yeah. That could be really interesting. He'd told her not to bring any clothes. He didn't say she couldn't bring some rope.

"WE'RE GOING TO LAS VEGAS?"

"What happens in Vegas stays in Vegas," Rand quipped.

Lord. She was in trouble now. Saturday morning had come in a flash, and really, she was god-awful nervous. She'd be spending more than twenty-four hours with him, sleeping with him, using the bathroom with him. It was terrifying to contemplate.

San José Airport was packed, queues of people going off in all directions, outside the Starbucks, clustered around each gate. If it was like this on a weekend, she hated to think about a weekday with all the business travelers. The security line had been hellacious, but at least they didn't have to check in; Rand had gotten their boarding passes online. She had a small carry-on with underwear and toiletries. The three-ounce bottle limit was a pain in the butt, and it was strange flying off with little more than a change of underwear. Oh, and the scarves. She hadn't had time to buy rope, but she'd been into scarves in the nineties, accenting every outfit with color. It was cheaper than jewelry. She hadn't worn them in years, but they would be perfect as a rope substitute.

Rand had a larger bag, which presumably held clothing for her as well. He'd taken her license and handed it to the security officer along with their boarding passes, so the first hint of their destination was when she'd read the flight information on the board outside their gate.

"So we're going gambling," she said. That would be the least terrifying possibility. She remembered his penchant for exhibitionism.

"Maybe a roll of quarters," he said as the boarding line inched forward.

"Cheapskate," she groused. "A show, then?"

He flashed her a smile. The best way to characterize it would be a shit-eating grin, but she was a lady and didn't use that kind of language. Except when she was having sex with Rand.

"Yes, a show," he said.

Good Lord. "Please don't tell me I'm going to be the show," she hissed at him in an undertone.

He grabbed her hand. "Don't worry, you're going to love everything I've planned."

Right. She'd hardly slept last night, her body humming with excitement and nerves. Rand wouldn't tell her a thing about the trip, but the week's evenings had been filled with one sexual escapade after another. He'd done her on his deck. Unfortunately the neighbor couple hadn't come out to bear witness, though without the lights on, it would have been hard to tell that she wasn't merely sitting in Rand's lap. She actually invited him over for dinner, and during dishwashing, he'd lifted her skirt, pulled down her panties, and had his wicked way with her right there in the kitchen. They'd had sex in every room of the house, except the boys' rooms, of course. Rand wanted to create dirty memories that would come back to her no matter what she was doing. She would never eat at the kitchen table again without thinking of what he'd done to her on it.

It was kinky, like an animal leaving his mark, but God, it made her feel sexy. She'd certainly crossed several lines she'd drawn in the sand for herself, though he hadn't spent the night yet. Vegas would be the first night they actually slept together.

After they boarded, he laid one hand on her ass to steer her to their seats. She'd worn her tightest jeans, and his hand molded to her flesh heated her through. He never missed an opportunity to touch her, but she had to admit, this one was particularly bold. What extra liberties would he take in Vegas?

He stowed their bags in the overhead bin, and once they were in the air, when the drinks were served, he ordered champagne for two. The glasses were plastic, and the champagne wasn't the best, but it tickled her nose and made her giddy. She had never been on a trip with a man she wasn't married to. This was somehow illicit and therefore all the more exciting.

Rand leaned in. "I have a goal to make sure we have sex at least six times and you have at least twice that many orgasms."

His breath was sweet with champagne, and he set her pulse racing. She'd make him wild when she turned the tables on him with the scarves. Yet she did wonder how far he'd push her tonight. Sex in public. God, what if Vegas had orgy clubs? You see everything on TV, but who knew if any of it was true.

"Remember," he said, tipping her chin to force her to meet his gaze. "What happens in Vegas stays in Vegas. No one ever has to know what we do there."

The hottest part of the flame was blue, and it was all blazing in his eyes.

Oh yeah, he was going to push her. Rachel wondered how far she would actually go for him.

EXCEPT FOR THE DOOR, THE ELEVATOR WAS A WALL OF MIRRORS ON every side. Rachel couldn't avoid seeing herself. Good God, she was practically naked, and Rand was taking her out like this into the Las Vegas nightlife.

The afternoon had been fun. He'd booked them into a hotel with a premium location on the Strip. After checking in and dropping their bags off in the room, they'd walked the crowded Las Vegas Boulevard. Rand set a brisk pace, wending through the throng with her hand tightly clasped in his. It was unusually windy, at least that's what the concierge at the hotel had said, but it was fairly warm by San Francisco standards. They'd gambled a little in Monte Carlo, admired the butterflies in the Bellagio's conservatory, sipped mochas outside a French café in Paris, taken a gondola ride along the Venetian's Grand Canal. Then he'd made her ride the roller coaster at New York New York. Oh my God! She'd screamed her head off and enjoyed every moment.

Rachel couldn't remember having that much fun since they'd taken the boys to Disneyland years ago. Come to think of it, Disneyland hadn't been all that fun, because Nathan had gotten sunburned and Gary had been pissed because she'd forgotten the sunscreen.

Do not think of Gary.

They'd had supper at the Rio's seafood buffet. She was terrified of eating too much because Rand had yet to show her the clothes he wanted her to wear. She didn't want any bulges to show if he'd brought her something tight.

She needn't have worried. He'd chosen a flirty black skirt that was short enough to be sexy, but not too short for a woman her age.

"You look fucking hot," he murmured, holding her hand, looking at her in one of the elevator's mirrored walls.

Thank God they were alone, because he made her actually look at herself as they descended the thirty floors. And really, it was a sight to behold. Rand stood slightly behind her, dressed all in black in stark contrast to his blond hair. He was mouthwatering in a button-down shirt and fitted slacks that were designed to hug and emphasize every delicious part of him. She felt petite beside him despite the shoes he'd bought her. She'd never had a pair like these—four-inch red spiked heels—not for Rachel the mother; these were for Rachel the hot, sexy lover he couldn't get enough of.

"You can see my nipples," she whispered, looking in the mirror, breathless, excited, nervous.

"Men will have to do a double take to notice."

Which is exactly what he wanted them to do, she was sure. He'd bought the shoes to match the blouse, a lacy design of sheer red that didn't effectively cover the strategic body parts beneath. It was the kind of garment meant to be worn over a camisole or at least with a bra. Rand had brought neither. Just the see-through red blouse. With every move, her bare flesh played peekaboo through the lace. If anyone looked closely, they would see her beaded nipples.

And what no one but she and Rand knew was that under the skirt, she was bare except for the black fishnet thigh-high stockings he'd bought for her.

26

RAND HADN'T BROUGHT PANTIES FOR HER. THE KNOWLEDGE GAVE
Rachel a sexy little rush. Standing at an angle beside her, he stud-
ied their reflection in the mirror as he raised a hand and lightly
stroked her nipple with his palm. "There," he murmured, his
breath sweet against her ear, "if they look hard enough, a man
will see those gorgeous nipples of yours."

Rachel shivered in anticipation. "I can't believe you're making
me do this."

He stepped back to survey her, arranging her hair to fall art-
fully over her shoulders. "I give you permission to return to the
hotel room and change back into the shirt you had on."

A T-shirt, nothing special; it simply made her feel sexy because
of its tightness across her breasts. Did she want to wear that? Or
could she handle something a little more risqué? *What happens
in Vegas stays in Vegas.* She wore dark red lipstick, making her
lips plump and kissable. She wouldn't spoil the look or the sexy
red shoes with a T-shirt. "I'll wear this."

He laughed. "I knew you could be a naughty slut for me."

She raised her brow and tipped her shoulder seductively. "Just watch out that I don't choose someone over you." She wasn't going to let him do all the directing; she'd have her own fun, too, and keep him guessing.

He raised her hand to his lips as the door opened to a group of men, laughing loudly, shoving good-naturedly, and slightly worse for wear in the alcohol-consumption department. They let her step off the elevator first. There was a moment of complete silence, then one of them whispered, "Holy shit." Another muttered, "I'd love to suck those titties."

Rand winked at her, a gleam in his eye. It was starting. She felt a rush of power and turned. "Thank you, gentlemen." Then, squeezing Rand's arm and dropping her voice, she added, "Tonight it's his turn." She winked, just as Rand had. "But you boys can look for me tomorrow night. I'll be around." Looping her arm through Rand's, she gave an exaggerated sway of her hips as she strolled away.

The elevator doors closed before any of the men even stepped inside.

"Tease," Rand murmured.

"Isn't that what you wanted?"

"Oh yeah." As evidenced by the bulge in his slacks. The man had an impressive package, and while she displayed hers, he certainly garnered a few of his own double takes from the women as they left the elevator lobby. And from some of the men, too.

The casino was only slightly smoky, considering that smoking was allowed indoors, and alive with voices, laughter, the bells and whistles of the slot machines, even the electronic sound of coins dropping when someone cashed out. She still thought the old-fashioned arm you pulled and the clink of your winnings in the tray was more fun, but these days it was all push-button. She loved the penny slots, though, where you could throw in twenty dollars and make it last two hours, which was about the same cost as a movie, popcorn, and a soda these days.

Rand led her down the center aisle, slowly heading to the front of the casino. "Let's stroll," he said. "I want to make sure everyone sees you."

Despite the presence of the same kind of sweet, young, bikini-clad nymphets they'd seen that afternoon, Rachel was getting her own share of attention. The women stared to make sure they were actually seeing what they thought they were. The male gazes never made it to her face, fastening onto her nipples, eyes glazing over. It should have been degrading, yet it was Rand's air of possession and his delight in the show that made her skin hot and her body wet.

She wasn't Rachel Delaney, thirty-nine-year-old mother of two. She was sexy, seductive Rachel, ready for anything this hunky man had in mind. Vegas was a party town, and she could get away with being loose and wild.

"Men love to look at you. Do you like it?"

She tipped her head to lean lightly against his shoulder. "I never thought I'd love being ogled." Because she'd never *been* ogled, and because everyone told you it was bad to be nothing more than a sex object. She was realizing that sometimes a woman *needed* to be a sex object.

Call her shallow, but it wasn't the overweight drunk ones that gave her the glow. It was the occasional hot dark-haired young stud, or even the still-sexy gray-haired used-to-be stud.

Rand obviously loved displaying her. Would he actually try giving her to any of these men? She wouldn't like that, but she loved his cocky, possessive smile.

"Where are we going?" she asked as they hit the marble lobby and he maneuvered them to the front doors. People were still checking in, even this late at night. Vegas certainly never slept.

228 • Jasmine Haynes

"Patience," he said. Outside, they queued for a cab. In less than five minutes, they were in the backseat. Rachel snuggled close, hanging on Rand's arm like a besotted lover.

"Where to, sir?" the cabbie asked with a guttural German accent.

"The Bordello," Rand answered.

The cabbie's expression in the mirror said it all. Rachel saw both eyebrows go up, then he cocked his head and shot a smirk over his shoulder. The Bordello. It had to be something very interesting.

"What are you planning, honey bunch?" she asked in a coquettish voice, her lips almost against his cheek. She molded herself to his side and slid one foot up his leg until she crossed her knee over his.

"It's a surprise, darling. Don't you worry your pretty little head about it." Then he winked into the rearview mirror as if he were sharing a big secret with the cabdriver.

"I'll take the backstreets to avoid the Strip traffic," the cabbie offered.

"Perfect." Then Rand ignored him, cuddling her closer. The show was already starting, and it was for their driver.

Rand undid another button on the see-through blouse and trailed a finger from her throat to her cleavage. "Very nice," he said, his head down, inspecting her. He hitched her leg higher on his, and her skirt rode up to reveal more thigh. If he moved it just a little farther, their driver would see that she wasn't wearing panties.

Stopped at a light, the cabbie adjusted the mirror down for a better view. Both she and Rand pretended not to notice. She held her breath, waiting for Rand's next move, then said, "So tell me more about this bordello."

The cab made the left turn as Rand caressed her thigh right up under the skirt, cupping her butt, squeezing her bare skin.

"It's a couples' club. Scantily clad waitresses, nude dancers, posh atmosphere."

"Naked women doesn't sound like a *couples'* club, honey bunch." She pouted for him.

Removing his hand from beneath her skirt, he trailed along the outside of it, up the center buttons of the blouse, then rested his fingers along the underside of her breast, stroking her nipple with his thumb. She was sure the cabbie had seen far more explicit things, but to her, this was sexy and daring.

"Watching a bit of pole dancing and whispering dirty things in each other's ears can whip up the erotic emotions, my dear."

The cabbie nodded vigorously in agreement.

"It would be more helpful to me if the pole dancer was a man." She pursed her lips, blew him a kiss. As Rand teased her through the blouse, Rachel decided it was only fair to tease him, too. She moved her leg, up, down, caressing him through his slacks. Something was definitely heating up down there. He paid her back by slipping right inside the blouse this time.

True to his word, the streets the cabdriver took were far less crowded. Rachel figured it gave them more time to play and him more time to watch.

"This is how it works," Rand said, pinching her nipple.

Rachel moaned, loudly for the driver. "That's definitely working, sweetie."

"I'm talking about The Bordello. We watch the dancers, then I say I'd love to see you dip down like *that*, or I'd love for you to sit on my lap making *that* move."

"Ah," she said dramatically. "So we go elsewhere and act it all out."

He smiled. "You're starting to get the idea."

"I certainly am. We'll do a private pole dance later."

The cabbie raised the rearview mirror to exchange a glance with Rand. "Something like that, my sweet," Rand answered.

God. He didn't expect her to pole dance for him in public, did he? The man had another thing coming, but she'd get into the rest of the game. Thank God this was all staying in Vegas.

Then, at last, they pulled up in front of an innocuous-looking building off the main Strip with small clothing boutiques and jewelry shops. The stores were open, but the sidewalks were far less crowded, and the patrons appeared to be dressed less casually than what you saw out on the main boulevard.

The cabbie double-parked, and Rand helped her out. Leaning into the window as he paid the man, they exchanged a few words and some manly laughter before the cab drove away. Rachel knew it was something rude. It was all part of the game.

A windowless establishment with a narrow brick facade and wooden, brass-handled door was sandwiched between a dress shop and a jewelry store. There were no identifying markings except a large *B* branded into the wood.

Rand knocked; the door opened. A burly man even taller than Rand looked them up and down. Rand handed him a business card, or it could have been a ticket. Bald, muscles bulging under his tuxedo, the man glanced at the card, handed it back, then held the door wide, flourishing a hand to indicate a set of stairs.

Rachel followed Rand in. She ascended the wide hardwood steps with one hand on the polished railing, the other through Rand's arm, until they reached another door at the top, this one padded burgundy leather. Rand tugged the gold bellpull beside it.

"This is fancy," she whispered. "How did a mere high school principal hear about it?"

"Ask the Internet," he said, "and ye shall receive."

"That's scary." The Internet was a whole lot of trouble for a mother of teenagers these days. But she wasn't a mother right now. She was a seductive lady on a very sexy man's arm.

The door was opened by a man in a flashy tuxedo, this one looking less like a bouncer and more like a maître d'. He eyed

Rachel's nipples appreciatively, then ushered them into a carpeted hallway with dark wood paneling and several ornate doors up and down its length.

Without a word, Rand handed him the card, the man read it, then returned it with a smile. "Welcome to The Bordello. What room may I show you to?"

"We'd like The Saloon."

"Excellent choice, sir. Right this way." The man turned, crooking his finger for them to follow, his shoes soundless on the carpet. Slender but tall, his dark hair was cut short, and his tuxedo and grooming added to the ambiance.

The Bordello was housed along the top of the shops and therefore was much larger than Rachel had first imagined. She counted six doors spaced fairly far apart along either side of the hall. Their host led them to the third door along and opened it, the noise overwhelming as he ushered them inside.

"Sit anywhere you like," he said, leaning close to be heard.

Rachel clung to Rand's arm after the man left. "I can't believe you don't even hear all this out there." There were so many indistinct voices, the cries of gamblers winning, laughter, and music like something out of an Old West movie. The noise wasn't ear-splitting, just surprising after the quiet of the outer hallway.

The large room was set up like an old-fashioned saloon, with an intricately carved wooden bar, card tables, roulette wheel, and a craps table. At least she thought the dice game was called craps. The waitresses wended their way through the tables. Dressed like saloon girls, they wore bustiers tied tightly to push up their breasts and short skirts with stiff crinolines that held them almost straight out to the sides, like a ballerina outfit. A wide wooden stage ran down the center, with several poles for the dancers. Bar stools ringed it, the girls just out of reach. The dancers weren't scantily clad, dressed instead in elaborate saloon-singer costumes, albeit with slits high up their thighs and deeply plunging necklines. They dipped and twirled on the poles, their sequined dresses sparkling in overhead lamps, which were shaped like vintage gaslights.

The dress code was upper-crust, Rand being one of the few men in the crowd without a tie. The women primarily were adorned in evening gowns, very few as revealing as the blouse Rachel wore.

Despite the noise level, it was not so crowded they couldn't find a spot. Rand led them to a wide curved bench of red leather with a small table at one end for drinks. Just as he'd said, it was a couples' club, and there were very few single males drooling over the pole dancers on the center stage.

They'd been seated less than a minute when a waitress stopped by to take their drink orders. She didn't dip at the knees but leaned down to ask what they'd like, and Rachel feared her nipples might pop right out of the bustier. She was young, pretty, and stacked—almost anyone would be in that outfit—but Rand simply turned to Rachel. "What would you like?"

"A chardonnay," she said.

The girl began listing the different chardonnays, and Rand said, "She'll have the Cakebread. I'll have a Campari and soda."

Smiling, the girl straightened, saucily flipped her little crinolined skirt, and headed back to the bar without writing anything down.

"This place is kind of fun," Rachel said.

Before Rand could answer, there was a burst of applause center stage. The four dancers wore identical dresses in different colors: green, red, blue, and gold. Twirling in unison, they kicked high, wrapped around their poles, then with a flourish, they each tore off a layer of sequined skirt, revealing a shorter skirt beneath. The crowd around the stage hollered as the girls tossed the material high, each managing to land it on a man's head.

She grabbed Rand's arm, pulled him close. "We should be sitting over there."

Rand shook his head. "I like the view better here." He glanced down to her breasts beneath the lace. "So do some other men." His gaze traveled around the room.

Sure enough, she noticed several pairs of eyes focused on her lacy peekaboo top.

"You're the show tonight, sweetheart." In the guise of caressing her thigh, he eased the skirt up. "Cross your legs for the men."

She suddenly understood his plan. They were seated on a bench with the small drink table to one side.

The next time she crossed her legs the opposite way, she'd be giving her audience a shot à la Sharon Stone in *Basic Instinct*. Sharon hadn't been wearing panties either.

27

SHE WASN'T THE YOUNGEST WOMAN HERE TONIGHT, NOT EVEN the prettiest, but she was the hottest. Rachel was a MILF. Every man wanted a MILF, a mom all dressed up and ready to fuck. Rand wanted her badly, but he also hoped for a little sexy fun with her first. Just like in the cab, touching her in front of the driver. It made him rock solid in his pants.

He loved showing her off, teasing other men. That blouse had been an inspiration. He'd taken a trip to the lingerie shop at the mall, where the saleslady offered silky negligees and high-cut panties. He'd spied the see-through blouse and known immediately it was perfect. The whole idea came to him while imagining her in it. Imagining other men watching her. She'd drive them crazy.

The waitress brought their drinks and despite the wiggle and the preponderance of breast pressed almost into his face, all he could think of was the next show he'd make sweet Rachel give.

"Do you like the club?" he asked conversationally, so when he offered up a new command, he'd take her by surprise.

"It's actually quite classy."

Hell yes. He'd done an exhaustive Internet search for just the right venue. It was pricy and exclusive with a higher caliber of patron than a peep show or a downtown strip club. He hadn't wanted sleazy; he'd wanted elegant. Just like her.

The pole dancers ripped off another layer of dress and tossed it into the revelers around the stage. They were down to bustiers, ruffled bottoms, and fishnet stockings.

He arranged Rachel's hair, which smelled of some flowery shampoo. Then he leaned down. "Cross your legs again."

In the midst of all the whooping over the dancers, Rachel recrossed her legs slowly, parting her thighs a tiny bit more than necessary. Most watched the stage, but a select group watched Rachel. And she liked it. Her breasts rose and fell, and beneath the lace, her nipples were tighter.

"Do you like your wine?" He leaned across her to retrieve the glass and handed it to her.

"Mmm," she said after a long swallow. "That's delicious."

She was delicious. He wanted her tipsy and willing, and liked that she didn't slouch, at ease with the see-through nature of her blouse.

He kissed her ear, then licked her lobe, blowing a breath against the moist flesh. She squirmed on the seat. "Stop that," she whispered, and batted at him ineffectually. "You're getting me all wet."

He ran a hand up her thigh, raising the skirt a little more. "I want you very wet."

She laughed. "I meant my ear."

He knew exactly what she meant. He knew exactly what she wanted. Holding her chin for a quick kiss, he then trailed a finger down her throat and straight across her nipple.

"You're very bad." But she didn't push him away.

He tested her limits, palming her breast. She'd allowed him a few liberties in the cab, but they'd had only one witness. Here, they had a whole audience.

Her nipple was hard, her lips tantalizingly red, her eyes a smoky hot hazel as she held his gaze. Then, dropping her voice, she said, "Pinch me. I want to make sure this is real."

Most people would take that to mean their arm. Rand understood it was another step. Her nipple was already peaked beneath the delicate lace. He gathered the bud between his thumb and forefinger, giving her a hard tweak.

She pressed her lips together, smoothing her lipstick. Her eyes shuttered, then she let out a whispered, "Oh."

The sex wasn't overt. While some of The Bordello's rooms displayed rampant sexual activity, he hadn't chosen that for Rachel. He'd planned something milder, a taste of being naughty that would delight and mesmerize her, and have her begging for more. That whispered *Oh* was exactly what he'd hoped for.

She opened her eyes, smiled directly into his before her gaze flitted around the room to determine who had been watching. "Filthy man," she said, pushing his hand away and raising her arms to fluff her hair. The move drew her breasts high and displayed her beaded nipples.

Oh yeah, she liked the brazenness of it. Vegas gave her freedom.

The piano rose to a crescendo, and the girls onstage kicked high and twirled, then slid down to do amazing splits. After a hearty round of applause, the piano player began a series of old-time melodies, and the dancers gracefully stepped down from the stage to prowl the room in their tight bustiers.

The brunette in blue trailed her fingers over a man's shoulder, leaned down to murmur in his ear. He slid his hand across the ruffled bottom of her lingerie, then slipped a bill beneath the lace edging of the bustier right over her breast. His hand lingered a moment, tracing her flesh just above her nipple. Pushing his straight back chair away from the small table at which he was seated, he helped her climb aboard his lap. Spreading her legs over him, she snuggled close, wriggling, laughing, her hands on his shoulders, her hair cascading down the back lacings of the bustier.

The other girls were searching for lap dances as well.

They'd arrived relatively early, and the action would get rowdier. How much sexier, Rand wasn't sure.

Rachel leaned in, her scent surrounding him. "Pay one of them to give you a lap dance."

Now, that wasn't something he'd expected. He'd taken her for a woman who wouldn't share. Perhaps, though, her confidence in her own charms was growing; she'd let him have the dance, but knew he'd be back to her for the real thing.

"Which one?"

"The gold one."

The girl was tall, her blond hair matching the gold of her bustier. Just as Rachel spoke, she found a willing victim, an older gentleman with graying hair. After receiving her tip in the top of her stocking, she climbed on top of him.

"We'll watch how good she is, then decide if she's the one," he said. But he mused about something even better.

There were three centers of attention, the gambling—even sexy play on the dance-hall floor didn't distract a gambler—the girls giving their lap dances, and Rachel. Yes, several male gazes surveyed her reaction to the dancers as they did a sexy bump-and-grind with their partners.

Rachel leaned against Rand's shoulder, her hand on his chest, caressing him, teasing his nipples lightly. She laughed, whispered naughty things in his ear, sending shivers down his spine with her warm breath. His balls began to ache with need as she clung to him. He didn't think she had any clue that it wasn't the girls but her proximity that made him hard.

The piano player banged out a jaunty tune as the gold girl gave her man a hell of a wild ride. She rolled on his lap as if he were a bucking bronco trying hard to throw her off. Her heels on the floor, her thighs tight around him, she rocked and rolled, thrusting her breasts into his face.

"He's either licking her or she's suffocating him," Rachel said.

"Whichever it is, he's enjoying it." Rand stroked her knee, the skirt rising ever higher.

The man raised his head, holding the girl's breasts in his hands, squeezing them as she bounced on his lap. The four girls were giving their paying partners equal opportunities. The red girl with black hair did a slow and sinuous dance on the lap of a guy in his midthirties. His face flushed, he wore suit and tie, his brown hair cut short, a young executive type.

Rand nudged Rachel. "Look at that one." The exec's hand was between the red girl's legs. He could have been playing her, or stroking himself. Either way, they were both glassy-eyed.

"I didn't think they'd get to put their hands down there even during a lap dance."

Rand laughed. "I'd wager at least one of them will come from the ride."

"Oh my God, look at her." Rachel's voice was hushed and seductive against his ear as she pointed with her chin.

He followed the line of her gaze. The green girl. Her chestnut brown hair flowed over the man's hands as he held her breasts. Rand couldn't see his face or determine his age; the girl's torso was in the way. She sat backward in his lap, facing the stage and all the people watching. She rode him as if she were fucking him, her legs spread wide over his lap, her hands braced on his knees.

Rand thought of Rachel the night he'd taken the video of her, fucking him, legs wide for the camera.

"Does that remind you of anything?" he asked. A hand on her knee, he suddenly pulled her leg over his, spreading her, and let his hand wander up and down her thigh, the stocking silky against his palm.

Her sweet pussy visible to anyone who chose to look, Rachel was so close, her tremble shimmied through his body. "The video," she murmured.

"You never showed it to me. I need to see it. I want to watch you doing that to me. It was so fucking hot."

"I want you to do it to me while we watch." Her voice was breathy, excited. Damn, he wished they'd thought to bring the video card with them.

Even over the music, the laughter, the shouts at the craps table as someone won big, he heard the man grunt as the girl rode him. The guy was in climax, his body jerking, and he wasn't even inside her.

"Maybe you need *her*," Rachel said.

He turned then, grabbed her chin, held her for a long moment until finally he spoke, softly, almost deadly. "Is that what you really want? For another woman to make me come while you watch?"

"I—" She blinked, swallowed.

He laid her hand on his cock, pressed her hard, stroked himself with her fingers. "I need to come. I need it now. Do you want her to do it?" He paused, making sure she understood every word. "Or do you want to do the honors?"

Parting her lips, she mouthed the word *How?* without a sound.

"Give me the lap dance," he whispered, seduced.

Trapped by his gaze, she reached for her glass and took a long drink of wine. Setting it down, she hung there a moment, halfway between this decision and that one.

Then she squeezed his cock and whispered the magic words. "I'll do it."

And she climbed onto his lap.

* * *

RACHEL STRADDLED RAND ON THE BENCH SEAT, TUCKING HER LEGS beneath her on either side of his thighs. Putting his two big hands on her butt, he snugged her close until his cock was hard against her center.

"Fuck me through my clothes while they all watch." His eyes were a deep ocean blue.

She moved on him as if he'd hypnotized her, but Rachel was aware of every touch, every sound. She wasn't his student's mother; she was his lover. And she wasn't going to let some pole dancing floozy take her man.

She'd only said it to test him. This was what she'd really wanted, his hot gaze on her. Looping her arms around his neck, she rocked against his cock. "I'm wet," she whispered to him.

"I know." He closed his eyes, breathed deeply. "I can smell you."

"Undo my blouse," she ordered. She felt wild. Did they arrest people for doing this kind of stuff in a club? She didn't know what the rules were, and she didn't care. She wanted *this*.

Rand slipped the buttons loose on her blouse until her breasts were free.

"Don't touch," she warned him. "You can only look."

Beyond his shoulder, at a bench along the wall, she met another man's gaze. He could only watch, too. Rachel liked it. Here, she was free to be crazy.

Rand hitched her closer still, and she rolled against him as if he were inside her. "Oh, that's good."

She leaned her head back, her hair swinging as she moved, her blouse falling open to completely bare her breasts to Rand, to the other man. As she closed her eyes, Rand wrapped his hands across her spine, holding her as she simulated sex on his lap. It didn't feel fake as her need rose, her skin turning warm and fragrant for him.

She opened her eyes, turned her head, and other men were watching her, too. So many men. Women, too. She moaned.

One hand on Rand's shoulder to steady herself, she cupped her breast, pinched her nipple for him.

"Give them a show, baby. That's what they want."

She moaned again, writhed on him. A twenty-dollar bill floated down onto the bench beside her. The man from the back bench was closer, moving in on her. The twenty dollars fueled her. She wondered how much the gold girl had gotten in her stocking.

Then Rand's hand snaked beneath the skirt, on her thigh, higher, higher. Until he touched the moist lips of her pussy. She should stop him. Instead, Rachel released his shoulder and molded both her breasts. She moved slowly on top of him, eyes wide open, her gaze locked with his.

"Beg me," he murmured. She wasn't even sure she heard the words, or merely saw them on his lips.

A fifty fluttered down into the lap of her skirt. Rand's hand was beneath. Yet he hadn't moved. There was only the friction of her own rocking.

If she wanted more, she'd have to beg.

If the small crowd gathered round them wanted more, they'd have to pay to see it.

"How much is it worth?" she asked Rand, asked them all.

Someone tossed a hundred.

"Touch me," Rachel whispered to him. "Please."

Rand's finger slid over her clitoris.

"Oh God," she murmured, closing her eyes. She didn't hide from the sight of people watching her; it was Rand, the pure pleasure of his touch. She didn't need to see, only to feel.

He stroked her. "You're so fucking wet."

She rode his fingers, rubbing herself on him, forcing him to a harder rhythm. "Oh yes, yes." She loved his hard muscles between her legs, the tinny sound of the old piano, the cheers at the gambling tables, the raspy breathing of the men around her. She wanted to come. Her body was all that mattered, the sensations, the heat of her flesh.

"Make me come, make me come," she said over and over.

He fit a finger inside her, held his thumb on her clitoris. And she rode him. She fucked him. She took her own pleasure from him. Her nipples were tight beads between her fingers, and the harder she pinched, the greater the intensity of Rand's touch between her legs.

She was letting him touch her in front of strangers, letting him push her to climax, and Rachel loved it.

In that moment, for the first time in her life, she felt wholly feminine, a complete woman. It was the sexy red shoes, the see-through blouse, the people watching, and it was Rand. The orgasm shot straight up from her center, and Rachel cried out, long, loud, and clear for everyone in that room to hear.

28

"I CAN'T BELIEVE YOU MADE ME DO THAT." RACHEL SHOVED through the hotel room door before he even had a chance to open it for her.

She'd remained silent the entire cab ride back. In The Bordello, she'd been as hot as Hades, coming in his arms for damn near two minutes. As he'd held her close, she tipped her head back, smiled, then kissed him dreamily.

Until she'd abruptly gone menopausal, jerking up in the seat, shoving him away. "I'm leaving." And she'd marched out. Just like that.

He'd shrugged at her rapt audience as if to say, *Women: can't live without 'em, can't kill 'em.* He'd followed her out, leaving the bills she'd earned on the bench, unsure if he was supposed to gather them up like her pimp. He didn't know if she'd wanted only to see how much she was worth, or if she'd actually wanted to be paid. In his gut, however, he believed that with the cash in hand, she'd start having regrets later, and he wasn't about to let there be any regrets over this weekend.

He understood teenagers better than he did women. Nah, not true. She was pissed because he'd gotten her to do more than she'd intended.

She threw her handbag on the bed, then paced over to the table and chairs near the window. Her knuckles whitened as she fisted them across the top of the nearest chair. "Somebody could have videoed us and by morning, I'll be on the Internet."

He didn't mention that nobody would recognize her. With the makeup, the outfit, the hair, she didn't resemble Rachel Delaney, mother of two teenage boys.

She looked like the sexy MILF in *American Pie*. But he wouldn't say that. Big mistake.

"Video cameras aren't allowed," he said reasonably.

"Someone could have used their phone," she stormed, pulling the chair away from the small round table. She didn't sit, however. Instead, she stomped to her overnight bag on the valet tray and unzipped it. Rooting around inside, she stopped suddenly and pointed at the chair. "Sit," she ordered. "And don't say a word."

He didn't smile. He'd never seen her in such a temper, and it actually turned him on. She'd done a number on him when she came in The Bordello. Maybe it was the residual effects because he hadn't had his own climax. Whatever the reason, his slacks were tight across his groin as he sat.

She bent to her task again, tossing things around in the small case. She couldn't have carried *much*, but carry *something* she had, because she smiled maliciously when she found it.

Not *it*, *them*, he saw when she held up the prize. Two scarves, one a plain yet sexy red that matched the fuck-me heels he'd bought her, the other red with tiny swirls of black in it.

"Put your hands behind your back," she demanded.

Rand barely kept the smile off his lips. The little wench. She wasn't angry; she'd planned this charade. He played along, crossing his hands behind the chair back.

She had the angry stomp down pat, then she pulled a scarf tight around his wrists and tied it off.

"What are you going to do?" he asked.

She whirled on him, standing right in front, leaning down until her nose was in his face. "Payback time," she whispered. "Remember what you did to me in my very own house?"

"Fucked you until you begged," he muttered.

"Raped me," she snapped.

Oh yeah, this was payback. And he was going to love it.

She covered his eyes with the second scarf.

"You will be at my mercy," she said softly. "I can do anything I want to you."

She should have undressed him first, but he didn't mention that. This was her show. She'd been fucking hot in The Bordello. She was hotter now. He loved that she wanted to take control. She'd thought it out, too, came prepared with the scarves. Then she was on him, straddling his lap as she had in The Bordello, but with the chair instead of the bench, she was so much closer, so much more in control, her thighs taut along his.

She held his chin in her hand. "I am going to fuck you. I am going to ride you for as long as I please. You will not come until I'm done with you. Do you understand?"

Christ, he understood; she was going to kill him with need.

"If you feel close to climax, you better tell me so I can stop until you have yourself in hand again."

"What if I don't?" he tested, just to see what she'd do.

She pinched his nipple hard through his shirt. Heat shot down to his cock, started it throbbing and his balls aching.

"I will punish you," she whispered. "You won't like it."

"I'll do whatever you say." He'd love it. No teenage boy, he could hold off his orgasm, drive her absolutely crazy, until she was begging to feel the pulse of his climax inside her.

Reaching down between their legs, she cupped his balls,

squeezed. His eyes damn near rolled back in his head. Then she touched herself, the back of her hand caressing him. Maybe she *was* going to drive him crazy.

Slowly, she drew her hand out, and he smelled her scent as she raised her fingers to his lips, rubbing her moisture over them.

"Lick it off," she whispered. "That's me. Taste me."

Robbed of sight by the scarf, his other senses seemed stronger, and she was ambrosia, sweet, creamy, sexy. "More," he begged. Christ, he could drink her.

She slapped his cheek, not hard, merely a tap. "Don't ask for anything. You only get what I give you."

She loved the power; he could feel it on her, smell it like perfume. "Yes, ma'am."

This time when she put her hands down between them, she unbuckled his belt, undid the buttons of his slacks, and pulled down his zipper. "Good boy." Her voice was soft, melodious, as she reached inside his briefs to wrap her hand around his cock.

She stroked him slowly, rubbing the tip with her thumb, slipping in the pre-come that had gathered there. "Look at that. You're ready. I didn't even suck you. You're such a slut, you already want it."

"I've wanted it all night long."

"Right," she drawled, squeezing him tightly. "That's why you wanted one of those girls to give you a lap dance."

"I didn't want them. You asked for that."

She slapped her hand over his mouth, her scent still rising up from her fingers. "Don't you say a word. Don't try to deny it. You're a man, and you took me there hoping I'd let you screw some other woman in the heat of the moment."

Clearly it had been a fear. It had never been his intention. He'd gotten exactly what he wanted: her.

She dropped her hand from his mouth, trailing her fingers down his shirt to his pants again. "I'm going to do you so well you'll never look at another woman."

Didn't she know that had been true for weeks now? She was his only focus.

She moved slightly. He heard the tear of foil. A condom. She'd obviously brought her own, made plans. He loved games. The fact that she was making up one of her own shot him higher.

Rising over him, she took his cock in hand. "I'm going to fuck you," she said softly as she rolled the condom onto him. He was so hard, it made the job easy.

"Fuck you," she whispered, and he loved the word on her lips. He loved it when she let herself go and talked dirty.

Then she lowered herself onto him, her thighs taut as she controlled the movement. Even through the condom, she was slick and hot.

"Oh." She rubbed his crown in her heat. Then, one hand guiding him, the other braced on his shoulder, she slid down quickly, taking him deep. "Oh yes," she said on a quiet breath. "Yes." She stopped, held, flexed her muscles around him.

Christ. He wanted to touch her, see her, revel in the sight of her, feel the texture of her skin against his fingers. That was the torture in this; he couldn't see or touch.

"I'm going to fuck you," she said again, and began to rise and fall on him.

Fuck, yes. He loved that word in her sexy voice. Her body gripped him on the inside, worked him. She always did that, an unconscious clenching that heightened the effect she had on him.

"Fuck you, fuck you," she cried out. Behind the scarf, he saw her as she'd been in The Bordello, lost to everyone around them, aware only of his hand beneath her skirt, touching her, making her wild. Him, only him.

"Fuck, fuck, fuck." She took him on the wild ride now, the slip-slide of his cock in her, his harsh breaths rasping in his throat. He liked talk, touch, feel. She was killing him by denying him, and yet it was so damn hot, the come built in his balls, throbbed through his cock.

She wrapped her hand around his neck, dug her fingernails in, chanting that special word at him, her breath puffing across his face, her taste on his lips, her scent clouding his mind. When her body began to spasm on him, he couldn't hold back. Letting go. Losing himself in her. Lost.

RACHEL HADN'T SLEPT WITH A MAN OTHER THAN GARY IN ALMOST twenty years. Rand didn't snore, but he was big, and he took up more than half the bed. She couldn't see the clock so she didn't know the time, but with the curtains open, she knew it was still dark outside. She estimated she'd been awake about half an hour.

In the strip of moonlight that made it to the bed, Rand's profile was breathtaking. He was a beautiful man, the contours of his face strong, his body solid. The orgasm she'd had as she rode him had zonked her for the night. She'd untied him, undressed, then they'd poured themselves into bed. She couldn't remember the last time a man had held her as she fell asleep. She wished she'd been able to lie awake longer to savor it.

She liked this, lying here with him, watching him, remembering the things they'd done. It wasn't frightening, her nerves of yesterday long gone. She'd loved playing the angry mistress, tying him up, not allowing him to speak, taking him. She didn't need the audience to come hard.

But he was a dangerous man; he was becoming important to her. She was starting to want more. She dreamed about more nights sleeping in his arms, waking up in the morning to his lovemaking. If somehow their relationship was revealed, if she was forced to make a choice, she didn't believe she could give him up. It was a sobering thought.

Finally, she couldn't lie there anymore. She needed the bathroom. As she passed his side of the bed with the clock on the table, she noted it was almost six. After washing her hands, she thought about crawling back into bed for that morning lovemaking. So delicious. Then she thought about how there were things she should never get used to. If you didn't have it, you didn't crave it. Once you'd tasted the forbidden fruit, however, you were hooked. You couldn't give it up. Best not to start. So she turned on the shower and stepped beneath the spray.

He was still sleeping when she opened the bathroom door. A towel wrapped around her, she tiptoed to her bag and scooped out a fresh pair of panties and a clean T-shirt she'd dropped in at the last moment, since she wasn't sure Rand would provide anything for the return trip.

He slept soundly. Like the boys. A herd of hippos wouldn't wake them.

Once she was dressed, her hair drying on its own, and her makeup applied, she slipped out of the room. Though early morning patrons were few, the sounds of slot machines assaulted her as she stepped off the lobby elevator. There was already a line at Starbucks, so she headed up the ramp to the food court. At McDonald's, she purchased two coffees. Casino hotels did not have coffeemakers in the rooms. They wanted to you downstairs where you could buy their food and play their machines.

At one of the other fast-food places, she snagged a Danish to share, then headed back up. It was seven. Surely he couldn't still be asleep.

He was, despite the sunshine now spilling through the bank of windows. Removing the top from the large coffee she'd brought him, she set in on the bedside table, wafting the steam with her hand. Maybe the coffee scent would penetrate.

He moved like a snake striking, grabbing her wrist and tumbling her onto the bed across him. His lips were on hers before she could utter a sound or complain that he might have made her knock over the coffee. He tasted sweet and minty; he'd obviously already been up. He was also up beneath the sheet, his cock hard along her thigh.

"I wanted to wake you up with a spectacular fuck," he muttered against her mouth.

That word. She'd said it so many times last night. It got to her, so elemental, so physical. His hands were already tunneling down between her legs. She was wet. "I needed coffee," she said, trying to sound composed.

"Sex is more important than coffee."

"Not to an addict."

"I *am* addicted." He bent his head, bit her nipple through her bra and T-shirt. An arc of electricity shot through her. "To you," he finished.

God. He made her melt, with his words, his touch, his desire. She needed to be wanted. "But what about our flight?"

"There's plenty of time to make you come at least twice before we have to check out." He lifted his head, held her gaze. "I don't get you for another week so I'm not going to waste one single minute."

He tugged on her belt, her zipper, then yanked her jeans all the way down her legs and tossed them off along with her shoes.

"I need to be inside you," he murmured at her ear as his fingers slipped all over her hot, wet, needy places.

Fuck me, fuck me, fuck me. The words reverberated in her mind. She needed this. She would never stop needing it.

She was addicted, too.

29

THE FLIGHT WAS LATE TAKING OFF. MECHANICAL FAILURE. FOR the first two hours, they were stuck on the plane itself, then, when it looked like it was going to take another two—and the air-conditioning wasn't working—they were allowed to deplane for the duration. Rand felt the tension vibrating through her as he held her hand.

"I have to call Gary," she'd said when they weren't sure they were ever going to get out of Las Vegas.

He'd listened to her end of the conversation.

"No, I don't know when the flight will take off." She pursed her lips. "I don't need to tell you when I go out of town." Her fingers drummed on the armrest. "You have my cell number, and you can call it anytime." She glanced at Rand, her teeth gritted, then turned slightly away from him as if she didn't want him to hear.

Fuck that, he thought. They might have secrets from everyone else, but she didn't need to hide anything from him.

"It isn't your business whether I went away with someone or not," she snapped into the phone.

It had been so good. Doing the tourist thing yesterday, a couple of hours of gambling, shopping, then The Bordello and burning-hot sex. He'd even liked being tied up, because she was having so much fun. Then this morning, ah, the deliciously languid sex, twice. She'd been pliable, hanging all over him in the security line, snuggled up against him while they waited to board. Yeah, he could get used to it.

Now this. Fuck. Everything ruined because of her asshole ex. If it had gone according to plan, he'd have had her home by three. Now it would be more like seven. She'd had to tell the asshole, of course. Rand understood that, but he still resented the guy's intrusion. He was dating, so what the hell did it matter if Rachel was, too? Because she went away? Because she was secretive about it?

Whatever. Four hours late, they finally took off. When they arrived, it took half an hour to deplane, get on the long-term parking bus, and retrieve his car. Finally, when he was afraid her head might explode with the tension, they were headed to her place.

"Drop me at the corner," she said.

"I'm not dropping you at the corner."

"Don't be difficult, Rand." She sounded like she was talking to Nathan.

"I'm not one of your boys, and I don't just drop a lady off at the corner."

She turned in her seat, her face set. "I already have enough issues with Gary. I do not want him to recognize you. So if you will please help out and allow me to walk from the corner to my house, I would appreciate it."

He realized he no longer liked being a secret. He didn't want to barrel in and start taking over like her husband was so obviously good at, but neither did he like being forced into a one-eighth slice of her life. He wanted to take her away for weekend trips. Or out to dinner. Without worrying about who might see them. He wanted to pick her up at her door, to have more nights with her in a bed, all night, and long into the morning.

Good God. He actually wanted a relationship. Something beyond just sex. He didn't know exactly when it had happened, though he was sure it had started brewing the moment she'd walked into the principal's office and was no longer his mystery woman.

"Please, Rand."

There were obstacles, of course, Nathan being the biggest one, since the kid hated his guts. But they were workable.

For now, however, he had to acquiesce. "I'll let you out at the corner, but I'll watch to make sure you get in the house safely." He pulled over at the end of her street.

She touched his arm. "Thank you."

He wrapped his hand around the nape of her neck and pulled her in for a kiss, her lips sweet beneath his. "Next Sunday." He paused for another kiss. "Dinner at my place." Yeah, he could actually cook. "And bring that little video with you. I feel like watching a movie together."

He felt her smile against his mouth. "You're such a dirty man."

"And you're a slut, which I love. So bring it with you."

She nuzzled him a moment. It was sweet. He liked the closeness. He didn't want her to go.

"Thanks for this weekend. It was incredible."

He had to agree. "I want more weekends like that. I'll just make sure the plane works the next time."

She laughed softly. "And you should. You're the principal."

Then she pulled away, grabbed her small bag from the

backseat, and climbed out. He watched her all the way down the street, the sexy sway of her ass. He wanted that ass.

He was, therefore, going to have to make friends with her son.

GARY'S CAR WAS IN THE DRIVEWAY.

Dammit. Well, the cat was out of the bag anyway, so to speak, when she'd called him from the airport. Why oh why did that flight have to be late?

"You don't owe him any explanations," she muttered as she climbed the steps to the front door.

The door was locked. She had to get out her keys. She wished now she'd left the overnight bag in Rand's car. There wasn't anything in it she couldn't live without for a week. Maybe she could just toss it down in the hall as soon as she walked in, then take it back to her room later. It wasn't Gary; it was the boys. What on earth would they think? What had Gary told them?

The best-laid plans, that's how the old saying went. First the plane, now this. As she opened the door, Gary was coming out of the bedroom hallway, probably from the main bathroom.

"It's about time," he snarled. "I've been waiting an hour."

She felt herself flush with guilt, but she wouldn't let him see it. Instead, she glanced at her watch. "It's not even seven. And you didn't have to wait. Nathan and Justin are fine on their own for a couple of hours."

He looked pointedly at her bag. "Where'd you go, Rachel?"

"That isn't your business."

"The boys wondered why you didn't call them last night."

They probably hadn't even noticed. She ignored Gary's taunt. "Did you already give them dinner?"

"Of course I did. I do my duty."

He was baiting her. She wasn't going to bite. Instead she squeezed past him into the hallway. "Tell them I'll be along to see them in a minute." She assumed they were in the family room in front of the TV.

"What are you going to do, Rachel? Hide the evidence?"

The problem was she did have evidence in the bag. The sexy shoes and see-through blouse. The scarves. Although no one would really wonder about scarves. She should definitely have thrown out the rest of the condoms, though. "You can leave now, Gary."

In her bedroom, she threw the bag into the back of the closet. She'd empty it later, put the condoms at the bottom of her purse, take them to work tomorrow, and throw them out there.

Gary made her so angry. He had a girlfriend, for God's sake. The boys knew he was sleeping with Sherry.

She found her sons in the family room with Gary. "Hi, guys." She dropped a kiss on Justin's head. Nathan barely looked up from the TV. "Say goodnight to your dad," she said pointedly.

Gary stood. She wondered if he'd grilled the boys about what she did during their weeks with her.

After he left, she waited for one of them to ask her a question. *What were you doing, Mom? Why were you late, Mom? Where'd you go this weekend, Mom?*

Neither of them asked anything. In fact, the rest of the evening was quite pleasant. She started to feel like she could play the weekend over and over in her mind without feeling guilty. The boys didn't have a problem; only Gary did.

When they were in bed, she took her purse into the bedroom, buried the condoms deep inside it, then put the rest of her things away. For a moment, she held the blouse in her hands, fingering the lace, then she hung it at the far end of the closet. She touched the shoes, the gorgeous red shoes meant for a desirable woman. They made her feel sexy even now. Then she put them at the back, behind her more practical footwear. She folded the scarves, opened the drawer, and stopped.

Her heart began to race. The contents looked different. Her vibrator sat squarely on top of a jumble of panties. She shuffled things around, then started tossing them on the floor in a panic. Her upper lip began to sweat. Staring down into the empty drawer, her head was spinning. She couldn't breathe.

The video card was gone. It had been hidden under all the underwear and scarves. Right next to the vibrator. Someone had been through her things. Someone had found her vibrator and taken that damn card.

Gary.

RACHEL STARED AT THE CELL PHONE ON HER DESK. SHE'D PUT IT there the moment she walked into her office this morning. She'd been watching it for three hours. It hadn't rung.

Gary wanted to torture her a little longer.

She hadn't found the courage to call him last night, yet a million questions ran through her mind all night. She hadn't slept a wink. Why would he take the card? How could he possibly know something was on it? Because it was next to her vibrator? Why had he searched her drawers? What did he want?

She was a good mother. She'd been a good wife. Why was he doing this?

"Aren't you coming in to do the orders?"

Rachel jumped, almost shrieking out loud. Yvonne filled her office door, arms akimbo, her hair frazzled.

"Sorry," Rachel said. "I was finishing the cash receipts."

"That looked more like daydreaming."

Daydreaming implied something pleasant. Her thoughts were anything but. She gathered a pencil and pad to take more notes. "I'm coming."

Yvonne marched. Rachel followed. It was what she'd done all her life, marching to someone else's tune, following someone else's orders, trying to meet someone else's needs, hoping to keep everyone happy.

She screwed up the three customer orders she tried to do. Yvonne ended up grabbing the keyboard and making her watch. She requested a bio break and checked her cell phone.

No one had called.

After lunch, Dominic gave her a brochure to proof. She missed three typos. In the afternoon, the phone would not stop ringing, customers, vendors, solicitors, whatever. She transferred one of Erin's calls to Bree and lost one for Cam.

No one phoned for her.

She expected Erin to stomp into her office and ask what on earth was up, but Erin didn't, thank God.

Rachel was terrified, but she had to speak with Rand, tell him she'd lost the card. Oh God, his face was on that video. Gary could get him fired. At the very least, he could create a terrible scandal. He most certainly could tell Nathan he'd caught her in a compromising position with the principal.

Nathan would never talk to her again.

She left work ten minutes early. She could not stay there one more second. To call or not to call. Gary, that is. Preemptive strike, demand to know what the hell, yes, what *the hell* he was doing going through her drawers, her personal items.

Rachel didn't have the courage now any more than she'd had last night. Besides, he might have no clue how to use the video against her without making himself look even worse. He'd *never* tell the boys for fear it would backfire on him.

By the time Rachel was on her way home, she'd convinced herself of that and was feeling much better. Until she saw Gary's car in the drive. Naturally he was blocking the garage.

Her heart racing, she climbed the steps and found the front door unlocked. Good, the boys were home. She was safe. Gary couldn't say anything with them as witnesses.

Think, think, think. How could she fix this? She was a peace-maker. She knew how to get everyone to put down their weapons and make nice.

Except in the past few months.

Setting her purse on the front hall table, she was sure she could hear the TV in the family room. Her footsteps felt leaden. The farther she moved down the hall, the more recognizable the sounds became. Her ears were roaring, and she was sure she was going to faint by the time she stood in the family room doorway.

Gary was seated on the sofa, his gaze fixed, the remote in his hand.

On the TV screen, she saw herself, completely naked and fully exposed.

30

ON THE BIG SCREEN, RACHEL MOANED. RAND GROANED. HER LEGS were spread wide over him, her breasts bouncing as she rode him. She saw everything, his cock in her, the slickness of her pussy, the frenzy of desire contorting her face.

It had been so beautiful when she watched it by herself. Gary destroyed all the joy she'd had in it.

"What the hell are you doing?" She moved so fast, the toe of her shoe snagged on the carpet, and she stumbled. Catching herself, she made a grab for the remote. Gary held it out of reach.

And those sounds just went on and on.

"Stop it," she screamed at him.

Very calmly, his gaze on her, Gary pointed the remote and pushed a button.

The sounds stopped, the cessation so quick, her ears still hummed with it. But he hadn't turned it off. No, he left the freeze-frame right up there on the screen. Her. Rand. His cock deep inside her.

"Well," Gary said softly, maybe even snidely. "I guess I don't have to ask what you were doing this weekend or who you were with."

She felt utterly sick to the very pit of her stomach. Sick with fear. With horror. With loss.

"We need to have a talk, Rachel." He was so very calm, in total contrast to her roiling emotions. Of course. He had the upper hand.

She collapsed on the chair. "Where are the boys?" God, please don't let them be in their rooms. Gary would never do that. Would he?

"Sherry took them out to dinner."

She swallowed back the resentment. "What right did you have to search my things?"

He just smiled. "They're my sons. I have every right to make sure what you do doesn't taint them."

"What about you and Sherry?" she spat at him.

"Nothing happens when they are in my apartment," he said, holier than thou.

She wanted to smack him so badly, her body shook. "How did you even know it was important?"

He smirked. "Right next to your vibrator? *Tsk, tsk*, Rachel. I'm not an idiot. Of course it meant something."

Jesus. She should never have gotten the damn vibrator. It was the beginning of the end.

"Did you have that when we were married, Rachel?" he sneered.

She'd needed it when they were married, because she'd certainly gotten nothing out of him. But she wasn't going to justify anything. "What do you want, Gary?"

"It's simple," he said, speaking to her as if she were a child. "That"—he pointed, she didn't look—"if I'm not mistaken, is Principal Torvik fucking the hell out of you. Or should I say you're fucking the hell out of him."

Gary never talked like that. Her blood turned to dust in her veins, nothing moved, her whole body suddenly oxygen starved.

"I have a proposition." He waited.

She bit her lip. The bastard wanted her to ask. She had no choice but to play along. "What's your proposition?"

He smiled like a great white shark ready to take a big bite. She didn't recognize him. He couldn't be the man she'd slept in the same bed with for seventeen years, the father of her children. This was someone else entirely. Maybe he'd always had *this* man hidden beneath his facade.

"I won't show this video to anyone," he said. "Not his school board, not your employers, not my divorce attorney, no one."

He paused so long she was forced to ask, "If?"

"I want the boys full-time. You can have them one weekend a month."

She stared at his lips as if watching them move would make his jumble of words suddenly clear. "You want custody of the boys?" It felt like she was standing in the corner, looking on from afar, another woman saying those words, thinking her thoughts. "Why? You told me I couldn't go to school because you didn't want to have to take the boys."

"Sherry wants them."

"Sherry wants my boys?" It didn't make sense. She was young; Justin and Nathan were teenagers. It would be more likely that she'd want to get rid of them so she could have her own babies with Gary. "But why?"

"She doesn't want to go through childbirth, and she likes kids when they're older. She loves going to the basketball games and out for pizza or burgers."

"You don't have to have custody for that."

"She wants more time with them. She wants a family."

"But why *my* boys?"

"They're *my* boys, Rachel," he barked. "That's all that matters."

Maybe the questions were stupid under the circumstances. She just didn't get it. "But—"

He cut her off with a slash of his hand. "You're disgusting. Making a video anyone could see. Doing *that*"—he stabbed a finger at the screen—"and I won't have you corrupting our children. Give them to me or I will *take* them from you. If you make me go to court, you know the boys will eventually find out." He leaned close. She could smell his acrid sweat. Or was that her own? "Give them to me," he said softly, "and no one has to see this. You're safe. The principal is safe. The boys will never know."

She didn't know what to say, what to do. The worst had happened. She could lose the only important thing in her life: her sons. If she contested Gary in court, all he had to do was offer up that video. She could see it on the screen out of the corner of her eye. "Shut it off. Please." Her voice trembled.

He hit another button on the remote, and the screen went blissfully blue.

If she fought him, the boys would find out. Gary would make sure. He'd poison them against her. God only knew what he'd do to Rand.

"Can I have them two weekends?" she whispered.

Gary rose from the couch, stalked the room, then she heard the light mechanical whir as the TV ejected the card. He turned, pocketing it. "On occasion, I might allow that."

She was too stunned even to weep. "What will you tell them about why we're making this change?" Her throat ached just saying the words. Everything inside her ached.

He swept out his hand. "You're going back to school. You need to get an education to better yourself so you can take care of them. We'll say it's just for a few months."

Those months would segue into the years until they both

turned eighteen. They'd hate her for choosing school over them. But Nathan would *never* forgive her if he learned what she'd done with his principal. There was no way out, no easy choice. All she could do was hope to salvage whatever was left over during her one weekend a month, or two, if Gary was feeling generous.

She swallowed, feeling it stick halfway down. "Can I finish out my week with them?"

He considered her a long moment, then sighed. "I guess so." He stroked his chin like Freud considering a crazy patient. "It will be easier to transition that way. I can tell them about the change when they're with me." Then he smiled magnanimously. It came off looking smug. "Just think, now you can fuck anytime, anywhere you want." He winked. "Even in the principal's office after hours." He patted the pocket where he'd stowed the damning video card. "Oh"—he smiled—"I also fixed the garage door for you."

And Rachel hated him.

HER CELL PHONE DIDN'T WAKE HER AT ELEVEN-THIRTY THAT night. Rachel wasn't asleep. She might never sleep again. She'd been thinking about how she should throw out the rest of the evidence the way she'd tossed the condoms this morning. The naughty see-through blouse Rand had bought her, the sexy red shoes. She wasn't a woman who could carry off red spiked heels. No, that had been a fantasy. She wasn't that woman, could never be that woman.

The phone chirped softly at her. She'd turned it down as low as possible without going onto vibrate. She didn't have to look at it to know it was Rand; her intuition was in On mode where he was concerned.

Of course, it could have been Gary calling to grind home his point. But, no, Gary was most likely making nookie with his hot little tramp who wanted to take away Rachel's children.

The phone rang two more times. Another two, and it would go directly to voicemail. She'd planned on answering; that's why she'd left it beside the bed. She'd wanted to cry on Rand's shoulder, pour out her troubles, ask him what to do.

But then she'd have to tell him how idiotic she'd been, that she'd put his job in jeopardy. A part of her also wanted to rail at him. This was all his fault. *He'd* wanted to make that damn video. *He'd* wanted her to keep it so they could watch it together. Yes, yes, it was all *his* fault.

God, she needed to take it out on someone.

The phone stopped ringing. He was gone. She felt a rush of triumph for besting her neediness.

Rand wasn't the problem, though. He was just a symptom of her life falling apart; he hadn't caused it. Gary had. He'd gotten bored or depressed or maybe he'd even wanted someone like Sherry back then. So Gary had torn Rachel's world apart. He'd detonated an H-bomb on his sons' lives, too.

Now he wanted to ruin everything all over again, just as she was starting to feel good again. Because of Rand.

She needed that damn video back. She wondered if there was some space-age gizmo the government used in covert operations that she could drive by Gary's house with and erase the digital contents. Okay, she knew she was stretching.

The phone beeped, signaling a message. Rachel rolled to her back, taking the cell in her hand, its screen lit up. Keying in her password, she listened.

"Baby, my cock's hard for you. This weekend was better than anything. I'm going to jerk off remembering every moment."

His voice stole her breath and spread warmth through her. Just sounds, not even a touch, but suddenly he held her heart in the palm of his hand. He made her feel special, desired, wanted, needed. She couldn't remember the last time Gary had made her feel that way, if ever. Rand did it so easily, as if complimenting her and making her feel good was second nature.

It was like the masseur all over again, Gary telling her how terrible she was, how immoral. He was stealing away all her new-found self-confidence, her joy in her sexuality. That bastard. She couldn't let him win.

She wouldn't let him take her boys *and* destroy her relationship with Rand. There had to be something she could do.

Saving the message, she pulled the covers to her chin and hugged the phone to her chest. She might not have a device to erase it from a distance, but there were far less technical methods. Nathan and Justin both had keys to Gary's apartment, and it was empty all day long while he was at work.

She would search his place and steal the SD card back just the way Gary had stolen it from her.

31

ON TUESDAY MORNING, RAND FOLLOWED THE CURVE OF THE buildings past the rows of lockers. The second period bell had rung several minutes ago, and the halls were empty.

Walking empty hallways was good for thinking. He'd had his admin leave a note for Nathan scheduling a meeting just before lunch. Mondays were always full of to-dos, so he'd decided to start Operation Nathan Delaney today instead of yesterday. He would get the boy to like him no matter what.

Rand smiled at himself. How low he'd sunk, trying to get at a woman through her son.

He'd missed their phone calls on both of the last two nights. He'd missed *her*. One might consider him smitten. It was a pleasant feeling. She was such a varied mix of types, soccer mom as well as sexy slut, assured as well as vulnerable, submissive as well as dominant. He couldn't categorize her and thus everything they did was unpredictable, like the way she'd bound him with the scarves. He would never have expected that from her, and yet it delighted him.

Rounding the curve to C Building, an oddity pulled him out of his musings. Despite having been at the school only half a year, he knew these halls like the back of his hand. He was no longer alone.

Nathan Delaney stood motionless just outside the C Building bathroom, his shoulder against the door holding it slightly open. There was something furtive in his stance.

What was the boy doing? Why wasn't he in class?

Though he didn't see Rand watching him, Nathan suddenly pushed through the door and disappeared inside the restroom.

Rand sighed. Today's meeting was supposed to be about finding equal footing, coming to an understanding. Now he'd have to talk about tardiness and whatever the hell was going on in that bathroom. Smoking? Or worse? Drugs?

Rand did not want to have to call Rachel to tell her Nathan was using or buying drugs, or even selling them. Not Nathan. He hadn't pegged him for drugs, yet this could be the beginning of a downhill slide.

He covered the distance swiftly and quietly, then stopped outside the door, listening. Definitely voices within, so Nathan wasn't alone in there. Damn. If he had to catch them in the act, he needed a few more seconds to allow the contraband to come out of backpacks, pockets, wherever. For better eavesdropping, he pushed the door ajar an inch or two with his foot. It opened to a tiled wall hiding the urinals and stalls from outside view. To get out, they'd have to go around or through him. The boys were trapped inside with nowhere to go except past Rand.

They were so damn busted.

"LEAVE HIM ALONE, TOM." NATHAN'S VOICE, SOUNDING STRONGER and less sullen than Rand had ever heard it.

"Hey, Nathan, perfect timing. This moron"—Tom Molcini, naturally—"needs a lesson in being a man."

"Come on, guys, you've had your fun. Just let him up." Nathan paused, then added, "Get up, Wally. You can go now."

Jesus Christ, Wally was in there. Every muscle in Rand's body tensed to rush through the door, to rescue him, yet the purely unemotional side of his brain made him stand still. This was the thing Nathan needed, he knew it in his gut. Nathan needed to handle this crisis. He *could* handle it.

"Hey, asshole"—the ever-present Rick Franchetti, Tom's half-wit sidekick—"we're not done with him yet."

"Are you some kinda pussy, Delaney, defending a moron?" Tom sneered.

"He's not a moron, Tom. He's autistic. So just leave him alone. Come on, Wally. It's okay. You can get up."

Rand's heart actually turned over in his chest at Nathan's gentle voice, the kindness in his tone.

"Dude. You're making a big mistake. You don't wanna piss me off." Tom gave a snarl.

Nathan came back after a short silence, as if they'd all been moving in wary circles around one another, settling in for the clash. "You're pissing me off by picking on a kid who can't defend himself."

Rand had never been so proud of one of his students as he was in that moment.

"Well, then," Tom said, "maybe we need to pick on someone who *thinks*"—spittle hissed from his lips—"he's got some balls."

"Yeah, dude, you just think you got balls," Rick mocked, like a punctuation mark on whatever Tom said. He was just an ignorant follower. "We're gonna kick your ass."

"Yeah? You and whose army?"

Tom barked a laugh. "You're such a pussy."

It was time. Rand shoved the door open. "What the hell is going on in here?" His voice reverberated off the walls.

Tom and Rick jumped, turning to face the Rand. They flanked

Nathan, obviously intending to come at him from both sides. But Nathan stood his ground, hovering over Wally protectively, his fists bunched in readiness as if he were waiting for a free-for-all to break out. Tears streaked Wally's face, a wet spot stained his jeans, and his backpack lay in a puddle beneath one of the urinals.

Jesus. Maybe he'd waited too long to come in. Except that Nathan *had* handled it. He'd gone to bat for Wally. He was willing to fight for him.

"This creep," Tom said, stabbing a finger in Nathan's back, "was giving poor Wally a bad time."

"Yeah," Rick said, sounding like the drone he was. "Look how he threw poor Wally's backpack in the piss puddle."

"Are you all right, Wally?" Rand asked.

"Fine, fine, fine," Wally chirped, but he huddled down on the floor.

"Molcini and Franchetti," Rand said very softly, "get out of here and go to your classes."

"Yes, sir," they said like chipper parrots.

The door whooshed closed behind them, but Rand could still hear their laughter outside. If he wasn't a principal with a sworn duty, he'd have beaten their heads together. Instead, he'd take care of them later, within the confines of his mandate. Which meant no physical violence.

With the imminent danger over, Nathan reached out a hand to help Wally up.

"Don't touch him," Rand barked. There was no telling how Wally would react if touched right now, even when someone intended to help him.

Nathan froze, then glanced over his shoulder, his eyes dark and angry. He didn't understand; Rand didn't have time to explain.

"Come on, Wally, get up." Rand stepped around Nathan to grab Wally's backpack out of the puddle. Carrying it to the sink, he ran water over the bottom of it.

Wally rolled to his hands and knees. "Yes, sir, yes, sir, yes, sir." Then he got to his feet, turned to the wall and zipped up. Dammit, they'd attacked him with his pants down. Rand's blood boiled. When Wally turned, the dark stain on his jeans was a stark reminder.

Nathan grimaced. "You can't send him out like that, Principal Torvik."

Rand was silent a long moment. "I'll take care of it, Nathan. Go to class." His voice came out more harshly than he'd intended, but he didn't have time to deal with Nathan's feelings. They'd have to discuss it later. "Be in my office as soon as the lunch bell rings."

Nathan stared at him a moment longer, emotions—anger, bitterness—flitting across his features, then he stomped across the tile floor, grabbed his backpack, and slammed through the door.

Maybe he should have explained, but Nathan's needs at the moment were secondary to Wally's.

RAND HAD NOT TAKEN HIS SEAT BEHIND THE DESK. INSTEAD, HE turned the chair beside Nathan's to face him. Sitting, he assumed a relaxed posture.

Nathan wore his usual sullen demeanor, eyes down, head lowered.

"Wally's fine," Rand said. He'd scrubbed off the bottom of the boy's backpack. Nathan had been right; Wally couldn't walk around school in those clothes. Rand had taken him to the locker rooms where Wally's mother kept a cache of extra clothing. Not that Wally wet himself as a matter of course, but his mother was one of those women who was always prepared.

The boy was fine. He was a remarkable sort. After his progress over the last six months, Rand was hopeful that Wally would someday find his perfect place in society, especially with the end of Molcini's and Franchetti's tyranny.

Then there was Nathan. Rand had been planning his tête-à-tête with Rachel's son, then he'd walked into the restroom and it had all been blown to hell. This was no longer about Rachel, or about getting on the good side of her son so he could keep fucking the boy's mother.

This was about Wally and Nathan.

"Do you remember the incident in the cafeteria when you knocked Wally's tray out of his hands?" Rand asked softly.

Nathan swallowed, then the muscles of his face tensed, and he clenched his fists on the armrests. "I told you I didn't touch him."

"Are we parsing words here? You didn't *touch* him, you bumped him. You can deny it all you want, but we both know I saw it, Nathan."

The boy was silent.

"What I fail to understand is why you rescued Wally from those two bullies today when less than a month ago you were pushing him around, too."

Nathan's head jerked up. For a moment he looked so much like Rachel that Rand's heart ached. Then the moment was gone, and he was Nathan, the student Rand couldn't seem to reach.

"Tom and Rick told you I was the one who pushed Wally down in the restroom. You believed them." His tone was challenging.

"I'm not stupid, Nathan." Rand decided to be completely honest. "I saw you go in, I heard voices, and was worried it might be about drugs. So I listened at the door to catch you all in the act." He raised a brow. "But what I heard was you going to bat for a kid who couldn't defend himself."

Nathan didn't say anything, but his cheeks colored.

"I was very proud of you, son." He waited for Nathan to meet his gaze. "You stood up to them, even though they were mad enough to beat the crap out of you for it."

Nathan actually smiled. "They were getting ready to."

"Why did you do it, Nathan?" Rand asked gently. "Was it because of your work in the special ed lab?" Rand didn't believe there'd been enough time for it to have turned the boy around this completely.

Nathan went back to staring at his hands, and Rand got it. The boy was ashamed. He didn't want to admit what he'd done, but he'd tried to make up for it in that restroom.

"You didn't push Wally down the gymnasium steps, did you." He didn't emphasize it as a question.

Nathan shook his head slowly.

"Did you see who did?"

Nathan shook his head again.

He was asking the boy to rat out his pals, but Rand needed to know. "You saw today that it can become serious very easily, Nathan. One of these times, someone could really get hurt."

He let the room sit in silence while Nathan thought.

Finally, the boy spoke. "I didn't see. Tom and Rick were there, and three or four of the other guys." He shrugged. "Then Wally was just falling."

"You don't think he was pushed?"

Again, silence. And again, Nathan finally answered. "He was pushed. Then they all ran away. I just don't know which one of them did it." He pressed his lips tightly together, and Rand suspected he might be fighting tears. "I should have told them to leave him alone then. But I just stood there." He paused a long moment as if truly looking at himself and not liking what he saw. When he spoke again, his voice dropped almost to a whisper. "I *always* just stood there and let it happen without even trying to stop them." He clenched his teeth a moment, then opened his mouth to drag in a deep breath as if he'd just bared his soul. "Sometimes, though, you just gotta draw a line and man up."

Rand realized what it must have cost the boy to admit he hadn't acted like a man until that moment in the boys' room. "You stood up for him today, Nathan, and that's what counts. The Wallys of the world need people like you."

Nathan's head swayed. "I did knock his tray out of his hands that day in the cafeteria." He took another deep breath, held it, then exhaled in a long, painful sigh. "And I called him a stupid retard," he said, his shame evident in the softness of those words.

Here's what Rand had been waiting weeks to hear. He let Nathan tell it.

"It was just supposed to be giving other kids crap. Like who's stronger or more popular, who's top dog, all that stuff." He sighed as if the weight of the world sat on his shoulders alone. "Then I started to see it was just about *those* kids."

"The special ed kids?"

He nodded. "It stopped being fun a long time ago and started being just plain mean."

"And you don't want to be mean anymore, do you."

Nathan raised his gaze to meet Rand's, and somehow his spine seemed to get a little straighter in his seat. "No. I don't. If that's what it takes to be on their team, I don't want to play."

Holy hell. Rand wanted to cheer. He couldn't have made up a better metaphor himself. "All it takes is awareness, Nathan. They aren't *those* kids. They're teenagers like anyone else, just with different needs." He lowered his voice conspiratorially. "They're special."

Nathan stared at the carpet, then nodded slowly. "Wally's actually capable of amazing things. I saw that in special ed."

His words were enough to bring a tear to Rand's eye. "Maybe we can help spread the word in small ways."

Nathan shrugged again in typical teenage fashion.

Rising, Rand clapped him on the shoulder. "By the way, many autistics don't like to be touched. That's why I didn't want you to help Wally up. It wasn't you personally."

"Really?" Nathan sounded hopeful.

He was a good kid. Rand had high hopes for him. "Really. Now, I'm going to need your help. Let me tell you my plan."

Nathan listened, nodding eagerly.

This could work. As an added benefit, it solved all Rand's problems with Rachel, too.

32

"WHAT DO YOU MEAN, YOU'RE TAKING AN EARLY LUNCH?" Yvonne's brown eyes snapped with ire.

This was *not* working. Yvonne wouldn't let her learn a thing, getting angry if she made a mistake, snatching the keyboard away. Rachel wasn't sure what half the mistakes she supposedly made actually were.

All she wanted to do was get out. She'd stolen Gary's key out of Justin's backpack this morning before school, and she wanted to get over there before lunch just in case Gary came home for a quick nooner with his little floozy.

God, she was turning into a judgmental bitch. Not to mention useless at order entry.

"I have a doctor's appointment." Now she was lying, too. Whatever, couldn't be helped, extenuating circumstances.

Yvonne merely huffed. "We're never going to get this done if you keep running off when we're right in the middle."

They had *months*, for God's sake. Rachel resisted rolling her eyes. If Yvonne stopped grabbing the keyboard every time Rachel made a teeny-tiny error, things would move a lot faster. "I'll be back before one. We can start again."

"I'll have placed all the orders by then," Yvonne grumbled.

Why was she being so difficult? Afraid Rachel would replace her, as Bree said? Whatever. "Perhaps you could leave me a couple of orders, and I'll enter them on my own. You can check them when I'm done." She could do it if Yvonne wasn't hanging over her, hemming, hawing, making her nervous and prone to mistakes.

Yvonne flapped a hand. "Go. Go." Then continued to mutter irritably to herself. "Silly girl," et cetera, et cetera.

Rachel was beyond caring. She stopped in her office for her purse, then made it to Gary's apartment complex much faster than usual, which meant she'd been speeding and could have gotten a ticket. Luckily, there weren't any cops around.

Gary's parking spot was empty, thank God. The development was huge, with apartments on three levels. Gary's was on the third floor because he'd wanted the vaulted ceilings, skylights, and balcony. It was nice, and since she got the house, she couldn't begrudge him a decent place to take the boys. Except right now when he was blackmailing her.

The front door opened into a small entry with a coat closet on one side. From there, you entered the living room, which had a sofa alcove. The room was bright with sun streaming through the skylights. To the right was the kitchen and eating nook and the hall back to the three bedrooms. The boys had their own bathroom, too.

She headed back to Gary's room. His bed was neatly made, all his clothes hung up or put in the hamper. Sherry's influence? God, she was still comparing. *Get over it.*

She stood in front of his bureau. Maybe he was as stupid as she was and had hidden the video card in the same place, the underwear drawer. She reached for it, a walnut bureau with three skinny drawers along the top for socks and underwear or lingerie.

She was here; she could search everywhere, find the video, save herself, save Rand. Yet now, when the moment was upon her, she couldn't get her hand to move. She couldn't touch that drawer.

What the hell was she doing? She'd lied to Yvonne about the doctor's appointment, gone through her son's backpack while he was getting ready for school, stolen his key, broken into her ex's apartment. Lying, stealing. What was next, murder? It didn't matter that she had a key, she didn't have permission. This wasn't like her; this was some other crazy woman. Gary had gone through her drawers, but was she as bad as him? No, she was better than that.

Rachel started backing out of the room as if she were afraid that something terrible would attack the moment she turned her back on the bureau. Or she'd change her mind and ransack the place.

And wasn't Gary a tiny bit right? Now she could have Rand. She wouldn't have to tell him she'd lost the video. He'd never have to know. He wouldn't get angry with her. They were safe.

She turned around only after she was out in the hall, the brightness of the freshly painted white almost blinding. Arms outstretched, both hands on the wall supporting her as she made her way back to the living room, she felt dizzy. Oh yes, she could have Rand. She could fuck him every night of the week. When she got horny, she could beg him to come over. They could play out all the rape fantasies they wanted.

All she had to do was give up her sons.

God, what had she been thinking when she let Rand make that video?

Maybe she could bargain with Gary. He could have the boys every weekend. She could take them during the week. Surely that would be enough to satisfy Sherry. Yes, yes, give and take.

But she'd still have to give up Rand. All of this had started when she'd let herself get carried away with him. She couldn't make everything right if she didn't put an end to it, if she didn't stop doing all the things that had gotten her into trouble in the first place. She had to return to being the staid, vanilla woman she'd been two months ago before she'd ever met Rand.

She had to tell him it was over and really mean it.

Before she lost her courage.

RAND DIDN'T GO OUT TO LUNCH ON A REGULAR BASIS. HE PRE-ferred having a sandwich at his desk, where he could take care of paperwork, and he often scheduled meetings during the lunch period, just as he had with Nathan earlier.

So he was pleased he was free when Miss Watson buzzed him and told him Mrs. Delaney was here. Perfect. Since he'd had Nathan in his office only half an hour before, there was nothing suspicious in his mother showing up.

He had visions of bending Rachel over the principal's desk.

He loved a really hot, sexy fantasy in the middle of the day. He'd tell her about it, get her all worked up. They could replay it tonight on the phone.

The visions died the moment he saw her face. She was pale, dark circles beneath her eyes, the hazel color now muddy with her roiling emotions. It couldn't be Nathan; everything was fine with Nathan, mission accomplished, except the last phase of his plan, which Rand would carry out this afternoon.

"Mrs. Delaney," he said for benefit of Miss Watson, "please, sit down." He leaned out the door. "Hold my calls." After receiving a thumbs-up, he shut himself in with Rachel.

She collapsed into the chair Nathan had occupied earlier.

"What's wrong?" Rand leaned back on the edge of the desk, propping himself so he could face her. He wanted to be close; the other side of the desk was too far away.

She clasped her hands in her lap and didn't look at him. "I have to stop seeing you."

His heart coughed like an engine that was on the verge of

dying. Then it kick-started. "What's happened? Is it something with Nathan?" Because *that* problem was solved.

She shook her head. "No."

"Justin?" It had to be one of her boys; there could be no other reason.

Again, she shook her head, then she swallowed. "It's not the boys. It's just that I need to do what's right."

He closed his eyes briefly. One day they were on; the next they were off. He was getting a little ticked at the roller-coaster ride she kept taking him on. Then he got hold of himself. She wouldn't look at him, so he went down in a squat before her. "Everything is good with Nathan now. We can work this out, let the boys know that we're attracted, that we'd like to see each other."

"I'm not telling them about us." Her eyes were wild.

Her sharp tone pissed him off as well, but he tamped it down since she was so obviously upset. "Rachel, it's time to start thinking in terms of a relationship, a future."

She simply stared at him like he'd suddenly shed his skin and turned out to be an alien. "This was casual. We have no future. No one was ever supposed to know."

"Is this because we arrived home late on Sunday?"

She clamped her lips shut. That was his answer; yes, it was about Sunday. Something had happened when she got home, which was why she hadn't taken his calls either Sunday night or Monday.

He covered her clasped hands with his palm. He realized he was springing this relationship idea on her. *He'd* thought about it; she might take a little bit longer. "This isn't about sex anymore, Rachel. It's become more important than *just* sex."

All at once, she yanked her hands out of his, shoved the chair back, and began to pace the office. Outside, teenagers marched— or shuffled—to and fro, but, for his students' privacy, he always kept the blinds slightly tilted so that it was difficult to see inside. Now it was for Rachel's privacy.

"I'm not letting you go without an explanation," he said softly, her back to him. "What happened on Sunday that has you all freaked out? Don't lie and tell me it's nothing."

She whirled on him. "I *do not* lie." Yet in the next split second, her gaze fell.

That obviously pricked a nerve. "Then tell me. Let's talk about this."

She buried her face in her hands. "Men don't like to talk." It came out slightly muffled through her fingers.

He gave her a gentle smile. "I'm an educator. I talk for a living. And I'm a good listener."

She was silent for several heartbeats, then finally she slid back down into the chair, perching on the edge of it. She smoothed her skirt down over her thighs. He didn't tower over her, but took up the other seat.

"Promise you're not going to get mad or freak out."

As much as he wanted to smile, he didn't. How many times had he heard those exact words in this office and all the other offices he'd had? He gave the same answer he always did. "I won't get mad."

"While we were in Las Vegas, my ex-husband found the video you and I made."

Instead of speeding up, his heart rate slowed to something like sludge. "Where was it?" He thought he sounded quite calm.

"In my lingerie drawer." She swallowed nervously.

"Does he feel he has a right to paw through your lingerie?" Yes, he was deadly calm about the whole thing.

"No, he just—" She stopped, as if fearing his reaction.

"He just"—significant pause—"what?"

"He wanted to find something on me," she said softly. "When he realized I'd been away for the weekend, he didn't think it was just a trip with the girls."

Rand breathed deeply, but found his fists clenched around the arms of his chair. He loosened them. He'd like nothing better than to beat Delaney to a bloody pulp. He advocated non-violence, but he enjoyed the image of crushing a few of the man's bones. "So he found our lovely video and told you that you had to break off our relationship or"—he spread his hands—"what?"

She shook her head, and he was struck again with the similarity to Nathan. Mannerisms were the tell between family. They pursed their lips the same, shook their heads the same.

"He doesn't care whether I stop seeing you or not." She dipped her head. "He wants me to give him full custody of the boys. If I don't, he'll go to court and use the video to show I'm an unfit mother."

He felt his anger rage until he was sure the whites of his eyes had turned red. "What did you tell him?"

"I said yes." Her eyes flashed, as if suddenly she had someone to lash out at. "What else could I tell him? He'll let me have them one or two weekends a month. Otherwise I might not get to see them at all."

The man definitely deserved a thrashing. Those boys were the most important thing in the world to Rachel, and that asshole ex of hers was hitting where it would hurt the most.

"He can also use it to get you fired," she said softly.

That did it. He couldn't ratchet back the ire, and he stood, turning on her. "We made a private video in the comfort of my home for personal use only. He cannot get me fired for that, especially as it was stolen property. This isn't about us. This is about you and the boys."

"I know," she said, her voice low, almost cowed. "His girlfriend wants more time with the boys. She wants to be a mother or something."

"Then tell her to have her own children," he barked, immediately regretting the harshness. This wasn't Rachel's fault. It wasn't even his for making the video in the first place. He didn't regret that for a moment. He regretted only that he hadn't yet gotten to watch it with her. What that man was doing to her was unconscionable.

He stood with his hands clasped behind his back. "He's bluffing, Rachel. He isn't going to show that video to anyone. If he intended to, he would have gone directly to family court without blackmailing you first."

She licked her lips, then looked up at him with pleading in her eyes. "I know. But I can't take that chance. He could try to hurt you. And what would the boys do if they ever found out?"

"I would enjoy having him take me on." He'd crush the asswipe. "But there's no way he's going to let your boys see that video or even hear of its existence. He knows it'll have the opposite effect and make them hate him for exposing it."

She pressed her lips together and gave him a militant glare. "You can't know that's how they'll react."

"I know teenagers, and they'll surprise you every time. They're far more tolerant than most parents expect. They'll probably think you're cool." Once they got over the idea of having their mom sexualized. No self-respecting kid *wanted* to imagine his parents having sex. But if the ex-husband told them about the video, they'd be much more likely to hate *him* because he was the one who'd asked for the divorce in the first place. It was the equivalent of waving a red flag at them and saying, *Yeah, I really was the asshole who dumped on your mom when she didn't deserve it.*

Rand pointed that out. "They'll blame Gary for doing this to you more than they'll blame you for making the video."

"They'll think I'm a slut," she muttered.

He was down beside her chair in a flash. "You are not a slut in a derogatory sense. You're beautiful, you're sexual, you're young, and you have a right to enjoy all the pleasure your body craves."

She rolled her lips together, smudging her lipstick. Then she dipped her head, trying to hide the tears he suspected were near the surface. "Please don't talk like that. I can't handle you being nice. It makes me want things I can't have."

He covered her folded hands just as he'd done before. "You *can* have them, Rachel. You deserve them. And you deserve to have your boys with you, too." He tipped his head to look up into her eyes and lowered his voice. "Call his bluff."

"I can't," she whispered. "I could lose everything."

"You've already lost it if you give him full custody without a fight."

She sniffed. "You don't understand."

He wanted to shout at her. She was giving in to her husband, giving up her kids, and giving up on him because she was afraid something worse would happen. He understood fear. He just didn't understand letting it completely control you.

"Maybe things will all blow over," she offered meekly. "Sherry could decide she doesn't want the kids all the time. Something will happen."

Something would happen. Nathan and Justin would think she'd abandoned them. "What excuse are you going to give the boys?"

She flapped a hand as if it didn't matter. "That I'm going back to school."

He sighed. "You're handing your ex-husband all the cards. Your kids will blame *you*. This is wrong, Rachel."

"I don't have any other choice."

She did. She was just afraid to make it. He rose, hearing his knees creak as if in the space of half an hour, he'd aged a decade. "I want you, Rachel. I'm willing to stand by you if you want to challenge him. You haven't done anything wrong. He violated your privacy. Now he's trying to make you into the villain. Don't let him."

He knew her answer before she said it. "There isn't any other way."

"There's always another way." He waited. She didn't answer. He could go to her ex-husband, force the man to back down, but Gary would find another way to get at her. Unless *she* stood up to him. "I can't fight this battle for you, Rachel. You have to do this yourself. You have to refuse to give him your kids."

He'd wanted more from her. He wasn't going to get it. For years, he'd taken care of his students, listened to their problems, counseled them, gotten fulfillment out of their successes. Yet he realized now that he'd lived his life one step back from true involvement. For the first time, with Rachel, he wanted to risk it all, dive headfirst into the murky waters of a real relationship. Only to find she wasn't willing to take the same risk.

THERE SHOULD HAVE BEEN A GRAY SKY TO MATCH THE PALL HANGing over her. Yet the sun was so bright Rachel had to put her sunglasses on to drive.

He didn't get it. He could be dispassionate about it because he wasn't a parent and didn't have to worry about what his kids would think of him, that they might possibly hate him. That's why he was willing to fight. Because he had less to lose.

He was wrong, though. Gary *would* use that video against her, and the boys would hate her for it. She had no choice but to end the relationship once and for all.

But she hated herself for not being a fighter like he was.

33

"SINCE THERE'S NO WAY TO PROVE WHO DID WHAT TO WHOM AND when," Rand said, "I'm holding you all responsible."

This counted twice today that Nathan had been called to the principal's office. The group sat across the desk from Rand, Nathan on the right, Molcini and Franchetti in the two chairs closest to the window.

Rand glowered at them all, waiting for a response. No one said a thing. So he did. "I'm not suspending you. Instead, I'm offering you an opportunity."

He didn't rat out Nathan, but instead made it sound like he was punishing them equally. It was the only way the plan would work, and Nathan was fully on board with it.

"I'm assigning all three of you as Wally's bodyguards."

Tom snorted. Rick grumbled. Nathan said, "Just what does that mean?"

When Rand unveiled his plan, they hadn't rehearsed what they'd say, but Nathan was falling in with the correct dialogue. Making them bodyguards would accomplish two things. Wally would be safe, and it afforded the other two boys the opportunity to discover that Wally was an awesome kid, just as Nathan had during his time in the special ed lab. Perhaps that was wishful thinking—Molcini and Franchetti could well be lost causes—but the beauty of the plan was in giving Nathan a chance to redeem himself in his own eyes. He would take this duty seriously.

"It means," Rand said, "that I will hold all three of you responsible for Wally's well-being here at school. If anyone hassles him, you will all defend him."

Tom cocked his head. "And, like, what, we gotta come and rat to you if anyone gives him a bad time?"

Rand stared him down. "I expect you gentlemen to handle it on your own. Without fighting. I assume that once you've established your authority, no one will bully Wally again."

"So, like, all three of us have to hang around the kid all day long?" Rick gaped. He looked like an ape.

"It won't be necessary to sit in his classrooms. To and from class, to and from the bus, and during lunch period will suffice."

"Geez." Rick rolled his eyes and drooped dramatically in his chair. "That's every freaking minute of the day. When do we get to hang out with our friends?"

Rand raised one eyebrow. "The easiest thing would be to include Wally."

Tom let out a noise that was half a disgusted snort, half retching. "You gotta be kidding."

"I'm simply giving you the responsibility for ensuring Wally's welfare with all the latitude of deciding how you three will accomplish that *together*." He enunciated clearly to make sure the boys got it.

Nathan played his role superbly. "But if we don't have to rat on each other or anyone else, how are you going to know if we screw it up?"

Rick snickered.

Leaning forward, Rand eyed them all. "I'll be watching."

It was democratic in that they could decide how they managed the assignment, and autocratic because they had no choice but to try. Rand hadn't asked Nathan to report on the other two; he'd simply tasked the boy with making sure Wally was good to go. He'd taken Nathan into his confidence with the plan, trusted him to carry it out.

He might have lost Rachel, but he wouldn't lose her son to a pack of bullies.

IT FELT LIKE THE MORNING AFTER. AND IT WAS; RACHEL HADN'T slept well. But she'd been a damn good mom this morning, letting Nathan drive to school without once stomping on her imaginary passenger brake. Funnily enough, he hadn't become furtive and embarrassed about having to drive the dreaded *minivan*. He'd even waved good-bye. Justin had hopped out of the car after accepting a quick kiss, and run across the street to the middle school.

She hadn't bugged Nathan about his homework last night, hadn't asked how working in the special education lab was going. She didn't want to mention Rand's name, both for herself—the pain was too raw after that showdown in his office earlier in the day—and because she didn't want to start a fight with Nathan. She was done with fighting for now. If she did everything right, maybe they'd tell Gary they wanted to see her more than one weekend per month.

It was going to be hell no matter what happened. Somehow, someday, she would make Gary pay for this.

At work, Yvonne was her usual self—in other words, totally impossible. To be fair, she'd only been so since starting to teach Rachel the order entry system—*start* being the operative word, because they certainly hadn't made any progress. Rachel wasn't going to talk to Erin about it either, no way.

"Not there. Here." Yvonne stabbed the screen as Rachel entered the customer number. "You have to do the lookup first."

"I already know the number so I don't have to look it up." It was written right on the piece of paper from which Rachel had been keying.

"But if you don't do the lookup, it won't pull all the customer information."

Before Yvonne could snatch the keyboard, Rachel typed the last number and hit Enter. The screen populated with all the correct customer information. "See, it worked."

Yvonne glared. "I know it *works*," she said waspishly. "But it's inefficient to look it up and handwrite all the customer numbers *first*."

"I didn't look it up. I remembered it from the last time."

Yvonne narrowed her eyes until they were slits, then breathed deeply as if trying very hard not to scream. "You could have gotten it wrong, then you might have put the whole order against the wrong customer. Some of the names are very similar."

Oh, for God's sake. "I always check the details before I finish entering."

Yvonne said nothing for several moments, just continued the devil glare. "This isn't going to work," she finally said. "I'll tell Erin we need a temp, someone who's dedicated to this task and isn't flitting around answering phones, doing data entry for accounting, or proofing Dominic's sales brochures."

"I *am* dedicated, Yvonne, to this company and to doing the very best job I can."

Yvonne ignored her. "My mind's made up. You're just not good at learning this stuff."

"If you'll—"

Yvonne turned her face away and held out her palm in a talk-to-the-hand gesture.

She stared at Yvonne's hand. This is what Rachel always did:

shut up, tried to please, made nice, knuckled under, did what everyone told her to do. What had it gotten her? She didn't make enough to support her kids, Nathan hated her, even if he had been reasonable this morning. Gary was stealing the boys, and she'd dumped a man who made her feel better than anyone had in years. Now this—Yvonne ripping this latest opportunity out of her hands for no good reason. Dammit, this was the end of her rope, the straw that broke the camel's back, and any other cliché she could think of.

She wasn't going to take it anymore. "I am the mother of two teenage boys," she said calmly, but with a razor's edge in her tone. "And when they are failing, I don't simply look at what *they* are doing wrong, I look at the teacher to see where he or *she* is failing." She leaned in close, lowered her voice. "Even if it's me doing the teaching."

Yvonne narrowed her eyes. "What are you saying?"

"I'm saying you need to look at your teaching methods in addition to my learning capacity."

"Well, I never," Yvonne said, suddenly haughty.

"You're right, Yvonne, you've never taught anyone how to do this. And the way you're teaching isn't working." She waited a second for that to register, but not long enough to allow Yvonne to jump in. "Bree taught me receivables and payables with no problem at all. Orders are just as simple."

"Order entry is the backbone of all—"

Rachel held her hand in Yvonne's face. "I'm not finished. I was saying you need to give me the orders, let me enter them on my own, without hovering over me, then check my work and we'll discuss what, if anything, I did incorrectly. That's"—she stabbed her chest—"how I learn. I am not stupid."

"I never said you were."

"Then give me a chance. I can cover for you while you're gone, and I can even help you out at month-end when you're trying to get everything shipped. You know, this could actually be a very good thing, Yvonne. I'm not trying to steal your job."

"I didn't say you were," Yvonne replied stiffly, but she'd dropped her gaze and was now shuffling papers on the desk.

It was the moment to soften a little. "Let me help out, Yvonne. You won't be sorry."

Yvonne's throat worked as she swallowed. Then the papers were all straightened, and finally Yvonne looked at her from the corner of her eye. "I'm sorry I've been hard on you. I just don't want to have to worry about everything falling apart while I'm gone. I don't want to come back to a big mess."

Rachel chose not to resent Yvonne's sentiments. "I'll do my very best to make sure everything goes smoothly. Erin and Bree are here to answer any questions I've got while you're away."

Yvonne nodded. "You can call me, too." Then, slowly, very slowly, she slid the pile of orders to Rachel. "You go enter these. I'll check them this afternoon. Next week, I'll start doing some of the order-taking on speakerphone so you can listen in and learn that part, too."

Rachel didn't punch the air in triumph. She simply said, "That would be good. We'll make this work, Yvonne."

Later, when Yvonne checked Rachel's work, there wasn't a single error. Rachel also took two orders, one from a distributor, another from a performance racing customer.

It was powerful to stick up for yourself. You didn't necessarily get slammed down.

Rachel thought about that all afternoon. Which meant she couldn't help thinking about Rand and what he'd said.

Was she giving in because she was afraid to fight, afraid of the consequences? Because really, what *were* the consequences? If she called Gary's blackmail bluff, she might lose the boys. But if she didn't, she'd lose them anyway. Two days a month wasn't enough to be a good mother to them. Even two weekends wasn't going to cut it. She couldn't repair the damage to her relationship with Nathan in two short days a month, and for Justin, that could be the tipping point. *To hell with you, Mom.*

No. Rachel stood up. She hadn't fought to keep Gary; she'd let him walk away from his responsibilities to her and to their children. She'd let him dictate about Nathan's driver's permit and where she'd live and paying half of expenses she didn't authorize and couldn't afford. Now she was about to let him dictate when she could see the boys.

No way. He was screwing his little floozy, and she had an equal right to screw whomever she wanted—and make a *personal and private* video of it if she wanted to. Goddammit, Gary could not simply walk into her house and search her drawers.

It was time to stop being a peacemaker and make a stand. If she was going to lose everything anyway, she sure as hell wasn't going to throw away her self-respect at the same time.

34

RACHEL MADE THE BOYS DINNER AND LEFT THEM TO DO THEIR homework. "Nathan, you're in charge. I have to see your dad. I'll be back in about an hour."

"Sure, Mom."

She looked at him askance. He was pleasant. He was actually *nice* to her. He *smiled*. What was up with that? She didn't ask because she couldn't start worrying about one more thing.

"What are you going to see Dad for?" Justin wanted to know.

"Some legal stuff with the divorce." It wasn't a lie, and that's all they needed to know. "By the way, I borrowed your key to your dad's apartment." She dug in her purse, handed it back.

Justin held it in the palm of his hand, staring at it. "Why'd you need his key?"

"I had to pick up something of mine that he had," she said in a tone that brooked no further questions. "Please make sure your homework's done before you start watching TV."

Before lunch, she'd slinked up the stairs to Gary's apartment, looking over her shoulder like a frightened mouse. This time, she marched up the three flights and knocked loudly.

Gary opened the door still dressed in his white shirt and black pants. No tie. He worked semi-casual. When he saw her, he backed up, and Rachel felt a thrill of power. She'd expected to feel butterflies or nerves or to stutter or *something*, but instead she stepped into his hall and closed the door.

"First of all," she said, "I am not changing the custody arrangement we have with the boys." He opened his mouth; she didn't close hers long enough for him to interrupt. "Second, I want the key to my house."

"It's not your house; it's ours for the time being."

Leaning forward slightly, she got in his face. "I'm living in it, and you don't need to have a key."

"Rachel," he said, spreading his hands, getting ready for the let's-be-reasonable speech.

She didn't let him make it. "Third, I want my video back. You searched my home, went through my personal possessions to find it, and I want it back."

"Rachel, we've already talked about this."

She stepped closer; he stepped back, stumbling slightly over the edge of the living room carpet.

"*You* talked. I only got to listen. Now I'm through listening to anything you have to say."

He glanced over his shoulder, holding his hands up again to ward her off. "We can talk about this later. You're not reasonable right now."

"I'm very reasonable," she said. "I've simply decided that I will not allow you to appease your girlfriend by taking my children from me. I'll fight you. You'll have to take this to court. If you try to use that video, you'll have to admit you searched my bedroom to find it." She heard her own voice and was amazed at the strength of it. Power pulsed through her.

Gary stepped into her space, trying to get her to back up, but she wasn't moving. On the edge of her peripheral vision, something moved, a shape darkened the kitchen door.

"What's the matter, Gary?"

Sherry, pretty, trim, young, with an apron tied at her waist and a wooden spoon in her hand. It was only then that Rachel caught a whiff of spices, something Italian.

"Nothing," Gary snapped without turning. "Rachel was just leaving."

"What did she mean about trying to appease me?" She sounded little-girl sweet, but Sherry had fire in her eyes.

"Nothing, Sherry. It's just divorce stuff."

Rachel stared at him and felt the spark of victory rising in her chest, heating her through. "Sherry doesn't know what you're trying to do, does she?"

Gary swallowed, his Adam's apple seeming to get stuck for a moment on a very large lump in his throat. "This isn't about Sherry. It's about you and me."

"It's about Justin and Nathan and who they're going to live with," she said flatly.

"But they live with you for a week, then with Gary for a week," Sherry said to Rachel as she looked at her suddenly shrinking weasel of a boyfriend.

"Gary wants them full-time because—" Rachel stopped, glared at him. "Why don't *you* tell Sherry why you want them full-time?"

He opened his mouth, but his tongue seemed to stick to the roof of his mouth. Finally, for Sherry, he managed, "You said you wanted to spend more time with them, sweetheart."

Rachel tried to remember what endearments he'd used on her and couldn't. They'd long since lost all that.

"The boys are wonderful," Sherry said, staring at Gary as if she didn't know who he was anymore. "But Rachel's their mom. I don't want to take them away from her. How could you even think I'd want that?"

The girl wasn't so bad. Maybe clueless, maybe not, who knew, but she wasn't evil.

"What have you done, Gary?" she whispered in a guileless voice that Rachel believed completely. Sherry didn't know anything about the video or the blackmail or Gary's plans.

"It was just a discussion," he said softly, his brown eyes pleading and pathetic. "I just *asked*."

Rachel couldn't stand another word from him. "You didn't ask." She narrowed her eyes on him. "You stole from me." She held out her hand, palm up. "I want the video card back. Now," she added through gritted teeth.

"Gary," Sherry said.

Gary's gaze shifted between them as if he didn't know who posed the greater threat.

Then he huffed out a breath, reached into his pocket, pulled out the precious video card, and slapped it onto Rachel's palm. "There. You've got it back. Now you can leave."

Rachel smiled, feeling so damn good, she wanted to dance. "I have one more thing to ask."

"What?" he said, his voice strained, a very sore loser.

"Not from you. From Sherry."

"What?" Sherry asked sweetly.

"Would you guys take the boys tomorrow night? I have a friend I need to mend some fences with, and I'd really appreciate it if you'd take care of my sons for the night."

"Of course, Rachel. Anytime." Sherry smiled. "They're wonderful boys, and you've done a great job raising them."

"Thank you, Sherry. I'll drop them off after dinner, about seven." She smiled at the woman, turned to leave.

"One more thing," Sherry said.

Rachel raised a brow. The girl could possibly give as good as she got.

Sherry held out a hand to Gary, palm up. "You've got Rachel's key. You need to give it back."

Oh yeah. In her moment of glory, Rachel had forgotten all about it.

Gary muttered something Rachel couldn't hear, then dug his key ring out of his pocket and slid off the house key. He laid it in Sherry's hand, and Sherry handed it to Rachel.

Whoa. Gary had met his match. Perhaps if Rachel had done the same kind of thing years ago, taken charge when it was needed—like telling him he was ridiculous about the whole massage episode—their marriage would have been entirely different.

Not that it mattered anymore. The only important thing now, besides the boys, was seeing Rand.

WHEN SHE ARRIVED HOME FROM WORK THE FOLLOWING EVENING, Rachel packed a small overnight bag and stowed it in the minivan. Then she made dinner for herself and the boys. She hadn't called Rand to tell him she'd be showing up on his doorstep. He might very well slam the door in her face, but she'd worry about that when it happened instead of coming up with the worst-case scenario before she even started.

"So why are we going to Dad's?" Justin, he always had to question. He'd end up being a lawyer. Or a reporter.

Rachel wasn't going to lie about tonight's outing, and she wasn't going to pussyfoot. "I have a date, and I'm not sure when I'll be home." She was hoping she wouldn't be home at all tonight, if things went well.

Justin stopped, a spoonful of minestrone halfway to his

mouth. "*You're* going on a date?" His eyes were round with wonder as if he couldn't believe a woman her age could find a date. Then he caught himself. "I mean, who are you going out with?"

The moment of truth. She looked at Nathan, who was eating his soup without an overwhelming level of interest in the conversation. In for a penny, in for a pound, as her mother said. Rachel dove in. "I'm going out with Nathan's Principal Torvik."

Nathan's spoon splashed into his soup. "You're kidding."

She could handle this. She could explain. She could win him over. "Yes. I rather liked him that time we met in his office." She took a breath. "And it seems he liked me, too."

Nathan picked up his crust of Parmesan bread, bit, and chewed, his gaze unfocused as if he were reviewing all the ramifications in his head before he said anything.

He'd want to know if she'd called the principal or if he'd called her. If she was checking up on Nathan far more than she'd ever told him. How it all went down. She should have rehearsed her answers. Of course, she couldn't tell the *whole* truth, but she would minimize the necessary falsehoods.

Then Nathan smiled. "That's cool, Mom. He's an okay guy."

Rachel felt her jaw drop. "I thought you hated him."

Nathan shrugged. "I was just angry. I'm over it."

He was *over* it? Just like that? All her worrying for nothing? "Did something happen at school, with the special ed lab or . . . ?" she trailed off. She couldn't believe it. This was too good to be true.

"I like tutoring in the lab. The kids are pretty cool once you get to know them."

Who was this young man? He'd stolen her son's body. Teenagers. They were so changeable; one minute, their life was absolutely terrible and they were *dying*, the next, they couldn't even remember what they'd been so upset about. "And Principal Torvik's cool, too?" she tested.

Nathan shrugged. "He's not as bad as I thought. We had a long talk yesterday—"

"Yesterday?" Before or after she'd crawled miserably into Rand's office?

Nathan seesawed his head. "Once just before lunch, then again after school. He's asked me to help Wally get acclimated to the student body and make sure no one causes him undue distress."

Acclimated? Undue distress? Nathan was parroting Rand, she was sure. Rand had fixed everything, just the way he'd said he would. "Well, I'm sure you'll do a fine job helping Wally." The responsibility would be good for him. That's probably how Rand had planned it. Yet he hadn't said a word yesterday. Not that she'd given him much of a chance. "I'm proud of you, honey."

Nathan smiled and started slurping his soup again.

She still couldn't believe it all. *Nothing* could be this easy. She didn't trust her luck. "You're both sure you're okay if I date the principal?"

"Dad's dating Sherry," Justin said as Nathan nodded, his mouth full again. "And if he gets to date, you get to as well."

"Thank you for being so fair, Justin." She'd have liked to ask how they felt about Sherry, but she didn't want to interject herself into the middle of that relationship, especially since Sherry now had her vote of confidence.

Some people would quit while they were ahead, but Rachel was on a roll and figured she might as well check in on their feelings about something else, too. "What about me going back to school? Are you sure you're okay with that?"

Nathan gave her a look. "I'm old enough to be in charge a couple of evenings a week, Mom," he drawled.

Justin wasn't about to be outdone. "And I can be in charge of him when he's being a dick—" Justin stopped when Nathan gave him a mock punch to the arm.

Someone needed to pinch her because, honestly, she must be dreaming. Could things actually work out? Really, truly? Well, yes, they could. It might very well be as simple as finally making a stand.

Now she had to see Rand and beg him to forgive her for doubting him and throwing him aside. He'd been right about everything.

WHEN HIS DOORBELL RANG WEDNESDAY EVENING, RAND KNEW IT was Rachel. The law of attraction; he'd wanted her here, and here she was. He opened the door to her, feeling neither triumph nor anger, only relief. He'd planned a trip to her house Sunday evening after seven when he knew the boys would be gone. At that time, he'd fully intended to show her how ludicrous it was to give in to her husband's demand. Tie her to the bed, take her, and when he was buried deep inside, he knew he could convince her of anything. If that didn't work, well, he'd just have to pay the asshole ex a visit himself.

But Rachel had come to him instead.

"Come in," he said, his heart jackhammering despite the sense of relief. He'd invited women into his house, but never into his life the way he had with Rachel.

Of course, she could be here only to discuss Nathan. Yet she wore a delicious little sweater top that was unbuttoned down to her magnificent cleavage, the flirty black skirt he'd bought her for Las Vegas, and the red high heels. Christ. Those sexy shoes. His heart began to race, and his cock pulsed to life.

The other indication that she wasn't here about her son's school activities? The overnight case she'd used on their trip.

She clutched the bag two-handed in front of her as if she were a little unsure of her reception. "Thank you for what you did for Nathan."

"I've always believed he was a good kid." Rand smiled, thinking of those moments he'd stood with his foot propping open the restroom door. "You raised a son you can be extremely proud of. I admire the way he defended Wally. He was ready to take a beating for the boy."

She tipped her head. "He was?"

"He didn't tell you the whole story?"

She snorted. "Nathan didn't tell me anything. He just stopped calling you a dickhead and said you were an okay guy."

Rand laughed. Sometimes he *was* a dickhead. "I'll tell you all about it. But right now we have something else we need to talk about."

She abruptly put a finger to his lips, her hand scented with flowers. "Shh," she said.

He nodded, and she removed her hand. Although he would have loved for her to keep it there. He could have licked her fingers, worked his way to the crook of her elbow, then higher to the hollow of her throat . . .

She put her bag on the entry floor, squatting beside it. He could see straight down the unbuttoned sweater to the swell of creamy breasts. He needed to lick her. Now.

She unzipped the bag and held up the two red scarves she'd restrained him with in the Vegas hotel. "I've been very bad, and I need to be punished for being so stupid, Principal Torvik."

35

HEAT SHOT FROM THE CENTER OF HIS CHEST TO THE TIP OF HIS cock. "What have you done that you need to be punished for?"

"I told you that I didn't want to see you anymore and that I wouldn't tell my ex-husband to go"—she rolled her lips between her teeth, then licked them—"to go screw himself."

"Have you done that now?"

She nodded her head, her lips parted invitingly. He adored looking down at her, wanting her as she squatted beside the bag. It might be nice to have her here on the hall floor. It would be so damn nice to have her anywhere. "Did that work for you?"

She nodded again, something lighting in her hazel eyes. He'd get the whole story later; now there was something else he needed badly. "Good. But you need to be punished for being such a willful bitch."

She fluffed the scarves at him. "Do you want to tie me up, Principal Torvik?"

A new game. He loved new games. He loved that she wanted

to play them. There were so many fantasies to fulfill, they would keep themselves happy for a very long time.

Towering over her, he dropped his voice. "In my office." He pointed down the hall, past the stairs to his home office. "I'll be there in five minutes. Then I'll decide what to do with you."

"I've never been called to the principal's office before." She rose, leaving the bag where it was, the scarves clutched in her hands.

"And you'll pay for your disobedience. So go."

She left him with an exaggerated sway to her hips that made his heart pump blood straight to his cock. Her toned legs in those fuck-me red shoes sent his blood pressure soaring.

"And remove your panties," he called after her.

She glanced over her shoulder with a coy gaze. "I'm not wearing panties, Principal Torvik," she cooed.

"You dirty girl." His balls ached, he wanted her so badly. "Maybe I should fuck you right here in the hall."

She fluttered her eyelashes at him. "Oh, Principal Torvik, you are a very bad man."

"You're about to find out just how bad, Rachel. Now go, before I change my mind." He counted to ten once she'd entered his office, then climbed the stairs to his bedroom and his stash of condoms. Back down in less than three minutes, he couldn't wait a moment longer.

She stood by his desk, her hip jutted out, ankles crossed. The room was his favorite, polished wood paneling, built-in bookcases, hardwood floor, long windows with an expansive view of the backyard, a big walnut desk. And his reading chair, her scarves a splash of color on the black leather. There were a lot of things he'd enjoy doing to Rachel in that chair.

"It's time to rewrite the rules, Rachel," he said sternly.

"Yes, Principal Torvik." She pouted at him.

He gathered the red scarf with the tiny black swirls in it. "Hold out your wrists."

She laced one over the other. He wound the silky material around, over, under, through, and tied it off. "Lean over the chair."

The high heels were so tall that her ass rose pertly in the air as she braced her forearms on the back of the chair.

"Now put your feet together." He grabbed the second red scarf as she followed his instructions, and he bent down to bind her at the ankles, tying it off in a neat bow. Like a gift ready to unwrap. "Perfect," he whispered. Rachel brought out his best and naughtiest fantasies. "You need a spanking for being so bad."

"Oh no, Principal Torvik, please don't hurt me."

"It's the only way you'll learn your lesson, Rachel." He raised her skirt, pushing it up to the small of her back. The creamy flesh of her bare ass was exceedingly inviting. He slapped one firm globe.

She squealed. "Principal Torvik." Her scent rose then, sweet, musky, sexual.

"I will list the rules for you, Rachel. If you don't immediately accept a rule, I'll give you another smack."

"Oh, sir, please don't."

He spanked her again, then couldn't resist slipping down to the crease of flesh between her legs. She was deliciously, fragrantly wet. "Don't argue, Rachel. Or you'll get more of it."

"No, Principal Torvik." Her voice was laced with laughter, yet throaty with desire.

"First rule. You'll spend the night at my home. All night. In my bed."

"Principal Torvik, you know I can't do that."

He swatted her other cheek, leaving a mild red mark, and again, couldn't resist following the line of her ass to that sweet wet spot between her legs, caressing. She moaned.

"I told you not to argue, Rachel."

"All right. I'll spend the night, sir."

"I forgot to add that we would only do that during the weeks you don't have the boys."

"Yes, sir."

"Good girl. Next rule. We'll go on dates. I'll pick you up at your house. I will meet your boys, and you will tell them I'm your boyfriend."

"My boyfriend?" she said with an exaggerated high-pitched squeak.

This time he spanked her right on her center. Her body seemed to gush with her pleasure. She groaned, pushed back against him, and he delved deeper to find her clitoris.

Leaning over her, he whispered close to her ear. "Your boyfriend," he repeated.

"Yes, Principal Torvik." She panted as he massaged her. "You're my boyfriend."

"We're having a relationship, Rachel."

She clenched her fingers spasmodically over the back of the chair, squirming against his touch. "A relationship, Principal Torvik? Oh, but we can't do that."

He slapped her ass again, then once more. She put her face to the side, eyes closed, biting her lip, and a small sigh of pleasure escaped her.

Rubbing along her wet and greedy pussy, he said again, "A relationship. Not a few dates. Not casual sex. But real."

She opened her eyes. "Yes," she said softly. "Nothing casual. Something very, very important."

A warmth spread through his chest that had nothing to do with sexual desire. "We won't be merely fucking, Rachel. It will be so much more." He slid a finger inside her.

Her body welcomed him. "So much more, Rand. I need you."

"If you have problems with your ex, you'll tell me, and we'll deal with him together."

She pushed back against his hand. "Yes, Rand."

"We'll deal with everything together."

She moaned and rocked. "Yes, Rand, everything." She gasped as he hit her G-spot. "Together."

"Am I missing any rules, Rachel?" he said softly.

"Yes."

"Tell me." He withdrew his hand, unzipped, and rolled on a condom.

"The one about naughty fantasy sex."

"Yes, I forgot that one." She was wet; he was so ready. He held her hips and plunged deep. Christ, with her feet tied at the ankles and her legs together, she was so fucking tight around him. "Yes, Rachel, we're going to have lots and lots of dirty, filthy fantasy sex."

For so long, he'd remained one step back in all his affairs. But no more. With Rachel, he was fully involved, fully committed.

RACHEL GASPED AS HE FILLED HER. HER BUTT WAS SLIGHTLY TENDER from the spanking he'd given her, and the sensations made her feel luscious and desired. "I need to be spanked in the principal's office. A lot." She panted as he began to move inside her, grazing her G-spot with slow inexorable strokes.

He held her hips, thrust deep. "You liked that."

"God, I love everything you do to me," she admitted, in thrall, her body filled yet needing more. "I need you, Rand."

"No more than I need you," he whispered, leaning down, wrapping himself around her.

Her mind floated free, the tension rising, pushing her higher, the relentless stroke of his body, the heat of his skin, his male scent filling her head. "I don't know what I'd do without you now."

"You're mine, baby. I'm yours." His body covering her completely, he reached beneath to put his finger to her clitoris as he took her.

"I'm sorry," she moaned. "I was so stupid. Oh God, oh God, Rand." She could barely say the words; maybe she didn't say them, only felt them.

"We're together. We're so good together." He clenched one hand on her shoulder, a little pain, so much pleasure.

"Do me like this all the time, Rand. Want me like this. Need me like this."

He was all around her, in her body, her mind, her heart.

"Always like this, baby." Then he groaned, pulsed and throbbed inside her, his body slamming into hers one last time, holding fast, pushing, pressing, and they went under together.

Always together, from now on.

"I meant it," he said moments later. Or minutes, or hours. They were seated in the chair, she on his lap, cradled in his arms. She didn't remember exactly how they'd gotten that way or when he'd untied the scarves.

"What?" she murmured dreamily.

"We're together. This isn't casual. No more walking out when things get tough."

She leaned her head back against his shoulder, stroking the line of his strong chin with her index finger as she held his gaze. "I was wrong about so many things. I'm not cut out for casual sex, or for keeping secrets from my boys. I want you in my life, I've told them, and I'm not running away again."

"Long haul," he whispered.

"Long haul," she repeated.

"I've never wanted that before. But I want it with you." He kissed her forehead. "How did Nathan take our being together?"

She laughed. "Like I said, you've been elevated to the status of cool. I don't know what you did for him, but he's like a different kid."

"He just needed to solve a few issues for himself. Yesterday he did that, taking on Tom and Rick. He settled things with them."

Tom and Rick. They must be the so-called friends. "I think you gave him a lot of help getting there."

"I'd like to take credit. But he did it himself. We always think we need to tell them what to do, how to do it, force them to see the light as if somehow they aren't capable of doing it on their own. But they are." He stroked her hair. "You gave him the building blocks to figure out what to do, Rachel. You've raised an incredibly amazing young man."

He was a good man, never self-aggrandizing, always sharing the credit, and his praise warmed her through. She burrowed into his chest, trying to make herself a part of him. "Gary gave me back the video card."

"I never doubted for a minute that you'd win."

But she would have knuckled under without Rand. He'd made her see the light. He was good for the boys. He was good for her. He was just plain good all around.

She tipped her head back against his shoulder again, looked up at him, smiled. "I brought it with me."

"The video?"

She nodded slowly, then bit her lip, and finally said, "I think we should put it on your big-screen TV and watch it together."

"Now?"

"Right now. And then"—she nuzzled his cheek—"you should do some naughty things to me."

"Sweetheart, I'll be doing very naughty things to you for a very long time to come." He kissed her hard, lips, tongue, his whole body, stealing her breath, then he backed off just as quickly.

"We were meant to be together from the moment I rescued your orange juice in the grocery store."

She laughed. And she remembered that moment, when he'd awakened her like Prince Charming.

"It's why Nathan was *my* student, not some other principal's at some other high school. Because we're all connected. We all needed each other. And I'm not letting you go."

"I'm not letting *you* go." Not ever. She traced his chin with her finger, breathed in her fill of him. It was finally time. "Let me tell you about this really hot fantasy I've had for a very long time," she said softly, using his words. "I should have told you weeks ago. Because there's a story behind it." She should have trusted him to understand how it had affected her. She trusted him now, completely, with everything. "It's about a massage . . ."

ABOUT THE AUTHOR

With a bachelor's degree in accounting from Cal Poly, San Luis Obispo, Jasmine Haynes has worked in the high-tech Silicon Valley for the last twenty years and hasn't met a boring accountant yet! Okay, maybe a few. She and her husband live with numerous wild cats, one of whom has now moved into the house. Jasmine's pastimes, when not writing, are speed-walking in the Redwoods, watching classic movies, and hanging out with writer friends in coffee shops. She is the author of classy erotic romance and the popular Max Starr paranormal romance mystery series, and also writes quirky laugh-out-loud romances as Jennifer Skully. Visit her at jasminehaynes.com and jasmine haynes.blogspot.com.